Some Days Suck;

Some Days Suck Worse

A Collection of Short Stories

by

Michael A. Kozlowski

This book is a work of fiction. Names, characters, places and events are products of the author's imagination or have been used fictitiously. Any resemblance to persons living or dead, actual events, locales or organizations is entirely coincidental.

TABLE OF CONTENTS

DEDICATION

There are a lot of people to thank for getting me this far in my writing; my family, editors who saw something worthwhile in the words of an unknown author, other writers who encouraged me whether they knew it or not. I'll miss a bunch of people who should be named here but know that I couldn't have done it without any of you and, just because I'm shit with names and I have the memory of a gnat, I love you all.

Here's some that I can remember:

My supportive and patient wife, Laurie.

My boys, Aaron and Connor, who keep me young and full of wonder.

My parents, Ruth and John, who have always been there and made it seem like reading was as natural a thing as breathing.

My brothers, John and Danny, who often tortured me but stopped short of causing any permanent damage (at least that can be directly traced back to them) and who each inspired me in their own way.

Various authors, some of whom I've had actual conversations with and some who needed only to speak to me through their books, including: Stephen King, Neil Gaiman, Jonathon Maberry, Brian Keene, Jay Wilburn and Weston Ochse (who were both kind enough to blurb the book and/or write a review), Joe Hill, Ray Bradbury, Richard Matheson.

Friends and first readers (not only for the stories in this collection but for various works): Jennifer Harrison, Donnitta Williamson, Julie Cassar, John Kachnowski, Melissa Barth, Natalie Buckler, Tammy Pineda.

And always to those who support me (family, friends, fans), collectively known and loved as The Faithful Few.

THE LAST CALL

The Last Call was your typical, small, neighborhood bar. The lighting was purposefully bad to disguise the fact that the décor hadn't been updated in at least twenty years and to hide the decidedly lax attitude toward general housekeeping. Every now and again rumors would circulate among the regulars that someone new was considering buying the place and, in fact, the bar had switched ownership several times over the last decade, yet it remained stubbornly unchanged. Jack, the bartender, and the small crew of waitresses (never more than one on duty at a time, and usually sitting at the far end of the bar reading a magazine and smoking a cigarette) were as much fixtures of The Last Call as were the grime darkened, stained glass table lamps that hung from tarnished chains over the row of booths along the wall casting a soft, if rather dim, glow on the tables below them.

At 10:30 that Thursday evening, Ed Carter walked into the bar through the once red, now brownish, vinyl clad door, its window blacked out to repel the garish light of the real world. The smells of stale beer and cigarette smoke that had leeched into the very walls of the dim tavern offered a familiar welcoming. Fresh off his shift as a salesman in the appliance section of the Tredmont Department Store, he took his customary seat on the third stool from the far end of the Formica topped bar. Two stools to his left sat Charlie Halfert, staring into the last dregs of a warming glass of Budweiser. The stool between them sat empty, awaiting the arrival of John Cabbitzn, who was regularly referred to as "Spider" for reasons lost to time, and who would be sure to join them within the hour, as he did every night. To Ed's right sat Wild Bill McGentry, who was not especially wild and, despite his surname, was primarily of Polish descent. Grunts were exchanged in lieu of formal greetings and Jack delivered a longneck bottle of Labatt Blue to Ed without his needing to order. While Ed was not especially preferential to the Canadian import, he secretly harbored the opinion that drinking it made him slightly more refined than his Budweiser swilling counterparts.

There was no conversation exchanged between the three men. At some point over the past several years they had silently, but unanimously, determined that any conversation taking place prior to the arrival of the whole foursome was time wasted as it invariably had to be rehashed to bring the later arrivals up to speed. It could have been just as easily determined that the weight of these conversations rarely held any significant information that any of them couldn't have done without.

Spider arrived at 10:45 and, after allowing him an appropriate amount of time to settle into his stool, procure his beer and carefully arrange his cigarette pack, lighter, keys and wallet on the space of bar in front of him, the group fell into their usual murmurings. Local sports teams, the depressed economy and the incompetence of elected officials constituted the bulk of the conversation.

At 11:30, in the midst of a diatribe by Spider about how the clutch on his 1976 Trans Am was acting up and the anticipated cost of repair, the door to the street opened up and Wild Bill, situated farthest from the door and at an angle which gave him the best view of anyone coming or going, held up his hand to stifle Spider's rant. The generally accepted process for indicating that one was about to comment on a current topic was to nod or shake one's head thoughtfully, slowly take a drink of beer, and make a few "tsk, tsk" type noises. Wild Bill's abrupt breach of etiquette caused the three other barflies to glare at him with both incredulousness and anticipation. They gathered that something abnormally important was about to be revealed.

"Boys," said Wild Bill, nodding toward the door, "take a lookie here."

The other three men turned toward the door, expecting to see nothing less extraordinary than a three-headed dog or a chicken on roller skates. Spider's anticipation, as the offended party of the interruption, was the highest. None were disappointed.

Standing in the doorway was a young woman who may or may not have been old enough to legally drink but certainly had no business in a bar like The Last Call. She wore high-heeled, leather boots that came up to her knees. The ample amount of her legs still visible between the boots and her short, black skirt, were clad in fishnet stockings. There was rip in the stocking on her left leg, which if not there by design should have been, revealing the milky, white skin of her thigh. Her white tank top was covered by a dark, flimsy tunic. The men could see a glimpse of the red bra that was pushing her healthy breasts up and out for display. Raven hair, with crimson streaks dyed through it, fell down across her shoulders and was swept from right to left across her face, almost but not quite concealing her dark eyes. She was dressed for a night on the town, perhaps at one of the hip dance clubs. She stuck out like a full moon in a starless sky as she stood in the dingy bar.

Megan, as that was what she was calling herself this evening, stood for a moment inside of the bar while her eyes adjusted to the lack of light. Besides the bartender, she saw four, no five, figures at the bar. She had nearly missed the women at the far end playing the table top video game. All the booths, and the few tables spaced between the bar and the booths, were empty. She made her way along the thin corridor formed by the bar on her left and the tables on her right. The men gaped openly at her. It was their opinion that this was their bar and anyone intruding upon the premises invited full examination.

As the young woman passed the men, she gave them a brief glance and a half-hearted smile. The scent of coconut danced on the air, trailing behind her, temporarily masking the smell of beer and cigarettes. She continued to the very last booth in the rear of the room and sat with her back to them. The waitress, Betty, a 48 year old, divorced, mother of two, let loose an audible sigh and snuffed her cigarette out in the ashtray next to the video game. With effort, she pushed herself off her stool. She was several credits down to the video poker machine and she loathed walking away from it, anxious to scratch her way back to, at least, even.

Betty walked over to the booth and took the girl's order, never bothering to ask for I.D. Charlie, Spider, Ed and Wild Bill remained interested spectators, having spun on their stools in a half circle as they followed the girl across the room. Even Jack, the bartender, kept an eye on the back booth while idly wiping glasses that would never be truly clean again and restacking them on the shelf behind the bar. The men's attention followed Betty back to the bar and switched to Jack as he began mixing a Screwdriver to fill the girl's order. They exchanged glances trying to determine if any further course of action was required. This was an unprecedented occurrence. A non-regular in The Last Call was an oddity, if not entirely unheard of; a lone female was a blue moon occurrence; an attractive, young woman on her own was pure lunacy. Sly smiles were flashed and eyebrows were raised in acknowledgement of the girl's beauty. Heads were nodded to convey that they each shared thoughts about what they would like to do with the unexpected arrival. Then they lost themselves in their own thoughts, taking sudden interest in their beer glasses, cigarette packs, fingernails or the flecks in the Formica bar top as they each gradually reminded themselves of the truth of their social abilities and prowess with members of the opposite sex.

Spider, deciding the silence was overwhelming, began to revive the story that had been cut short.

"So, anyway, the clutch is probably gonna cost me…"

He stopped when Ed stood up suddenly, just as Jack was bringing the Screwdriver over to Betty.

"Hold on, Jack," Ed said. "I got this one."

Ed pulled a crumpled five dollar bill out of the pocket of his slacks and laid it on the Formica.

"And I'll deliver it, as well," he said to Betty, his chest swelling noticeably.

The other three men stared at him as if he had grown another head and was breathing fire out of it and smoke from his asshole. Spider flushed a little red at having been interrupted a second time but, again, buried his annoyance and deferred to the gravity of the moment.

Ed straightened his black tie and worked on securing the white dress shirt (standard issue for Tredmont salesmen) back into the waist of his pants, a slightly more difficult task than he liked to admit given the size of his growing, if not yet large, beer belly. In his mind he wondered just what the hell he thought he was doing and what he was going to say when he got over to the booth, but he had impulsively decided to play the Alpha male, that he knew he was not, and felt he was too far gone to turn back now. Stuck in limbo by his momentary bravado between the ridicule of his peers should he back down and the inevitable embarrassment waiting for him across the room, Ed grabbed his beer and the Screwdriver off the bar, turned, took a deep breath through his nose and exhaled hard. Putting one tremulous foot in front of the other, he began moving toward the rear booth.

Worse case, he thought, *I'll be able to tell those pussies that I had the guts to make a move and I'll probably never see this chick again, so who really cares how badly she shoots me down.*

When he arrived at her booth, the girl looked up at him through eyes the color of tar; deep and dark. She offered the same half-hearted smile she had flashed as she passed by the bar. Ed stammered for a moment, taken aback by her beauty and questioning, for the second time in as many minutes, the intelligence of his aggressive play.

"I, uh, brought your drink," Ed said. He placed the Screwdriver in front of her, flashing his own half-hearted smile.

"Thank you," she said. She stared down into the pale orange liquid in her glass, held it with both hands and ran her thumbs along the sides, streaking the droplets of condensation already forming there. Ed noticed how the light from the dim bulb above the table caught little specks of sparkle in her blood red nail polish.

Ed stood, unsure about his next step. He had hoped she would invite him to sit down. He felt a bit silly standing there next to her, staring at her, taking in the smell of her. He could feel the eyes of Charlie, Spider, Wild Bill, Jack and even Betty, boring into his back. The girl looked up just as Ed was shifting his weight to turn and face the jeering.

"Would you like to join me?" she asked.

Ed thought she look resigned, maybe even defeated, as if he had played a silent game of chicken with her and she had flinched first. But, despite the felling that her offer was made with little to no enthusiasm, he quickly accepted and slid into the booth opposite her.

After quick introductions, they fell into general small talk. Ed exaggerated his position and importance at work, Megan feigned humility at any compliments he sent her way. He told her he had never married; had no family close by. She said she lived in an upper flat she rented, she was originally from a small town out west. She was attending classes a couple nights each week deciding what to do with the rest of her life. She told him how she had been at one of the clubs across town, gotten into a fight with her date and had been walking home when she passed the bar and decided to have one last drink; a few minutes to feel sorry for herself and cry into her beer because she didn't have close friends or family nearby either. Ed reminded her that she was preparing to cry into a Screwdriver instead of a beer and she laughed at the joke; Ed never felt more victorious and vital than in that micro-second before she laughed and he saw her eyes sparkle and knew she was going to laugh, felt it like the tingle before a sneeze, and knew he was the one responsible for making her happy, if only for that moment.

Ed told her he was five years younger than he really was; Megan told him she was five years older; it still left them several years apart. She told him it was nice to talk to a "regular" guy. He bought her another drink.

Ed surprised himself with the ease in which he found he could converse with her; was amazed at his own wit and charm. When, as 1:00 am rolled around, Megan said she had better get going because she still had a bit of a walk, Ed quickly offered to give her a ride home. She hesitated, just enough so as not to seem anxious, and then accepted. Jack offered a smile as Ed escorted the girl to the door. Charlie, Spider and Wild Bill watched open-mouthed in disbelief as

Ed paused to grab his keys from the bar, said "See ya tomorrow night, fellas" and headed out with his hand low on the girl's back. Betty was engrossed in the Poker machine.

It was a couple of miles to Megan's place. There was an awkward silence in Ed's rusted Buick as they drove. Her perfume mixed with the smell of the old, fast food bags in the backseat. Ed decided he was glad McDonald's didn't sell a coconut flavored shake; it probably wouldn't sit well with a Big Mac. He rolled the windows down half way to let some fresh air in or some stale air out; either way worked. He was still trying to figure out how in the world he had gotten this far. Megan was deciding how far it would go.

When Ed pulled up to the curb in front of the dark house, he put the car in park but left the engine running, He didn't want seem like he was making assumptions.

"I appreciate the ride," she said.

"It was my pleasure," he replied.

Megan looked out the passenger window and Ed wondered if she was waiting for him to make a move. He thought about lightly cupping her cheek and turning her toward him, kissing her softly but passionately. He thought about it but, being an almost middle-aged, generally socially inept appliance salesman, he *only* thought about it.

"Well…" he started.

She turned to him quickly and spoke just as fast; as if she were pushing the words out before she changed her mind, "You wanna come up for a cup of coffee?"

Ed hesitated. He wanted more than anything to go up to her flat with her but suddenly he was sixteen again and telling Janice Hemington that he really wanted to see the movie because he was too nervous and anxious to fool around in the back row of the theater. He was twenty and in the backseat of his car with a girl from his biology class at the community college. It had taken three weeks for him to get up the nerve to talk to her, two more to ask her out, and about twenty seconds of anticipation before he wasted the opportunity before he could get his pants off. He was twenty two and laying in his apartment being told by his first serious girlfriend that it was okay, it would be better next time; twenty five and knowing it wasn't better; thirty and being laughed at by the young lady that had just bought a washer and dryer combo from him, because she wouldn't go out with a guy that sold washer and dryer combos for a living. Now he was thirty five and spending every night in a bar, nursing a beer belly to full gestation, with three other guys who lied about their sexual exploits and occasionally picking up a hooker behind the Bowl-O-Rama, embarrassed to be paying for it but glad he could at least last long enough to feel he was getting his money's worth.

"Yeah," Ed swallowed hard, "I'd love a cup of coffee."

Through the entry door on the porch, up a flight of stairs and through the door that opened into the flat, Ed followed Megan. When he was able to pull his focus away from what he determined to be the most magnificent ass he had ever seen, he thought about the situation. He was proud of himself that he had acted with such impulsivity at the bar; very unlike him. He was pleased that he had been clever and smooth through their conversation and, a few "ums" and "ahs" aside, right up until now; remarkably unlike him. Just the same, he knew he was out of his league. Hell, he wasn't even playing the same sport.

As they entered the living room, Ed was struck by a new odor; one that overpowered Megan's perfume. It could have been flowers, a new room freshener or potpourri. For some reason the word "jasmine" jumped into Ed's mind, though he wouldn't have been able to tell you what "jasmine" smelled like or differentiate it from any other flowery fragrance. Beneath that smell, Ed thought he detected another. Maybe the smell of unwashed dishes lingering in the sink or a wastebasket that needed to be emptied. It was hardly noticeable; briefly invading his senses and then vanishing like the smell from somebody's backyard barbecue rolling down the street in the middle of summer; just the powerful, flowery, perfume smell remained

The front room was tidy, though sparse in adornments. There were no pictures on the plain, white walls, no picture frames on the end tables, no spread over the back of the couch, no colorful throw pillows. The furniture was simple, clean and in good shape, though clearly not new or expensive. He remembered Megan saying she was taking night classes and thought that the flat looked typical of a student's apartment; functional.

"Nice place," he said.

"It's not much," Megan replied, "but it's cheap."

She directed him to the couch and walked off to the kitchen to put on a pot of coffee, then joined him in the living room. Ed had positioned himself in the middle of the couch, thinking it gave her no option but to sit close to him. If she chose to sit on the chair opposite him, he would consider it a sign that coffee was as much as he was going to get out of the evening. Megan sat perched on the arm of the couch, confounding Ed's plan and reasoning alike.

"I'm glad you asked me up," he said.

She smiled; that same half-hearted, shy smile she had been flashing all night. Her eyes were cast downward and Ed wondered if she was toying with him.

"I'm glad you accepted."

She slid off the arm of the sofa and next to him; their thighs just touching. Ed cautiously placed his hand on her knee, careful only to set it there and not to stroke along the fishnet stocking. He was trying to make his move, but slowly, afraid to rush it.

She met his eyes and leaned toward him. Swallowing hard, his heart beating like a drum, he kissed her. It began as a soft, gentle, tentative, searching kiss; a kiss that asked permission. She accepted it, encouraged it by opening her mouth slightly and inviting his tongue inside of her. His trembling hand moved up her thigh, Megan's hands cupped his face and she kissed him more aggressively as their breathing quickened.

She stood, pulling him up with her, and began backing toward a door to the left. It was open and Ed could see the bed within the room.

"Are you sure?" he asked

"No."

He searched her eyes. He thought he saw tears gathering. She smiled softly, almost sadly.

"C'mon," she whispered.

Fuck it, Ed thought, maybe she's got some kind of low self-esteem thing going on. And thinking about how she looked, how he looked, he decided there was no "maybe" about it.

She pushed him, gently, down on to the bed and closed the door behind them. The darkness of the room was complete. He felt her weight on the bed, then on top of him. He smelled her, the coconut lotion or perfume that reminded him of strippers at one of the downtown clubs. It mixed in his nostrils with the scent of the flat (jasmine?) and he noticed that other, underlying odor; food left out from a midnight snack perhaps, a sweet but borderline rancid smell, just there, just underneath everything else.

Megan kissed him and he smelled only her.

"Just a minute," she breathed and he felt her get out of the bed, he heard a door open. The bathroom, he thought, probably getting a condom or some other type of birth control. He began stripping off his clothes, he heard the door close.

He felt the bed lilt as she climbed back in. Felt her weight and the presence of her body over him. He leaned forward, searching for her lips, felt hot breath on his face and was stopped by that rancid, decaying smell that now overtook all the other scents in the room.

The door to the living room opened and light spilled into the bedroom. All in the same moment he saw Megan, at the door, looking back at him as a tear ran down her cheek; he saw a thing above him, straddling him, it's flesh blotted and discolored as if it had been burned, thick, dark hairs in clumps here and there, fang-like teeth grinning at him, shiny wet with saliva, its face a grotesque jumble of features that had to be a mask. God, he thought, please let it be a mask.

The door closed and the darkness embraced the room. Before he could scream, the thing leaned into him and Ed Carter's last thought was how awful death smelled and then it tore his lower jaw clear from his face and skull. The pain and the fear left no more room for thought. It's hot, rancid breath brushed his neck. His awareness of the pain was blessedly brief.

Megan sat on the couch in the living room, trying not to listen to the sounds behind the bedroom door; the feeding. She wiped the tears from her eyes, tried to control her retching stomach, lost the battle and vomited on the floor; the taste of orange juice, vodka and bile lingered in her mouth.

She thought for probably the hundredth time that she couldn't do this again. How long would he, it, be satisfied with this offering? Two days? Three? Then she would have to feed it again or risk becoming its next meal. She considered running. Just getting up and going as far and as fast as she could, but she knew it wouldn't work. Hadn't her parents tried that when he, it, became more than they could face? And it had hunted them, killed them and brought her back to serve it. Why hadn't they killed it when they had the chance? Surely they could see what it was, or at least, what it wasn't. A parent's unconditional love? Surely there was a limit? And what of their love for her? Concern for her safety?

She staggered to the kitchen, the tears still coming, streaking mascara down her face. She pressed her hands to her ears but the sounds were inside her head. She flipped the switches on the stove, rummaged through the drawers in the kitchen, found what she was looking for and slumped down to the linoleum floor, her back against the cabinets.

She smelled the mixture of spring flowers; the smell coming from the dozens of air fresheners placed around the flat. She smelled the rancid, rotting meat smell; the smell of decay and fresh blood that was always there no matter how she tried to cover it. She smelled the new smell, the rotten egg smell that was growing stronger and stronger as she sat there, crying, hating the thing she had once, in another life, thought of as her brother, hating what it had made her become; a lethal Lolita, prowling bars and back alleys for men (or women; no difference to it) that nobody would notice were missing or look too long for if they disappeared.

With trembling hands she pulled a match from the box and inhaled deeply. The rotten egg smell of gas was strong enough now to block out all the others. This one had seemed like a nice guy. They usually didn't, but every once in a while…

She'd thought of trying to kill it before but knew she didn't have the strength. She thought of killing herself but that would just leave it to prowl on its own.

Coughing on the gas, she looked up as it appeared in the bedroom door. She had hoped it would be too engrossed in its prey to notice but it must have smelled the gas. It, he, stood there with its head cocked inquisitively, like a dog. She saw Ed's body behind it, ravaged and bloody across the bed. She met its eyes and dragged the match along the side of the box, hoping distantly that her landlady wasn't home downstairs.

Author's Notes:
I had a bit of a "Lolita" thing on my mind when I started this story; I must've been listening to the Police or something. As I wrote the first draft, I was sure that the girl was the monster, but she surprised me.
I really like the play with the different odors throughout the story. I think the power of the sense of smell is really underrated.

UNDER MY BED

1.

There is a monster under my bed. Believe me; I know how silly that sounds. I am not a pre-pubescent child who fears dark basements or bumps in the night so it would seem ludicrous for me to make such a statement. To the best of my knowledge I am neither insane nor suffering from a malady of the cerebral cortex which would cause me to imagine such things. In all manners of life and living I am a pretty regular guy.

Some may point out such things as my affinity for peanut butter and pickle sandwiches or a little habit of mine concerning the thorough washing of soda cans prior to drinking directly from them, for fear of microscopic vermin fecal matter, as proof that I am not necessarily normal. However, these and various other idiosyncrasies are matters of taste and hygiene which I do not feel cross the line of normal human behavior. Certainly there are many people out there much more peculiar than I.

It's possible, in fact likely, that monsters take up residence under many other beds around the world. Given the vast number of spaces available to them, I would imagine thousands, maybe hundreds of thousands, lurking among the dust bunnies in bedrooms around the world. I have no reason to believe I am a special magnet for such an occurrence. It's not something I bring up with people, just the same.

On occasion I have alluded to the monster when talking with the younger children of some of my friends, although I hesitate to relate specifics. More than once I have been present at the appointed bedtime of one of these young children and have heard them ask their father to do a cursory review of their bedrooms to ensure no monsters are present. At these times I wait, tense and nervous, afraid my friend, attempting to humor his child and taking the request in what could prove to be a regrettably light manner, may not return from his inspection. What if he runs into something untoward?

Invariably the child will wait in the presence of the remaining adults, unwilling to encounter said monsters should their father rouse them from their hiding places. Given the opportunity, as has happened more than once, I will quietly console the child and let them know I sympathize with their concern. I know what it's like to have a monster in your bedroom. To date, I am yet to be present in such a situation where a monster is discovered. I believe they are there but I am of the opinion they are especially good at hiding.

As I've said, I don't discuss my monster with other adults. I suspect they would not take me seriously, a man of thirty six years afraid of a monster under his bed. Quite possibly they would suggest that I seek "professional" help. By "professional" help they would mean a psychiatrist, even though I'd bet there are a fair number of other adults who are subject to the same situation as I. They probably try to pass it off as their imagination or some such. I wonder how they would react if they were to meet someone in a similar predicament? Would it be one of those "me too" moments?

The "professional" help I need is a monster hunter; someone like Abraham Van Helsing. Sadly, there are no listings of such occupations in the Yellow Pages. I've checked. I had considered hiring a ghost hunter, one of those paranormal experts, but I don't think their services would be effective. I am certain my monster is not a lingering spirit or other manifestation of a prior living being. It is not an electrical anomaly left by the life force of some deceased person who may have had a connection to me in some manner or another. No, my monster is a living thing. I've seen it. At any rate, I've glimpsed it.

I'm a creature of habit and my monster has been drooling beneath my various beds, in the various residences I have occupied in my lifetime, for something over thirty years. It knows me. It has had to adjust to my later bedtimes as I have grown and to the occasional variances in my nightly ritual, but it would seem to be entirely focused on me and my goings on and seldom caught unaware. When my monster does creep out of its lair, and I know that it does, it seems to be very alert and is almost always well out of sight by the time I enter the room. However, on occasion it would seem that I have surprised it.

Quite recently, for instance, I had fallen asleep on the couch in my living room while trying to fight off exhaustion long enough to watch the completion of a baseball game which had extended into extra innings. I awoke in the middle of the night, right around 3:00 a.m., and rather than brush my teeth, make the rounds of the house to check the door locks, shut off lights and have a drink of water from the kitchen tap, as is my usual ritual, I stumbled directly to my bedroom in a bit of a fog, my bare feet padding softly on the carpeted hall. Presumably, my monster was wondering what had become of me because, despite the fact that there is a terrible beast lying in wait and anticipation under the comfort of my queen-sized bed, I have rarely spent my nights sleeping elsewhere. Only just lately have I had cause to spend my hours of slumber in another location occasionally and it could be that my monster had determined I would not be returning to my bedroom on this evening and was taking the opportunity to explore the contents thereof, something I expect it does with some regularity and which would explain why midnight snacks, that are only half finished when I fall asleep, are often reduced to mere crumbs when I observe them the next evening having failed to remove them that morning. My monster seems to be especially fond of salami sandwiches but has yet to partake of my peanut butter and pickle fare.

When I opened the door to my bedroom on that particular night, a dark, hulking figure sped across my line of vision. The light from the living room, which I had neglected to extinguish, cast a dim glow down the hall and into my bedroom. My own body blocked much of this light from penetrating the room and sleep still clouded my eyes so I was unable to get a good view of the creature. Its movement startled me to alertness, however, and I was able to glimpse what appeared to be one of the monster's appendages as it clambered back to its hiding place under the cover of the Serta mattress and box spring set. I could not clearly discern if what I saw was a leg or an arm or some sort of tentacle, but it had a glossy sheen to it as if the creature excreted some sort of slimy substance from within itself.

The darkness obscured the color of the beast, though I would hazard to guess that it had a mottled greenish-brown skin. Wispy hairs covered the momentarily exposed body part, reminding me of the skull of a mostly decomposed corpse like one might see in a Halloween decoration display or on that cable show where the creepy looking puppet plays host to various scary stories.

On yet another occasion I happened to drop a particularly engrossing novel that I was reading, as I entered my bedroom. I had my nose in the book even as I passed through the doorway and stubbed my foot into the jamb, causing me to yelp, hop ridiculously on one leg for a moment and drop the book. As I bent to retrieve it, my knee gave out on me. This is something that happens with increasing regularity as I age; the lingering side effect of an old sports injury. The result was that I collapsed to the floor with my face only an inch or so from the carpet and turned so I was staring directly into the monster's abode.

It should be noted that I do not generally look under the bed for any reason. I will usually glance when I enter the bedroom in order to ensure no part of my unwanted roommate is extending beyond the edges of the bed and to judge the spot from which I must make my leap to most safely reach the bed while exposing myself in the least possible manner to the monster's reach. I will say the distance I can cover has become increasingly less comfortable, age and that knee injury are beginning to limit me, and the process of attaining the relative safety of the covers is hindered dramatically by my bad habit of bringing food and drink to the bedroom. That is neither here nor there for the moment; suffice it to say that the angle at which I usually view the underside of the bed affords very little view of the space directly beneath it. Should anything find its way under the bed, such as socks, loose change and various items are wont to do, they are forever dismissed and left to the monster. I imagine that it has quite an eclectic collection of articles in its possession by this time, assuming that it retains any of this treasure.

On this occasion, I now found myself not only uncomfortable close to the dark, cavern-like space under the bed, but actually at face level with whatever had taken residence within. I saw two menacing red orbs, the monster's eyes glowing ominously from deep inside the darkness. It occurred to me the space beneath my bed seemed to have exceeded the rational limits that should be placed upon it by the workings of the physical universe. The monster's eyes at once seemed large and frightening while appearing to be a significant distance from me which would have placed the monster not only beyond the confines of the bed's frame but outside of the room, and perhaps the house, altogether. A glint of white alluded to the beast's fangs and I was sure that thick mucus was dripping from them as if this hideous creature was salivating at the thought of my tender flesh and sinewy muscle. It could have been anticipating a salami sandwich, I suppose, as I do not pretend to know the inner workings of one of hell's own spawn but the inference in those piercing, red eyes was of a more sinister intent.

I was momentarily frozen in place and deduced, shortly thereafter, that my continued existence had to do with the fact that the monster was probably as surprised to see me in this vulnerable position, as I have been steadfast through the years in my safety procedures, as I was to find that I was staring directly into its hideous face. I was able to regain control of my body and hurriedly scurry back to the safety of feather pillows and my down comforter before the monster could react. I have since occasionally tried to spy the monster from this vantage point, low to the floor albeit from the cautious distance of the hallway, and have not again seen the glowing red menace of its eyes. Perhaps it is sleeping or has retreated deeper within the lair that seems limitless in the evil space under my bed. Maybe the monster is wise to me and simply closes its' eyes to camouflage itself. Seen or unseen, I know it remains there.

2.

While the monster is surely a frightening thing to behold, even though I can only imagine the extent of its full repulsiveness, I believe that the images conjured up in my mind from these few glimpses and the noises it makes while doing whatever it is that it does beneath me at all hours of the night, are worse than an actual confrontation would be. H.P. Lovecraft once wrote that "the oldest and strongest emotion of mankind is fear, and the oldest and strongest kind of fear is fear of the unknown." One might think it unwise for me to read tales and essays regarding fear and monsters and horrors in general, given that I live with a monster under my bed. I believe, however, that it is my association with this creature that draws me to literary works of the kind. If I could but understand the "what" and "why" of the beast, perhaps that understanding would be enough alone to vanquish it or would allow me to find a way to do so.

I have recently come to the belief that the monster's life is predicated on my belief and fear in its existence. While it may pilfer the occasional half-eaten sandwich, partial can of soda or crumbs of chips, I am reasonably certain its sustenance is fear. It is this need for fear which restrains the beast from simply tearing through the box spring and mattress and pulling me with its' slimy, wispy haired, clawed hands down to an eager mouth. My death would be its' death, or at least precipitate a need for it to find other prey. This may have, in some small way, saved me from a gruesome fate on the occasion when I stared into the monster's face, although I think an actual confrontation would force its hand (or claw) and necessitate action on its part. I remain convinced that shock and surprise had a good deal to do with my continued existence.

Over the years I have given the monster plenty of food. My fear, while subsiding with age, is still immense. I would like to say I have come to terms with the monster and at times I believed I had, but given my theory of its need for fear, I think the beast has done whatever it found necessary to ensure that I could not simply drift off to peaceful slumber but rather have my fears rock me to sleep and fuel more nightmares. The glimpses of the beast may have been premeditated. Just as I was able to convince myself that the faint creaking was not the monster shifting position but the house settling, a shadow would sprint through my peripheral vision. When I determined the beast could not leave its lair under the bed, and that my only harm would come through the carelessness of proximity, the monster would prove its ability to wander beyond those confines. The very day that I proposed in my own mind that the monster could not interact with the physical world and existed only to cause fear, my cat disappeared.

My monster first came to live with me around my fifth birthday. I recall sitting with my father one summer evening, watching television. The local television station that carried the baseball games also aired a weekend horror movie festival. The show did not begin until midnight, and I was always safely in bed before the ghouls and demons and monsters began their celluloid rampages. On this particular evening, however, my father had fallen asleep in the chair prior to the Saturday night baseball game's completion. I was nestled comfortably in his lap, my head resting against his broad chest as his slow, rhythmic breathing sang to me like a lullaby. I drifted in and out of my own dreams, waking to the baseball game, then to an infomercial about press on nails and finally to the showing of the latest horror fare on the Midnight Monster Movie Madness Marathon.

I can't recall what horror features were playing on that night. I dozed in and out of sleep and only vaguely comprehended what was on the television screen. It's funny how the mind works, and even more so the mind of a child. I clearly remember the Lee Press On Nails commercial, although this could have been due to its regularity on television at the time. I know that the Detroit Tigers were playing that evening but only because they were our local team and would be the only sensible broadcast for my father to have been watching. This was some time before cable television, mind you. I do not remember who the Tigers were playing or the result of the game.

Whatever horror features graced the television that night, they left an indelible impact. It was shortly after this I began having nightmares and my monster came to live with me. As any child would, I asked my father to check for monsters in my room each evening and he would humor me by inspecting the closet and the drawers of my dresser and, of course, under the bed. He never found anything but I knew my monster was there. Only moments after my father would tuck me in and kiss me goodnight the monster would stir beneath me. It would, and still does, breathe heavily with a liquid sound. My monster growls in that deep, terrifying monster way; just barely audible. My monster also snores, or at least I think it is snoring. I find this both strangely amusing and helpful as I can ascertain when it is sleeping and make late night trips to the bathroom or kitchen much less frightening.

I know what you're thinking. My monster is a simple figment of my imagination; a childhood fear that I am yet to outgrow. To a degree, I would have to agree with you. I am sure my monster gained life somehow through my fears and nightmares and, as I've said, continues to feed on them. Believe me when I say, however, that it is real. It is as tangible as you and I. Is my monster special? I don't know. Do other children simply outgrow their fears and I am incapable of this? Or is my monster smarter than the average monster, and more capable, clever and tricky in being able to hold me at the precipice of fear?

In the end, I suppose it doesn't matter. I know the monster is there and what's worse, I believe I may have upset it.

3.

I've issued my monster an ultimatum. Just this morning, after I'd dressed and could foresee no immediate reason to re-enter my bedroom; I stood in the doorway at the hall and spoke to the room. A soft, morning light filtered through the curtains and the dust mites floated in the sun beams. The room looked very normal and anyone else would have never expected what was lurking within.

"You have to leave," I said. My words echoed in the hallway. I waited a moment, but no noise came from under the bed. I didn't really expect to hear any. Monsters are notoriously quiet during the daylight hours. I was sure it could hear me though.

"I'm not afraid of you anymore." I tried to sound convincing.

After thirty-odd years you might think I would have just accepted this peculiar relationship with my monster, but things change. I have recently met a woman with whom I believe I can have a long relationship. I've dated many women, as I've said, I am a normal guy, but this was different. I can see matrimony in my future and that means regularly sharing a bed with someone. I have shared beds with women but never my bed. My monster seems attached to whatever bed I use regularly, it doesn't follow me wherever I sleep. In the past, I have always made up reasons not to bring women to my home. Now it appeared that my bed was going to become her bed. I am concerned how this will affect the relationship between me and my monster. Will she be unaware of it? Will she be at some risk?

"Don't be here when I get home," I said. I was hoping to sound stern and firm but not too threatening. I imagined that it does not bode well to *really* piss off a monster. I closed the bedroom door and turned to leave for work. A loud thumping sound from behind me stopped me in my tracks only a few feet down the hallway.

I returned to the bedroom, hesitant to open the door. I knocked, just in case the monster was out and about. It seemed only courteous to allow it a moment to return to its hiding place. I had given the impression I would not be returning for a while, after all. I opened the door and found that the bed was askew in the room. It had been pushed or pulled or, perhaps, lifted and dropped given the sound I had heard. My nightstand had been shifted out of place and the alarm clock lay on the floor, the digital readout inverted so that 8:11 read as 11:8. Next to the alarm clock, a half-full can of Pepsi had tipped and emptied its contents on to the light gray carpet.

I wanted to believe the monster had decided to leave and disrupted the room during its exit, but I knew better. My monster was lashing out, throwing a bit of a tantrum. It seemed I would not be rid of him so easily and, quite frankly, I hadn't expected to be.

I spent my day at work in a bit of a daze. I found it hard to concentrate. I rarely think about my monster when I am not in my bedroom, save for the instances which called attention to it, such as the fears of a friend's child. Now it was forefront in my mind. I knew that this evening would be a moment of reckoning and I was not especially looking forward to it. It needed to be done; was well past needing to be dealt with, but I have little stomach for confrontation and the battle that I foresaw lying before me was enough to make me physically ill several times throughout the day.

My work day is over and I have made excuses to my significant other to avoid seeing her tonight. I didn't lie outright in telling her that I had been sick all day, I just didn't tell her the source of my illness. I've written this narrative as I sit in my dining room contemplating how to approach the problem in the bedroom. I have walked to the door of the room several times, waited and listened, held my breath, strained to hear movement of any kind. As of yet there has been none. Could it truly have gone? No. My belief and my fear tether it to this place, I am sure of it. It lives because I allow it to live. If only I could convince myself it is not real, but I know too well, after all these years, that it is real.

I've searched the internet several times, searching for tips on how to kill a monster. I have discovered an R.L. Stine story, in the acclaimed Goosebumps series with the title of How to Kill a Monster. It offers no real advice as the monster in that story meets its death due to an allergic reaction to humans. What a silly premise. Monsters wouldn't be monsters if they were allergic to humans, now would they? Besides, if my monster was allergic to me, surely I would have heard a sneeze or a sniffle from beneath the bed. I have gone several pages deep in my Google search and found nothing useful. If my monster were a video game monster I would be well prepared. If I had access to radioactive material or ridiculously powerful weapons like bazookas, I might have a chance. I don't think crosses or holy water or silver bullets will help me with my monster.

There is one prevalent theme beyond the gamers and horror movie buffs; beyond R.L. Stine's theory of allergic reaction which, I might add, can only be proven one way or the other by actual contact with the monster, at which point any back up plan would be far beyond implementing.

This theme is that to rid oneself of one's fear it must be faced. Of course, this falls right into my logic that my monster lives only through my terror and willingness to accept its existence. But more so, it suggests that perhaps my facing the monster, looking it in the eye and not backing down, would be enough to vanquish it. Then again, this plan seems perilously similar to hoping that the monster breaks out in hives, has its throat constrict and perishes through contact with my, presumably, toxic skin.

4.

I am in my bed now. I didn't bother to straighten it. The alarm clock and nearly empty Pepsi can remain on the floor. I tossed my laptop on to the bed from the door and made my leap from a good five feet away; hurt the hell out of my knee. I have a fresh Pepsi sitting on the nightstand. I had to throw it on the bed, as well, so I am waiting for the fizz to die down before I open it. The jump was still difficult as I had a peanut butter and pickle sandwich in my hand which I had to take care not to crush. It sits next to me now. I'll eat it when I am able to safely pop the top on my soda. It will be either a last meal or a victory dinner.

I have decided I have written this narrative for a number of reasons; I really wasn't sure why I had started it. It serves as a way for me to explore this situation. A type of self-therapy, I suppose. Somewhere in my mind I suspect I hoped I could convince myself this was all truly in my imagination. I did not succeed.

I also thought, perhaps, by exploring the situation I may have discovered a way to defeat my monster. Besides the obvious, just stop believing in it, the only thing I have come up with is, in recognizing its apparent aversion to my PB & P sandwiches, trying to force feed it some and hope that it chokes to death on it. Maybe the monster is allergic to pickles rather than humans.

Finally, I suppose I hope I can share this story with others who silently suffer with their own fears. Alert parents to the truth behind their children's fear so that they can take action early. Maybe if my own father had used "monster spray" to clear my room, becoming my ally and helping me to defeat the monster that terrified me rather than just satisfying himself that the room was clear of lurking beasts, my fear would never have developed into this salivating, red eyed denizen that waits for me now to make the first move in this dance of death.

As I shift to get comfortable, move to reach my Pepsi, I hear it beneath me. It matches my movements. I can picture it's great, greenish-brown body moving into position to lash out. I can hear it breathing. Its breaths are short and shallow, quick with excitement… or could it be its own fear. Yes, I think it fears me, or more precisely, it fears my increasing confidence. It lives because I allow it to live. It looks as I imagine it to look. My quickening pulse is its heartbeat.

My expectation of success grows as I continue to write these words. It is not the monster under my bed that I must defeat, it is my own mind. No longer must I let the darkness invade my thoughts. When I lay my head on the pillow I can allow my mind to search out happiness rather than terror. I will let the nightmares die with the monster. Its skin will dry out as it fades, no longer capable of excreting its toxic ooze. The wisps of hair will fall from it and become nothing more significant than the dust bunnies which it lies amongst.

Yes! I can feel it weakening. I can hear it growling, but these growls are those of a trapped animal not a threatening beast. It's scared!

My sandwich is delicious. The soda washes down the crumbs and frees the clinging peanut butter from the roof of my mouth.

For years and years I have lain in my beds, listening to my monster, taking care not to let my foot or arm hang over the edge for fear that it would reach up and grab me, pull me into the abyss beneath. No more!

The monster is angry. I hear the quick, sharp breathes coming faster. It is loud. I have never heard it so loud. My bed shakes. The monster's greatest strength, its most fearful quality was that it was an unknown. A glint of an eye that could have been a mere reflection, a low growl that was probably nothing more than the house settling, a soft scrape of claws across the bottom of the box mattress that, as I reflect now, sounded suspiciously like a scurrying mouse in the wall. My shaking bed is my own excitement. My own breath is quick and excited as I reach the moment of victory, not the breath of a monster.

I'll have another bite of my sandwich. Delicious! My Pepsi is empty but I have no fear of sliding my leg off the bed, dropping my feet to the floor and proceeding to the kitchen to get another. The monster is dead and, even now as I write, I am giddy at letting my feet dangle precariously out over the edge of the bed. I am wiggling my toes in the air, mocking my fear. I can hear breathing, growling but I am certain now that these are the noises of the house; my own breath.

Was that a sound under the bed? No, surely just the frame groaning as I wriggle with happiness. The monster can't be real, that would be ridiculous; childish. Did something slightly wet, with ticklish hairs, just brush my foot? I'd better stop typing for a moment and just check to be su

Author's Notes:

I don't care how often adults tell you that monsters aren't real. When you're a kid, you know adults are full of shit. Monsters just happen to know that kids are more tender and tasty and, generally, put up less of a fight. The only thing monsters find as delectable as small children is salami.

A friend read a draft of this story and asked why the protagonist didn't just place his mattresses right on the floor so that there was no space beneath the bed. I thought that would be obvious. If the monster couldn't retreat under the bed it would find another place to hide, like a closet, or it might just get really, really pissed off.

OBSERVATONS OF AN INDIFFERENT CORPSE

It took me awhile to realize that I was dead. At first, there was just darkness. I tried to blink my eyes but could feel nothing. Not the little twinge of muscle at the corners, not the feeling of my eyelids coming together or moving apart.

Then the darkness began to lighten a bit, turning to a sort of purplish haze. Streaks and swirls of yellow and white danced before my eyes. I recognized that my eyes were closed but that beyond the thin layer of skin, light was present. It seemed very matter-of-fact to me that I could not open my eyes. I wasn't scared or concerned in the slightest. I felt a general acceptance of the idea and, perhaps, even a bit of comfort in having resolved my momentary confusion.

It was then that I noticed an odor. It was a familiar smell and I recalled a neighbor on the street where I grew up. Her name was Fran. It's one of those names that have been largely lost to history, along with names like Ethel and Myrtle, and I was pleased I remembered it as I am notorious among friends and family members for my inability to retain the names of any but the most common acquaintances.

Fran was a friend of my mother's. She lived next door to us in a house which, like most on the quiet, suburban street, looked nearly identical to our own. As a child, I would accompany my mother on her daily visits to Fran's. They would drink tea or coffee and talk about the things that housewives talk about, as I sat in front of the television being entertained by the Sesame Street puppets, Mr.

Rogers or Popeye cartoons. This was prior to my school days and is one of very few memories I retain from that early age.

There was a particular odor to Fran's home. It seemed to have permeated the furniture, the drapes and the carpet. When Fran would visit our home, the odor would come with her. It was not unpleasant, but it did seem to me to be very unique to Fran and her home. In years since I have noticed that many people have an odor about them that seems to be all their own; some less pleasant than others.

It's curious, the power of a particular scent. I came to recognize, much later in life and through sheer accident, Fran's scent as that of a mixture of the powder and make-up she wore. Why it should be so distinguishable on her as opposed to many others who most certainly used similar products, my own mother included, I have yet to understand. At various times I have encountered a similar odor, as I was at the moment that most currently brought on this reflection, and always it was Fran that I was reminded of.

I could not describe Fran in any physical way. I have the vague idea that she bore the resemblance of a slightly older than middle aged woman who you might expect to be working in a diner. The type of diner with a long Formica counter and silver stools, with red cushiony tops that swiveled all the way around, bolted to floor along its length. She probably had a mole on her face. The reality of it is that I don't really recall what she looked like and I couldn't tell you what happened to her. She may have died or moved away but I have no recollection of her after about my turning the age of four or five, although I continued living with my parents in that same house until we moved elsewhere around my high school years.

As I ruminated on the odor and the memories that it invoked, I noticed a soft melody. It was quiet and felt somehow distant. It seemed that my senses were coming to me slowly, one by one, from whatever blackness I was emerging from.

It was then that I noticed the voices, as well. It was a din of conversation. I like that word; din. It seems to me to be one of those words that sound very descriptive of what it is intended to convey, an onomatopoeia. I recalled sitting in a school gymnasium, waiting for my daughter and her classmates to make their appearance before the gathered mass of parents and family members, to perform a play or a recital. This would have been many years passed as my daughter now is married and attending similar events for her own children. In that gymnasium there was a buzzing and humming of sound that floated up and over the audience. It was the various conversations taking place, each in their own small part of the room, mingled with each other into a single, indecipherable noise. What I heard at this moment was much the same, albeit quieter, as if all the conversations were taking place in whispered, reverent tones.

On occasion, a single voice would rise above the din, as if the speaker had moved closer to me. I was able to distinguish such comments as "at least he led a full life" and "I understand he died quickly, without suffering" and I understood that I was at a funeral. Of course the music made perfect sense in that context.

It was a few moments more before I recognized that it was *my* funeral.

I found that I was not scared, upset or even annoyed that I should be dead. Rather, I was curious as to how I was able to sense all that was going on around me if, as I seemed certain, I were a corpse. Suddenly, I could feel the weight of my body against the cushion beneath me. I could feel that my hands were lying folded at my waist. I hoped I looked nice and that my wife had chosen my black suit rather than the grey one, which I always thought had a funny cut and made me look a bit paunchy.

Of course, I was unable to move in even the slightest. I imagine that is a good thing as it would have no doubt caused a great deal of commotion among those who had come to pay their respects. Instead, I made a concerted effort to recall how I had ended up in this situation.

It took only a few seconds to recall that I had been driving back from a business meeting in Pennsylvania. It was snowing lightly but the roads were not in the least bit slippery. It was late in the evening; early March. Some snow had yet to succumb to the occasional warm days and covered the grassy median and ditches along I-90 in patches. It was a windy day and I found myself using the entirety of the lane in which I was travelling.

I was being lulled in to a nearly hypnotic state by the hum of the tires and the methodic flash of the lane markers as they sped past my car. I was driving faster than the posted speed limit, not an unusual occurrence, and was eager to be home. A couple of times I drifted a bit too far to my left, the growl of the rumble strip on the shoulder jarring me back to alertness.

I remembered that I was considering pulling off into the next rest area in order to stretch my legs, perhaps grab something to drink or even to catch a quick cat nap in the recline of my seat. The next thing I recalled was the growl of the shoulder as my tires again met the serrated pavement. This time, however, I must have really surrendered to my weariness as it was the passenger side tires eliciting the noise, my vehicle having traversed the entire width of the highway's shoulder. No sooner had I realized my predicament than the front, driver's side tire slipped off the shoulder and into the soft earth of the median, which grabbed at it greedily and pulled me even farther to the left.

Before I had time to react, I was trapped between two guardrails which had been strategically placed in order to restrict vehicles that may wander, or be forced, toward the median from colliding with the concrete support of an overpass. It was quite bad luck that I should find myself trapped by the very design which had been put in place to protect me. Had this occurred moments before or after the precise time that it did occur, I would have most likely been able to stop my vehicle or correct my heading. At worst I would have damaged the side of it as the guardrail restricted my movement any further left.

As it was, I was moving at an extremely high rate of speed toward a very imposing looking cement structure with no option of avoidance other than to bring my vehicle to an abrupt halt. Of course, all of this went through my mind in just a split second, the mind being

infinitely more capable than the body to react. I may have managed
to get my foot on the brake, I truly do not know, but it was obvious
by my current state that whatever reactionary measures I undertook
were woefully inadequate.

From the smell of the make-up and the recognition of the light
beyond my closed eyelids, I could ascertain that I had at least not
been horribly disfigured in the accident. I suspect a closed casket
would have been pertinent had that been the case.

And so I lay in state, as if I had other options, and listened to the
sobs and sorrow of friends and family. I heard the comfort that they
offered each other. I was struck again by my indifference to the
situation. It seemed that death had removed any feelings of sorrow or
joy, empathy or worry. I was left as a very cold and analytical being.
I thought of myself, at that instant, a bit like the unemotional Spock
character from the Star Trek series, observing the current events
from a purely logical standpoint.

I wondered how it was that I seemed to have no memory of any
time between the accident and the moment when I woke up in
darkness, here at my own funeral. I considered that this was
something I should probably be grateful for, should I have been able
to feel gratitude, as I am sure that being able to feel the pain of the
accident or the ensuing preparations of my body for burial, would
have been rather unpleasant.

I heard the voice of the priest calling everyone to attention for the
beginning of the service. This made me wonder how long I had been
in a state of nothingness and unknowing. It surely had to have been a

couple of days, at least. Time had little significance for me now, though.

As the eulogy began I wondered just why I wasn't with God in heaven, as the priest was assuring everyone that I was. Perhaps this was purgatory; being able to hear and smell and feel from within the shell that was your body. There were many nice things said about me, as I suppose is required at a such occasions, but they brought me neither joy nor comfort. I was an apathetic observer.

I heard the shuffling of feet and the quiet sobs as people filed past my body. I felt a hand or two on mine. I heard their prayers for me. I felt the wetness of tears as my wife kissed me softly on the cheek and I could taste their saltiness as they came to rest on my dry, cold lips.

I heard a soft creaking noise and the purple vastness in front of my eyes darkened to black as they shut the lid of the coffin. The white and yellow swirls of light remained; remnants of light dancing on the cones and rods of my eyeballs. I felt my body shift as I was lifted and carried to the waiting hearse. I could feel the bumps of the road as the hearse led the slow progression to the cemetery. I found it interesting that the driver was listening to a classic rock station during the journey rather than some Gregorian chants or something similarly suitable. I imagine that regularly transporting dead bodies eventually insulates one against the reverence and gravity of the whole death process though. And frankly, the rock music would have been my preference had I been asked.

Again, I was lifted and carried and then still. I could hear the wind blowing outside of my coffin. Some more words were said and then I heard the voices drifting away from me and the sounds of car doors slamming shut and vehicles starting their engines and driving off.

I lay there for what seemed like a long time. I was unsure if I had a real sense of time. I could hear the few, bravest birds who had returned early, bringing with them the hope of spring. The wind continued to whistle and howl about me. I felt a bit chilled.

After a while I had the sense that I was descending and ascertained that I was being lowered into my final resting place. I could hear the sound of heavy machinery above me and then the pounding of the dirt falling on top of the casket. It was reminiscent of a short, violent rainstorm; a burst from the clouds that lasted only a moment or two. As the dirt filled the hole and covered the coffin, the sound changed to a simple thump of earth meeting earth. The noise from the machinery faded to a dull drumming above me and then there was silence.

I lie here now simply waiting. Those who imagine me in some eternal paradise go on with their lives. Eventually their sorrow and grief will be a distant memory; an occasional remembrance brought on by a sight, sound or smell that reminds them of me. I wait to see what will happen next. I have no hope and I have no fear. I guess I am at peace or at least in as peaceful a state as I can imagine. There is no feeling of loss or grief or sorrow. There is no feeling of anything in particular.

Perhaps I feel just the smallest trepidation. Not a fear so much as a concern. If there is a heaven, I think I would like to be there soon. At the least, I think I would like for my senses to obey the physical laws of nature. My body cannot be functioning in any way that medical science would comprehend, so why should I be able to hear and smell and feel?

I can feel that it is warm here. Perhaps the insulating factor of the earth contributes to this and even the chemical reactions that must be taking place as my flesh decomposes. I do not expect it will pleasant to be able to smell my own body as it rots. Nor do I care to consider how long it might take for the worms and insects to find their way into my casket and what that might feel like. Perhaps I will be indifferent to all this, as well.

Author's Notes:

The idea of being buried alive ranks pretty high on most people's list of fears. So much so that, back in the day, coffins would sometimes be equipped with ropes attached to bells above ground, just in case the dead person wasn't so dead and happened to wake up after being entombed. Couple that with a natural fear of death and an uncertainty of what awaits us afterwards and you get this story.

The protagonist's cause of death was inspired by a road trip sighting of guardrails like those described in the story. What can I say? Sometimes I'm a bit of a pessimist.

Fran was a real person from my childhood and, every now and then, I catch a whiff of the odor that seemed to follow her (it wasn't necessarily a bad odor; it was just Fran's odor).

ROMEO'S CURSE

It's painful to love her.

It's not heart break because my heart has never had her; never been whole. Heart want? Would that be correct? She's so close to me, so often. Another brings her close to me, living the roll I long for, unaware.

We laugh together, we share the mundane moments of our lives; she has even discussed – in simple, unimportant ways - matters of love with me. Not my love though. It is a simple friendship borne out of proximity. And then, perhaps to her, it's not even that much. Nor more to her than a brief moment in time, a casual conversation caused only by a desire to avoid awkward silence when we are cast together by circumstance.

For me it is so much more. She smiles and I taste the victory of lightening her heart. A playful touch, one she may not even be conscious of, is like a warm embrace. I wonder what it must be like to be him. Does he appreciate these small moments? Unlikely. Those things are lost to time; blurred and erased by familiarity. Does he notice how the scent of her lingers long after she has gone? If she were mine would my feelings diminish, lose their strength and the power they hold over me?

These feelings should fade over time, but have not. What is this curse of the Creator? How cruel to allow such pain from desire. How torturous that such desire does not wane; does not succumb to the reality that the object of one's yearning is unattainable. Rather it burns hot, like a roaring fire, and then dims to an ember. And just when you believe that it has been extinguished, a slight breeze feeds it and the ember glows back to life and flares. And that breeze can be so small, yet so powerful. The mention of her name in conversation or the odor of her perfume as you walk by the cosmetics counter of a store can bring her bursting to life. The heat of the thought of her crashes into me and causes me to perspire, the image of her face filling my mind's eye and the sound of her laughter weakening me and making me nauseous with longing.

Is it love? It must be though I've had no chance to love her. I know her only through brief encounters, contrived conversations, the eyes of another and the dreams inspired by the confluence of them all and my own inflections.

Infatuation then. A silly boy's emotion. Yet it has gone on and goes on still.

Only lust, perhaps. No, I know it is much more than that. Perhaps, at the beginning, it was spurred by this primal want. Surely, it remains part of this aching inside of me. How soft I imagine her skin to be. Her face is radiant and smooth even though it is exposed to the same realities of life – wind, sun, worry, stress – that my beaten countenance experiences. Her thighs, her stomach, the shallow dip of her lower back must be silken. To feel that skin against my own would be overpowering. To kiss her lips, stare into her eyes as the heat of our love making melted us into one would surely cause my heart to explode from satisfaction and my body to collapse from sated hunger.

It is only in my dreams that I can have her. Only in a fantasy can I pull her to me and tell her how I long for her. In my imagination I lay with her, feeling her body breath within my arms. Even just to hold her in an embrace, her knowing how I feel and accepting it, would be so much.

I have thought that I must tell her. Oh how often I have dared to play it out in my mind! Forsake him! If I must be a pariah to him, to all others, I don't care as long as I have her. And if I cannot waylay her fears, what then? Would she consider a clandestine affair? If I can't have the fill of my desire, then I will take small sips, like a man in the desert searching for an oasis, water to immerse himself in and to drink his full, but grateful for even the smallest drop to wet his lips. Do I see it in her eyes? Does she, even in some small way, feel the same? Would she embrace me and tell me that she has felt the same and has been waiting for me to profess myself?

Fear has me suspended. For what if she is appalled? What if she thinks me horrid for casting the feelings of others aside in favor of my selfishness? If she does not return my feelings, could she understand that it is not that I want to love her, but that I must? I did not create her or ask that she should be brought into my life. How much simpler my life would be without these feelings; without her. I did not create myself, or these feelings within me. How many times I have prayed, with the same fervor that I should find a way to fulfill my desires, that I should be free of them.

Worse still, that she should let me know her heart has tormented her as well, but that she has overcome such fanciful wishes. For I expect, even if my love was returned to me, she is a stronger person and could put such things aside. For the sake of others she would repress her desires with the will of those men and women of the cloth who forsake all to their calling. Then I would know that the fulfillment of my dreams is ever so much more a reality but no more a possibility than it had been.

And whether sharing my feelings or horrified by them, what if she should then flee from me and avoid the situations that bring us together? Then I am left with nothing. Is it better to imagine and hope and dream? To see her smile, to inhale her scent, to hear her laughter, to touch her even in the most platonic of ways; if my senses were denied these small pleasures what would be left for me? Only the same, incredible ache that now tortures me, but with not even the smallest relief.

There are so many possibilities in which this want can cause me greater pain, and such a small chance at even the briefest fulfillment of my desire. Yet my heart screams in its agony, in its lust, in its yearning. And I think it may rise up against me, refusing to pump blood throughout my body in revolt, if I do not act. For the best, I think, for then I would be free of this pain. What of the afterlife, however? Did Romeo and Juliet find each other beyond the portal, free to love each other? Would she come to me there? And if that possibility exists, would it not stand to reason that if love can cross that threshold so can desire? I can only believe that death will free me. The alternative, an eternity of desire, is too painful to imagine.

Author's Notes:

Unrequited love; it's a bitch.

I know this story doesn't have anything supernatural or monstrous or evil, but sometimes life is horrific enough all by itself.

CROSSROADS

1

A light rain peppers the cracked windshield of the aging Cutlass. No sooner does Tom flip the windshield wipers on than he regrets the decision. Ripped and torn, the wipers leave streaks through his line of vision, making it more difficult to see than it was through the spattering of raindrops. The passenger side wiper screeches as it makes a slow, weak arc. The rubber has long since disintegrated and the metal of the wiper arm is threatening to mar the already damaged glass.

Tom squints as he leans forward over the wheel. The good news is that at 3:00 a.m. there are very few cars on the road; in fact the road is basically deserted. The bad news is that anybody driving at this hour is probably coming from a bar and shouldn't be behind the wheel. Tom is coming from a bar himself, he's had a few drinks but is fairly certain he could pass a sobriety test. He glances quickly to his left, then right, as he goes through an intersection, half expecting some drunken ass to blow through the stop sign and T-bone him.

Tom's knuckles whiten as he grips the steering wheel a bit tighter. He shifts in his seat, wanting to grab a Marlboro from the pack lying on the seat next to him, but deciding that he should wait until he reaches the stop sign a couple of blocks ahead. He glances in the rearview mirror to make sure nobody is behind him, and sees the deserted street falling away. Main street here is somewhere between big city and Podunk. Bars and restaurants line the road and the city has started trying to make this into a thriving, pedestrian-friendly downtown area. Most parking has been relegated to structures and lots behind the businesses.

His Marshall amp and guitar case peer over the seat at him. He sighs, feeling particularly tired tonight…well, this morning, technically. He'd run through four hours of music tonight at Slick Willie's. Jack, the owner, had insisted on renegotiating Tom's pay. Instead of the flat $300.00 and drinks that he had gotten for the last three gigs, he was now forced to take half the door and pay for his drinks.

He wasn't happy about the new arrangement but he was unable to scare up another gig this week, so he was pretty well stuck with it. With a band at nearly every bar on the strip, most of them playing standard covers that people want to dance to, there wasn't exactly a line forming to pay a cover charge to sit and listen to some guy playing the blues on his Strat. The crowd wasn't terrible, but the place was small. After paying his bar tab - a healthy chunk, granted - Tom netted a cool $50.00 for the night. He'd have to try a little harder on setting up something else.

He pulled to the curb as he neared the stop sign, in no hurry to get home; Mary and little Tommy would be long asleep. He lit his cigarette, leaned back into his seat and ran a hand through his longish, but thinning, blond hair. He thought about giving up on the music, for the hundredth time. The extra money, as little as it was, was certainly helpful but it was getting harder and harder to do a gig or two on the weekend and still take care of his responsibilities at home. He could probably talk to his boss at the factory and pick up a little overtime on the weekends, here and there, or even look for something part-time and steady in the evenings.

The dream of being a full-time musician was probably dead many years ago, but Tom was reluctant to admit it. The few demo tapes he would send off each year had never garnered much of a response outside of a form letter rejection and it wasn't very likely that an agent would be trolling Slick Willie's looking for new talent; "new" being a relative term for a 38 year old.

He put the car back into drive and continued homeward. A long, hot shower would make him feel better. Mary hated when he crawled into bed smelling of stale beer and cigarettes, anyway. Tomorrow was Saturday and he would get up early and take care of the yard work, maybe take Tommy down to the park for a game of catch or something. Jack had informed him that he'd *accidentally* double booked tomorrow night and had some cover band coming in so Tom's services wouldn't be needed. The fat, balding bar owner said he would call this week about next weekend's schedule. It sounded ominous to Tom.

Tom pulled into the little driveway that led to the little, one-car garage, which stood needing a new coat of paint behind the little, three-bedroom ranch. As he fumbled up the steps to the little porch he managed to stick his guitar case through the screen on the door.

"Great", he muttered, "one more thing to fix."

He crept inside as quietly as he could, shoved his amp behind the living room chair and leaned his guitar in the corner. As he started stripping out of his clothes he spied the two dinner plates sitting on the dining table. He could hear the familiar blues riff running through his head, as it so often did, and he started making up some silly lyrics in his head.

"Can barely pay the mortgage, and my house is a dump. So many nights I feel like a perfect, little chump. Don't see my wife and kid 'cause I'm trying to make a dime. But won't nobody help me 'cause they ain't got the time. Oh, I'm living those not quite middle-class blues."

With a slight, wry smile he made his way to the bathroom. So he wasn't Muddy Waters. Heck, he wasn't even slightly dirty water.

2

Tommy was riding his bike back and forth on the sidewalk in front of the house as Tom mowed the small yard. The boy waved as he rode past, his blond hair long and shaggy like his dad's. Mary was threatening that it was time for a back-to-school haircut, but they had let him grow it out for the summer to save few bucks each month. Tommy's smile was wide and bright, his blue eyes blazing in the late August sun. Tom envied his pure joy. No cares about money or work. He had a bike and sunshine and everything was right with the world in his mind.

Tom stopped the mower, wished he was six, and grabbed the half-full yard bag. He managed to get approximately three quarters of the grass clippings successfully transferred from the mower bag to the big, brown yard bag. He lugged it to the garage where it could sit and compost, probably destroying the bottom of the bag as it often did, until trash night on Tuesday.

Mary was in the back weeding the flower beds along the fence. He watched her for a moment. Her long, brown hair was pulled back into a ponytail and it fell softly over her shoulder. The back of her tank top shirt was damp between her shoulder blades and at the small of her back. Mary turned as if she felt his eyes on her.

"What?" she asked.

"Nothing," Tom smiled, "Just checking you out."

"Well, stop it," she grinned, just a hint flushed in the cheeks, "Get your horny butt back to work."

Tom laughed and did as he was told, grabbing the weed whip and the extension cord from the garage, stealing a glance down the driveway as he did, to see Tommy cruising by on his Huffy. His minor depression from last night was long forgotten. Life, he had reassured himself yet again, was not so bad. There were a whole lot of people worse off than he was. Sure, he had late bill here and there, wasn't able to take many vacations, but he wasn't so bad in the grand scheme of things.

With the yard work at least passable, Tom decided to see about getting the screen on the front door fixed. He called his son over.

"Go in back with your Mom. Tell her I'm running to the hardware store."

"Okay," Tommy said. "Will you get me something?"

"Sure. How about a box of nails?"

"No," said Tommy, giving his Dad the familiar 'you're such a goof' look, "some candy or a toy."

"I'll see what they have,' said Tom, ruffling the boy's hair.

3

Smitty's Hardware, the small Mom and Pop store that Tom liked to frequent, didn't have any screen in stock. Tom reluctantly decided to drive to the big chain store that had recently popped up in the new shopping center at the other end of town. He felt a little guilty pulling into the expansive parking lot of the shopping center, as if he were selling out to the national chains and leaving the folks at Smitty's to go the way of so many other small, locally owned stores.

The shopping center was anchored on one end by a Wal-Mart and on the other by a Home Depot, Tom's destination. The Wal-Mart and Home Depot stores stood alone with a strip mall sandwiched in middle. As he drove through the parking lot, he took note of the smaller retailers in the complex. There was a Chinese restaurant and a Hallmark store. A cellular place was squeezed between a pet supply store and a GNC. There was a dollar store and a clothing store, which looked to be just for women, and a Dick's Sporting Goods. What really caught Tom's attention though, was the music store.

It was the last store in the strip. The sign proclaimed the name as *The Crossroads* in plain, white block letters with a black background. The front display window was full of guitars. Tom decided to check it out after he took care of his business at the Home Depot.

It took nearly half an hour for Tom to get what he needed at Home Depot. A good ten minutes was blown just trying to find someone to help him. That someone wasn't really sure about the who, what, where, when or how of going about getting the screen repaired. Eventually Tom decided it would be easier to just buy a roll of screen and a roller to put the stupid, black rubber seal back in and fix the thing himself. Plus, it never hurt to have some screen and tools around for the next time.

After throwing the items in his car, he wandered over to the music store. The store was cluttered and haphazard. There were stacks of amplifiers, bits and pieces of drum sets piled on top of each other but unmatched, guitars leaning against walls, hanging on walls, sitting on stands and even leaning against each other in a teepee-like formation. Cords were piled on the floor like a den of snakes in an Indiana Jones movie. Band instruments – saxophones, trumpets, clarinets - were scattered throughout. Paths branched out from the front door and wound through the store like some sort of maze.

As he began picking his way through the place, Tom wondered how anyone could keep track of what was here and where in here it might be. Music books sat in piles everywhere and Tom considered that the store might not even be open for business yet. Maybe they were just starting to put the place together.

Eventually, he wound his way to the back of the store where he found a glass display case filled with pedals and other small electronic components, piled atop each other as if they had been thrown in there for temporary storage. A cash register sat on the far left corner of the case. The rest of the surface was covered with music books and various papers, so much so that he could see into the display case only from the front. Beyond the case, on the wall, was a peg board with various packets of guitar strings, picks and other assorted items hanging from it.

An open doorway led farther into the store, to what Tom assumed was a storage area. As Tom moved to get a better view into the back area, a body suddenly filled the space, startling him.

"Welcome."

4

The voice was deep, with a liquid quality to it. The man was tall, imposing Tom thought, probably 6'3" or better. His hair was jet black and slicked back on his head, hanging long in the back, not a touch of gray in it although his face was creased with age. He wore black jeans and a plain white t-shirt under a black suit coat; the sleeves pushed up on his forearms Miami Vice style. Black hairs were thick on his forearms and creeping across the top of his hands. His face was long, the cheeks shallow, his complexion pale.

The man moved forward, resting his long, thin hands on the top of the display case and leaning forward, "Can I help you find something?"

"I think it would be a small miracle if you could," said Tom, casting his gaze over the store. "I was just browsing really. Did you just open?"

The man smiled, his teeth stained yellow from nicotine, "Oh, I've been here awhile."

"The place just seems a little…unorganized," Tom said.

The man continued smiling but offered no explanation. Tom felt uneasy under the man's stare. He stepped back a step and scanned the display case, "Well, I could use a new pick up for my acoustic, the sounds a little flat. The one I have is sort of a cheapo."

The man said nothing, just continued smiling, waiting.

"Well, it could be me too, I suppose," Tom chuckled, trying to lighten the air between them, which felt heavy and thick. "Maybe I'm just a little flat."

The man straightened himself, pushing off the counter with an audible sigh. Six-four or six-five, at least, Tom thought. He craned his neck, rolling his head from one shoulder to the other, and Tom could hear the vertebrae crack as he did it, popping like bubble wrap in a kid's fingers. He held out his arm, offering his hand, the nails tapered and long. A fellow guitar player, Tom thought, and stepped forward again to shake it.

"Tom…Tom Drake," he offered as their hands met.

"Abaddon," the man said. As he grasped Tom's hand he closed his eyes and breathed in deeply, as if trying to savor a smell. Tom pulled his hand back, a little too quickly perhaps, but the man did not seem offended.

"Abaddon? That's an unusual name," Tom said.

"It's Hebrew," the man offered, "My friends just call me 'Bad'. It makes for a great stage name, like Slash or Edge or Sting."

Tom offered a smile, "Well, it's nice to meet you, Bad."

Bad walked around the counter and into the maze of instruments and equipment. Tom stood waiting, not sure if he should follow. After only a moment, Bad reemerged with a small box in his hands and handed it to Tom.

"This is an excellent pick up. It is particularly suited to a blues style," he smiled.

"That's just what I play," said Tom.

The tall, dark man nodded.

"Um…How much is it?" Tom asked.

"I don't think you're done just yet. You have what you've asked for, certainly, but not what you came for."

Tom frowned, "Like I said, I really was just browsing. I wasn't even looking to get this, but since I'm here…"

The man ignored him, walking back around the counter and into the back room. Tom stood waiting, again, thinking that this experience was getting a little strange. He turned in a circle, observing the mess of the store and wondering how Bad had managed to find the pick up so quickly. He hadn't even heard him moving things around; it was if it had been sitting right on top, waiting for him. After several minutes, Bad emerged from the storage room. He was carrying a beat up guitar case in one hand, with the other he swept away the books and papers on the top of the display case, letting them tumble to the floor, and then placed the guitar case on the counter.

"This is what you came for," he said, as he began unclasping the latches of the case.

"I really don't need another guitar. Besides, I don't have the money for one right now, anyway," Tom protested.

Bad did not look up at him, did not hesitate in his movements. He opened the case; the lid blocking Tom's view of what lay inside. For a moment Tom was certain that this absurdly tall, somewhat frightening looking man was going to pull a gun from the case, like in some old gangster movie, and cut Tom down right here in the middle of the store. Instead, the man lifted a guitar from the case, his long fingers wrapped around the neck. The overhead fluorescent lights reflected in the brilliant sunburst finish of the symmetrical body. The shape of it reminded Tom of the torso of a Rubenesque statue.

"This, my good friend is a 1928 Gibson L-1. Mahogany construction with an ebony fingerboard. It is in mint condition."

Tom stared at the guitar. It was beautiful, alluring, "That has to be worth a fortune."

"This guitar was made famous by Robert Johnson," Bad continued, "the Grandfather of the Blues. The great Eric Clapton, perhaps the only legitimate successor to Johnson, played it as well."

"Of course I know what kind of guitar Johnson played," said Tom. "Any bluesman worthy of the name knows that."

"No," said Bad, "you don't understand. It's not that he, or Clapton for that matter, played this type of guitar. They played *this* guitar!"

5

Tom looked from the guitar to Bad, then back to the guitar...then back to Bad, "You're trying to tell me that this is Robert Johnson's guitar?" He rolled his eyes and laughed, "In that case, I definitely can't afford it. It would be worth millions."

"Oh, it's worth far more than that," the man smiled, "but priced very reasonably."

"So do you have some sort of proof of authenticity?" Tom said. "I mean, it's a beautiful guitar, probably worth a few grand, no doubt, but really...Robert Johnson?"

The man smiled, those yellow teeth on display, and waited.

"Okay, how do you know this guitar belonged to him, or even to Clapton?"

Bad closed the lid of the case, setting the guitar on top of it. He leaned forward, and as he did his eyes changed from a dark, hazel shade to a pure black, as if the pupils had swallowed the color.

"Because I gave it to him," he said.

Tom stumbled backward, bumping into a pile of amplifiers that teetered and threatened to collapse. He stammered but said nothing.

Bad walked around the counter but to Tom it seemed as if he floated. His gaze never left Tom's, who stood there shaking, unsure of what he'd seen.

"Sorry about that. I know it's a bit disconcerting. It's really just for dramatic effect, you know."

Tom wondered if it had been a hallucination or if he was having some kind of dream

"It's weird," said the tall man, suddenly looking older. "I always find it funny when I reveal myself. People are quick to believe I am actively causing havoc all over the globe, influencing people to murder, steal and rape. Frankly, I find that sort of involvement unnecessary; humans are quite capable of those actions all on their own. Still, they are always amazed to meet me."

Tom could feel his heart rate returning to something resembling normal, "You're the Devil."

"The Devil, Lucifer, Beelzebub, so many names. And Abaddon, of course, is one as well. I wasn't yanking you're chain, son."

"You run a music store?" Tom asked, still hazy from the shock.

"For you, Tom. For *you* I run a music store. You see, despite the fact that I am not out in the world creating crime sprees or natural disasters, it is true that I am in the business of souls. The hard part about that is that I lose so many on their death beds. God…yes, He's as real as me and you…He has this annoying policy of instant forgiveness. So even when someone who has been one of mine for so long, has a change of heart, I lose them. It's quite a bitch."

Tom was now pretty convinced he was dreaming. And with that thought came a sense of calm.

"Anyway," the devil continued, "I do have a standing agreement with the "man upstairs" (he made quotation marks in the air with his fingers as he said it) that I can buy souls. Trade for them is probably more appropriate, although sometimes it is as simple as giving someone money. The whole contract thing I am sure you've heard of. I have the power to give people things, fame, and fortune, whatever. In return, I get their souls. And with the signed contract there is a no death bed salvation clause."

"And you want my soul," Tom said, regaining his voice.

"Of course," the Devil spread his arms, "I want everyone's soul." He leaned forward and winked, "It's kind of my thing."

"So, what's the deal?" Tom asked, feeling now as though he were bargaining for a used car. "I get the guitar, become famous and rich, etcetera, etcetera.

"Is that what you want?" the devil asked.

"Eternal damnation seems a pretty high price," Tom said and was surprised to find that he was thinking of how to work this bargain.

The devil pulled a pack of cigarettes from inside his suit coat and offered one to Tom, who took it, "Now watch while I light it with my finger."

The devil pulled a bic lighter from his pant pocket, "Just kidding," he winked again. He lit his cigarette and then Tom's. "The smoke does remind me of home, though," and he laughed.

"Really," the devil went on, "it's not all fire and brimstone and pain. It's an absence from God. A loneliness of sorts. But you would have company. Lots of famous people. Just think of some of today's stars. Haven't you ever wondered how some of them managed to become famous with so little talent?"

"I'm not talentless," countered Tom.

"Oh, I didn't mean to offend. Some people just happen to ask for fame, no strings attached, so to speak. Two words for you, Paris Hilton."

Tom considered this, "What's the catch?"

"Your soul for all of eternity isn't enough?" the devil questioned. "Don't think of me as such a terrible being, Tom. You can't believe everything you read. Have a little "sympathy" (he made the quotes in the air again). Great song by the way."

"No, I'm talking about tricks. Robert Johnson ended up drug addicted and died young. If you're saying Clapton is on your team, how involved were you with his drug problems or his son dying?"

The devil smiled, "I only said Eric had this guitar for a while. Johnson, of course, is legendary for selling his soul, but with Clapton, I am sad to say, I didn't seal the deal."

"Just the same, you know what I'm talking about."

"I give people the ability to be what they want to be; in your case, a famous bluesman. With money or fame comes opportunity. Should you be of a nature predisposed to addiction, you just need to be mindful of that." The devil took a long drag from his cigarette and blew the smoke toward the ceiling. "Tell you what," he reached back and grabbed the guitar, extending it out to Tom, "Just give it a try."

Tom took the guitar and knelt on his left knee, resting the supple curve of the body across his right thigh. The wood was warm in his hands; he could feel the heat on his leg. He let his thumb strum over the strings. The sound was beautiful, each note blending seamlessly with the next. He let his fingers find their place on the frets, / G7, C7, G7 -/ C7 - G7 - / D7 C7 G7 -/

6

"One of my favorite songs," said the Devil as Crossroad Blues came to life, but his voice was distant in Tom's mind. Tom's eyes were shut.

He could see a theater full of people; he could feel the heat from the stage lights on his skin; small beads of sweat forming on his upper lip. The audience sat silent with rapt attention, soaking in the sounds from his guitar. They hung on every note and watch as his fingers dexterously flitted up and down the neck of the guitar.

A slight burning on his chest.

He heard the applause, ringing in his ears, as he finished his song; the audience standing, clapping and screaming his name.
His chest hot. He wonders if he's having a heart attack.

He makes his way back stage. Beautiful women reach for him. A man grabs him and leads him through a rear door to a waiting limousine. Inside there are two, young, gorgeous blondes. One hands him a glass of whiskey as the other moves up against him.

That burning still in his chest. He sees his arm; puncture marks; veins raised.

He's in a large mansion. It's a large party, beautiful people everywhere. Famous people. They all want a piece of his time. He laughs with them, the charming host.

A newspaper headline: Blues Star Divorces.

He's on a boat in the middle of a blue sea; so bright that he can't tell where the sky ends and the water begins. Another theater. No, an arena. Thousands of people chant his name. In the spotlight he can't see them but he can feel their energy. It's intoxicating.

Another headline: Estranged Son Commits Suicide. A tombstone.

Tom's eyes popped open. The Devil smiling. Tom's chest burning. The guitar was heavy in his hands and he let it drop. He stood and stumbled back through the clutter of the store, knocking over guitars, bumping his leg on a bass drum and falling to the ground. The Devil strode toward him, concern and confusion on his face. Regaining his feet, Tom felt for the door, backed into the window display and heard the guitars fall against the glass. He turned, spied the door; lunged for it.

Running for his car, Tom glanced back over his shoulder to see the tall man, dressed in black, leaning in the doorway, looking younger; looking like an ex-hippie who couldn't make it in the rock world and who now spent his days behind the counter of a small music store.

"Dude, don't you want the pick up?"

Tom fumbled for his keys, pressed the tab on the fob to unlock the doors. He collapsed into the seat, shaking, sweating, hardly able to catch his breath. He placed his hand on his chest over his thrumming heart. Tom felt a burning under his palm and pulled his shirt away to see the crucifix he always wears, the one Mary bought him a few years ago for Christmas. When he got home and jumped in the shower, saying only to Mary that he is not feeling well, he will noticed that the cross has left a mark on him, a brand.

Inside of the store, a man dressed in black picked a vintage guitar off the floor. He placed it softly in an old, battered case and carried it into a back room. He smiled, his teeth yellow from years of smoking, and looked toward the ceiling, "You're not playing fair."

7

It would be weeks before Tom would drive past the strip mall at the far end of town. He would do it only after convincing himself that the experience had been only a nightmare, something brought on by the sudden flu that kept him in bed for days. He could not explain the curious mark from the crucifix on his chest. Mary would say it was an allergic reaction, certainly odd not to have occurred over the years but maybe something to do with him being sick and his immune system changing. He refused to abandon the necklace, just the same.

As he drove past the strip mall he saw the Wal-Mart, Choo's Garden and the Hallmark store. The GNC was there, but the last store in the line, where Tom had expected to see a music store, was an antiques store called The Last Chance.

Curious, Tom pulled into the parking lot. As he walked toward the antiques store his heart began to beat harder. He opened the door and a collection of bells rang above his head. An older woman, late sixties, very grandmotherly in appearance, glanced in his direction. She was wearing a black knee length skirt, a black knit sweater over a white blouse. Her hair was gray and curly, cut short, and the glasses that hung from the beaded chain on her neck reminded Tom of a school teacher. She turned her attention back to the sandy blonde in front of her, mid-thirties Tom guessed, attractive in a bookish sort of way.

The store was cluttered, tables and chairs in no discernable order, lamps and bric-a-brac piled on top of any flat surface. The older woman was handing a small box to the blonde.

"I'm sure your mother will love this figurine, it will make an excellent gift," she said.

The blonde took the box, staring at it as if she wasn't sure what it was. Yes, she said, her mother would love it and wasn't it funny that she had just stopped in to have a look around, noticing the store for the first time. How convenient that she was able to find something she could use.

The older woman put a hand on her shoulder, "Did you say you were a writer, dear?"

Did she say? She must have. Poetry mostly, but she was working on a novel. The next great, American novel, she laughed.

"Well then," said the woman in black, "what I think you would really be interested in is right over here."

The older woman led the younger past a jumble of furniture and Tom had to move deeper into the store to watch them, feeling intensely uncomfortable, but unable to leave. The women stopped in front of a desk, the kind of sturdy, well-built desk you don't see any more.

"This desk belonged to Edgar Allen Poe. It is practically alive with history and stories," the older woman said.

The blonde gasped and put her hand to her chest. Oh my! It was so beautiful and, coincidentally, Poe was her favorite writer. But how expensive it must be!

"You'd be surprised at the price," the old woman replied, and she smiled, her teeth stained yellow.

Tom fled the store, wondering if the young woman happened to be wearing a crucifix.

Author's Notes:

Selling your soul to the Devil is an old, but entertaining, plot…and I really want to be able to play guitar better than I do…and strip malls scare the bejeezus out of me.

I've always thought that if the Devil does exist, he'd probably be kind of funny and a hoot to hang out with; until you were dead, anyway.

QUIET TIME

Geoff woke to the sunlight streaming through the slats of the blind on his bedroom window. Glancing at the bedside clock, he was both pleased and disappointed to see that it was 7:30 am. He was pleased because he had trained himself to wake up at this time each morning, having abandoned the shrill, buzzing alarm; disappointed because he really had no reason to be awake so early today and wouldn't have minded sleeping in a bit.

No birds chirping, no sounds from the street; Geoff heard only the sounds of himself. His breaths echoed in his skull, the thumping of his heart seemed to pulse just inside his ear canal and the dull hum that made him feel like he was living underwater remained a constant. Geoff found it still took a few moments each morning to adjust since he started wearing the ear plugs.

The water thrummed inside his head like a million fingers tapping a tabletop as he showered. Settling into his easy chair, coffee in hand and morning paper retrieved from the front porch, Geoff flipped on the television. CNN was reporting on the current status of the S.H.E. outbreak and Geoff read the ticker as it scrolled across the bottom of the screen, glancing up to the caption box to read what the anchor was saying. Geoff enjoyed trying to read the lips of the anchor to determine what he was saying while the caption box was catching up with its three to five second delay.

Three cases of S.H.E. have been confirmed this week in California. CDC officials have released a statement reiterating safety procedures that are suggested for the public. The total number of cases of Spontaneous Human Explosion in the U.S. has exceeded 100 for the month of March.

Geoff wonders how many people are actually listening to the anchor's voice and how many had taken to keeping their televisions on mute. Many people have brushed off the CDC warnings. Many would probably consider Geoff paranoid, like the people that walked around with surgical masks during the bird flu scare several years ago, but he doesn't care. He saw the effects of S.H.E. first hand and something like that tends to unnerve a person.

He would admit that when the first cases were being reported he was as skeptical as anybody. The idea that a person could just blow up for no reason seemed pretty ludicrous. The initial occurrences were assumed to be terrorist activity, some radical with an explosive device that went haywire. As more and more cases came in, the scientists started looking into it a bit more thoroughly. After all, it seemed unlikely that terrorism was involved when that kid in Des Moines blew up right in the middle of kindergarten during a class rendition of Twinkle, Twinkle Little Star. All of a sudden – POP! – and little Johnny was so much stew spread all over the classroom.

When 20 people burst at a Kid Rock concert in Detroit, things got real serious. At that point the CDC came in and was in panic control mode. Geoff had heard that an arm had actually landed on the stage, only a few feet from Kid Rock and that the bass player had taken a hit to the eye – WITH AN EYE! None of that was official, of course, but there was nobody questioning that the 20 people blew up and when the footage of the interviews afterward came out there was a curious swelling and noticeable redness to the bass players left eye. After watching the news for an hour or so, Geoff decided that there was no new information worth paying attention to; a few more cases, but no major occurrences. No new information narrowing down the cause, just the same old hunches he'd been hearing for the last month.

Spontaneous Human Explosion differs from Spontaneous Human Combustion in that the body actually blows up, or out may be more appropriate, rather than is incinerated. Spontaneous Human Combustion has always been met with skepticism as only 100 cases or so had been reported in the last few hundred years and most of those were dismissed upon further investigation. Spontaneous Human Explosion was a reality. Although cases were, thus far, relatively sparse – 10,000 in the United States over the last year – they seemed to be increasing and, given the population size, chances were exponentially better that you or someone you know would explode than the chances of, say, winning the lottery or being hit by lightning.

Geoff scanned the morning paper, not expecting any additional, useful information, and read, for perhaps the hundredth time, what the scientists had been able to determine thus far. Certain individuals (which they had no way of identifying) have a certain chemical makeup within their bodies (which they could not yet define) that caused them to explode within range of certain sound frequencies (which appeared to vary among cases).

Case studies suggested that people with poor dietary habits, those that ate a lot of foods with additives and preservatives and didn't process them well (fatties), were more susceptible to S.H.E. than others. This had a dramatic effect on the Ho-Ho industry, as one might expect. In the end though, the real bitch of it was that you just couldn't be certain if you were likely to be a human grenade or not.

Geoff was reasonable fit. He exercised regularly and ate fairly well, although he wasn't opposed to the occasional Ho-Ho. The current thinking was that the chemical anomaly that lurked within certain people was a result of a poor diet. It made sense to Geoff to think that the human body was changing based on the crap that we jammed into our food products, and thus ourselves, these days. You could look at any pre-teen and see the changes yourself. Geoff couldn't remember a single girl in his sixth grade class that had breasts. These days, you had to go training bra shopping before a kid's baby teeth fell out. It also made sense to Geoff in that all the cases of Spontaneous Human Explosion had occurred in developed countries.

For all intents and purposes, Geoff was at a very low risk for S.H.E. However, having seen somebody actually explode, he had decided not to take his chances and had been living in self-induced silence for the better part of three weeks.

He'd been at the supermarket and happened to be at the opposite end of the aisle from an overweight man who was piling a number of two liters of Diet Coke into his shopping cart. This man was significantly overweight, probably falling into the obese category although Geoff wasn't exactly certain what the rule of thumb was on that. He could remember hearing the Muzak cut off, an orchestrated version of some rock song or another, and one of the store advertisements coming on. Big sale on fresh ground chuck in the meat department, and then – Poomp! – the sound of someone jabbing a balloon with a safety pin.

Geoff had just enough time to glance down the aisle, see a mass of blood, tissue, skin, bone and clothing staining the linoleum with beams of goo emanating out from all directions like a water balloon full of paint and Jell-O had been dropped there. Bits and pieces of the guy coated the rows of soda on either side of the aisle and Geoff noticed what appeared to be pieces of skull and hair stuck to the ceiling. "Holy shit," he thought, "that fucker just blew up." Then the screaming started.

Whenever Geoff thought back about that day, he always found himself surprised at the relative lack of force the explosion caused. It explained, however, the fact that bystanders were rarely harmed when somebody did blow up. People blowing up was dramatic, for sure, but it wasn't as if it was a Roadrunner cartoon in which Wile E. Coyote fed them a bunch of TNT pellets disguised with a birdseed sign. As people exploding goes, it lacked a certain dramatic flair. Even at the Kid Rock concert, when those 20 people burst almost simultaneously during *Rock and Roll Jesus*, there were very few other injuries, barring those that got trampled in the ensuing chaos to get out of the place and the ironic injury to the bass player.

Geoff pulled a fresh set of earplugs from the industrial sized box he had bought at Sam's Club and rolled the soft material between his fingers. He quickly stuffed them into his ears as he pulled out the used ones, with a healthy coating of yellow wax on them, and flipped them into the trash. He grabbed the shooting muffs that he had laid on the kitchen counter, the ones he had bought from the sporting goods store just last week even though he didn't own a gun, and put them on as well. Picking up the radio that he once used for background noise while he did household chores, he went out to the porch and waited.

A week ago Geoff had gotten into a bit of an argument with his neighbor, Tom. Tom and his wife were in their forties, maybe pushing fifty, if Geoff were to guess. They were strange people who could seem fairly normal one minute, waving hello or complimenting him on how the current landscaping project was coming along, and in the next breath be throwing a hissy fit over something ridiculous.

This last argument began because Tom was unhappy that Geoff's grass clippings, from mowing the lawn, were defiling his driveway. There had been other arguments in the past. Tom didn't like when Geoff had friends over to barbecue in the summer, "making all kinds of racket and blaring the music" as Tom had put it. He'd gone so far as to call the police on one occasion and report Geoff as a nuisance – at 4:30 on a Saturday afternoon. That particular episode had not ended on a happy note for the neighbor when he spied the responding officer having a Coke and munching on a hot dog in Geoff's backyard.

During what Geoff liked to think of as *The Great Grass Clipping Controversy of 2014*, Tom had gotten very heated. Tom was not a small man. In fact, he weighed in at 320 pounds and his wife was pushing the three bill mark as well. During the yelling, Geoff had a brief moment when he thought that Tom may keel over from a heart attack right there on his driveway, falling face first into the offending grass clippings. Of course, Tom probably was yelling louder than normal to compensate for Geoff's earplugs. Tom and his family did not bother with any sort of hearing protection, despite the fact that they fell squarely into the profile of those most likely to be susceptible to S.H.E.

Over the next few days Geoff decided to run a few experiments. This was primarily a distraction to fill some of his day as he had opted not to go into work anymore. He was very ineffective as a salesperson due to his earplugs, anyway. The better part of his day was spent asking "What?" and "Huh?" and "Excuse me?" since he couldn't hear particularly well. Given the option to stay home or dispense with his safety procedures, Geoff had chosen the former.

Geoff brought several of his CDs out to the porch and, whenever he saw his neighbor, he would turn on the radio's CD player and look for a reaction. He never turned it on too loud; just enough so that he was certain Tom could hear it. The experimentation obviously held some inherent danger to Geoff himself, which is why he had invested in the shooting muffs.

This went on for three fruitless days. On the fourth day, however, Tom paused on his way down the driveway as the opening guitar riffs of AC/DC's *Highway to Hell* reach his ears. As the drums kicked in, Tom grabbed at his stomach, as if he was experiencing a sudden case of indigestion which, given the man's obvious dietary habits, wasn't entirely out of the realm of possibility. He belched loudly, shook his head as if clearing some cobwebs or the regurgitated taste of some bad takeout, and continued on his way.

Geoff, while not entirely convinced that AC/DC was responsible for the reaction, was still encouraged by the results. He really hadn't expected any reaction no matter how long he sat out on the porch or how deep he went into his CD collection.

Now he waited on the porch again, knowing that his neighbors would soon be making their way out of the house and into the car waiting in the driveway. Every Saturday morning they went out to breakfast; Tom, his wife and their teenage son who, like his parents, was grotesquely overweight, going 350 if he went an ounce. Geoff didn't have to wait long.

As the family members waddled their way toward the car, Geoff checked the volume control on the radio to ensure it was all the way up. As they squeezed into the car, the shocks and struts groaning their disapproval at the weight, Tom looked over at Geoff, probably wondering what in the world this idiot was doing listening to a radio with a set of ear muffs on. Geoff smiled at him and gave a quick "Hey, neighbor" wave that Tom responded to by glancing away and turning his nose up as if he was above interaction with Geoff. Geoff continued to smile.

Geoff pressed the play button on the radio and Angus Young blared from the speakers. Even through the earplugs and shooting muffs Geoff could hear the guitar and he had a moment of uneasiness. Feeling no ill effects, he returned his focus to the car in the driveway next door. All three of the occupants were staring at him, their faces scrunched in anger. Obviously they could hear the music even though the windows were rolled up.

Tom's look of anger suddenly melted away and was replaced with a look of perplexity. In the passenger seat – Tom's wife almost always drove and Geoff suspected it was because she had the least trouble fitting behind the steering wheel – Tom's hands moved to his stomach and his cheeks puffed out, staying there like he was vomiting but trying to hold it in. Geoff saw, rather than heard, the explosion this time. The car shook slightly side to side and the windows were immediately coated in gobs of skin, blood and what Geoff assumed were parts of internal organs.

He was surprised how much green was mixed in with the expected red and black. The whole incident looked a lot like what you might imagine the end result of mixing a puppy and a microwave might be.

The car shook again and it was obvious that a second explosion had occurred. Additional amounts of goo splattered against the window. Before the vehicle could cease its swaying, a third eruption was evident. Geoff sat on the porch, staring at the car, his smile gone, a look of dumbfounded astonishment in its place. His hand floated to the radio and, without removing his gaze from the car, he pushed the stop button. Again there was silence, save the sounds of his body; the thumping of his heart considerably faster than it had been when he had woke up.

Later that day, the CNN anchor reported the case of a family that had all spontaneously exploding in their vehicle. Scientists postulated that because they had shared similar diets, because the son in fact shared the same genetic makeup, it was not that unexpected that something like this could occur. In fact, it lent credence to earlier assumptions that the chemical makeup was similar in many people and that they would be affected by the same sound frequencies, as evidenced in the mass explosion at the Kid Rock concert.

In the evening, after the investigators had left and the vehicle and its gruesome contents had been towed off to some high security lab, Geoff fired up the lawn mower. He used to like listening to his iPod while he cut the grass but that wasn't an option these days. As he crisscrossed the lawn, the sound of the lawnmower faintly registered through his ear protection and in his head he sang a rock and roll song, paying no mind to where the stray grass clippings fell.

Author's Notes:

I've had some neighbors I didn't care for very much. This story is a little fantasy of self-indulgence. They pissed me off and I wrote this story as a means to vent. It's one of the best things about being a writer; killing people when you want to with no consequence.
It really did help; very therapeutic.

And neighbors, if you're reading this, writing the story relieved me of most of my anger...but I still think you're a whole family of flaming assholes...and I wouldn't mind seeing you blow up.

THE BLOCK

1.

"It's fantastic, Jake. But then…I wouldn't have expected anything less."

Jenna Shelley sat at her large, mahogany desk in her office on the twelfth floor of Black Sky Publishing. She swiveled in her plush, leather chair and looked out the window, seeing but not really registering the buds beginning to creep into the trees of Central Park. Trees that looked as though they had been plucked from the ground, flipped over and dipped in the cadmium green of an artist's palette and stuck back in place; the color dancing only on the tips of the branches. The manuscript of *Shared Heart* sat on the desk; the faint hum of distance spilled from the speaker phone.

"I'll have Caroline e-mail the edits over for your approval and start working on the legal mumbo-jumbo. Take some time to relax and I will get in touch with you once we have a timeframe for publishing, and to approve the cover art, of course."

At the other end of the phone line, Jake Stowe – whose Connecticut driver's license identified him as Jacob Stowinczak – basked in the praise from his editor. He could visualize her glowing in her office; an office his numerous best sellers had helped her attain. To be fair, however, she had dug his first novel out of the slush pile back when she was barely out of college and working at Dragonfire Press; a small, now defunct, horror publisher.

"I'm glad you like it, Jenna."

"Since you're last book is just starting its paperback run, we'll probably hold this one off until the Christmas buying season." Jenna swung her chair around, rested her elbows on the desk and her chin in her hands, leaning toward the speakerphone, "I swear Jake, I don't know how you churn these things out so quickly."

"I've told you before, sweetheart. They come to me in dreams."

That evening, Jake Stowinczak – because that was how he thought of himself regardless of the nine bestselling horror/suspense novels sitting on the shelf in his study, emblazoned on the spine with the solid block, gold lettering spelling out STOWE – sat in front of his television and checked his e-mail on his laptop.

After deleting the garbage that the spam filter missed, regretfully opening a dozen "jokes" from friends and family that failed to evoke the mildest laughter and saving messages that his website manager had forwarded with the implication that they may have a personal resonance of some sort or warrant a response directly from the author, Jake opened the pdf. file from Jenna's assistant.

In general, the edits were spelling errors that had slipped through the spell check program or grammatical issues. It didn't take long to breeze through the mark ups after he had printed them out, he and Jenna had been at this a while now and they were pretty used to each other. As usual, she wanted to delete all the commas – a trend that Jake found increasingly annoying with his editor as well as within the books he read. How the hell do you inflect a pause? How many times had he had to reread a sentence that didn't make sense because the words ran together? He compromised and allowed some of the commas to be removed, but held fast where he thought they were required. He smiled at the final note she had added to the last page – *What about the dedication?*

She'd thought it was a cute dedication for the first book. The second time, she'd asked if he didn't want to dedicate to his mother or father. The third time she'd grown a little angry, but what could she really say? By that time Jake had become a hot name and she had gotten a lucrative offer from Black Sky, contingent on bringing her rising star with her. It had been a no brainer. Dragonfire was struggling and didn't have the type of resources that a big, New York publisher could offer; they couldn't offer the fat advances, either.

Jenna had suggested that he dedicate the fourth book to his fans; something that he had no real opposition to other than that he felt the standard dedication was required and, quite frankly, he didn't see the need to mess with a good thing. After that, his editor didn't really pester him about the dedication anymore. Don't bite the hand that feeds you, and all that. It did, however, become a running joke between them. With each round of edits, Jenna would make a comment, generally on the last page as she did this time, in reference to changing the dedication. Each time Jake sent the mark ups back, he would include the dedication page; large, scribbled, capital letters spelling out *STAYS!;* underlined several times, next to the circled dedication reading *For My Muses.*

Jake piled the edit pages next to his printer, in his study. He would scan and e-mail them back to Caroline in the morning. He made a cup of instant coffee and spent a few minutes on the porch enjoying a cigarette and the quickly evaporating heat of a fine, spring day as night fell over his home. He had built this house after his fourth book had "gone platinum," as he liked to say. Just outside of a quaint New England town, on slightly elevated land that allowed him to see the roof tops of the stores and homes inside the town proper, it was exactly what his idea of an author's home should be.

He snuffed the cigarette in the butt bucket filled with sand that he kept on the porch; he didn't like the smell of cigarette smoke in the house. Draining the last of his coffee as he walked in the kitchen, he dropped the cup in the sink and headed up to bed with a collection of short stories he had been meaning to get to as soon as he had time. He knew, despite the coffee, that he would be lucky if he got through one whole offering before beginning to nod off, waking to reread the last sentence or two, nodding off again, and repeating the process until he finally put the book aside and succumbed to his dreams. He looked forward to the dreams though; looked forward to seeing his Muses.

2.

The first time they came to him was as he was struggling through his first novel. Jake had been pacing back and forth in his small, squalid, Detroit apartment, chain smoking cigarettes and cursing that the space wasn't large enough for him to even attempt to complete a full thought before having to turn in another direction.

He stalked into the tiny kitchen, the avocado-green paint, that had been applied when the apartment building was built in the late 60's, had faded to a pale jade where it could be seen through the years of dirt and grime that could no longer be cleaned away and had accumulated to become a part of the walls. He opened the refrigerator, stared in at the nearly empty shelves, considered grabbing the last Pabst on the bottom shelf, grunted, and slammed the door shut so hard that the floor trembled.

Stomping back to the living room, which also served duty as the dining room and his office, he dropped onto the couch and stared into the corner at the glowing monitor of his IBM computer. The cursor blinked mockingly at the end of an unfinished sentence. Jake ran his fingers through his longish hair, sighed, snubbed his Winston in the ashtray (that apartment smelled so bad that the odor of cigarettes was a blessed mask) and lit another.

He stood and walked to the window. The glow of the computer was the only light in the apartment; he saw it reflected in the glass. Outside, the neon sign of the liquor store across the street threw yellow, blue and red light across four figures. They were huddled close together, appeared to be passing something, or some *things*, between them. Drugs?Guns?

Jake considered returning to the kitchen for the beer, looked at the pile of empties next to the computer and thought better of it. The digital clock on the microwave reminded him it was almost midnight. He'd need to get to sleep soon. The first kids got to the school around seven; the ones that still cared to show up.

Only a year prior, Jake had been teaching English at Jefferson High School. Though he only had a handful of students that showed up regularly and his pay was well below the state average, Jake had enjoyed teaching, convincing himself that he was getting through to at least one or two kids each semester and, maybe, making the slightest difference that would help them escape the poverty-stricken, crime-ridden neighborhood. He had been laid off, indefinitely, just prior to the winter break. Merry fucking Christmas.

He'd spent several weeks trying to find another teaching job and had eventually settled for a "temporary" security guard position with a placement agency. He had been sent to a downtown warehouse to serve as a night watchman for two weeks, while the regular guard was on vacation, and then, ironically, back to Jefferson High to man the main entrance doors and listen for the metal detectors to alert him to anyone trying to sneak in a knife or a gun.

It was humiliating, seeing the kids he had taught and his ex-colleagues each day. It had spurred him to work on his book, the novel that he had been planning on writing for the last two years, but it still made his stomach churn and threaten to revolt each evening as he thought about walking into the school the next morning in his blue, A-1 Security jacket with the red badge sewn on the arm. The faculty members avoided his gaze and the students liked to ask him if the rent-a-cop business was better than teaching; just to get a rise out of him. In both cases, he would try to focus on the job as he felt the flush burning into his cheeks.

On that evening, eight years ago, ruminating on the sad state of his life, the job he hated but would trudge to the next morning anyway and the chapter and a half of a book that he really didn't feel was that good and that he couldn't find the words for to type another sentence, Jacob Stowinczak leaned over his avocado-green kitchen sink (which had, presumably, once matched the walls) and deposited the better part of a case of Pabst beer and hard, chunky bits of the day old pizza that had served as his dinner. He turned on the faucet, rinsed the mess away, washed his face with the cold water, rinsed, spit and wobbled to the bedroom. He collapsed on the bed, fully clothed, waiting for sleep to take him. He tried to muster up tears for himself and the sad state of his life – a twenty eight year old chain smoking, ex-teacher, rent-a-cop who could barely afford the rent on a shithole apartment in a seedy neighborhood, who had illusions of literary fame but not the will to write.

He hoped the release of tears would bring relief and that he could cry himself to sleep, awaking with renewed hope as he did when he was a child. The tears never came but, eventually, the sleep did; and the dream.

In the dream, three beautiful women floated toward him. They wore wispy silks about their bodies which flowed and ruffled softly in the wind he could not feel. He knew they were sisters though their appearances were not particularly alike. The first had hair like spun gold, or what he imagined spun gold to look like when his mother used to read him the Rumpelstiltskin fairy tale when he was a boy, and eyes so blue that it looked as if he were looking through them to the sky behind her. The second woman had long dark locks and coal black eyes to match, while the third was a redhead with shimmering green cat's eyes.

They surrounded him; caressed him. Their whispers were like a soft breeze and at once as if each were talking separately and at the same time as the others.

"Write for us," they whispered, soft hands stroking his cheek; fingers running through his hair.

"Write a story, a great story. For us."

With each whispered demand scenes of his novel played through his mind. The blonde leaned in to kiss his lips. As softly as a butterfly alighting on a flower he felt three sets of lips touch his own. Their silks fell away and he rolled with them in his dream, touching three; no, only one; then two. He felt himself melt into them.

"Write for us," they crooned.

"Write for us," they moaned.

"Tell us a story," they sighed.

When Jake awoke, the clock told him it was 3:00 a.m. He felt fully refreshed, alive and, for the first time in weeks, inspired. He nearly ran to the computer, wiped away the drivel he had typed and started anew. Three hours later, several thousand words were on the computer. His hands were shaking, sweat beaded his forehead and his heart threatened to thump its way out of his chest and into his lap. It took all his effort to tear himself away to go to work, but he did, and for the next several evenings he rushed home to his shit hole apartment and threw himself into the story, the words pouring out of him effortlessly. He had to force himself to stop in order to eat, and at those times he would reread what he had written.

His words seemed almost unfamiliar. As he read the work from each session he could hardly believe how magnificent it was. Historically self-deprecating, Jake could find no fault with the work. At the end of each night, though loathe to stop, he would retire expectantly to the bedroom to meet again with his Muses, for he was certain that that was what they were.

Nine novels later, Jake didn't work as feverishly as he did those first weeks, but still he was a prolific author. The Muses did not visit him each night, but frequently. He found that as he wrote the Muses became more affectionate, feeding on his words, gratifying him in his sleep as reward. He would make love to them in his dreams and awake sated, his sheets stained from his ejaculations. He thought of them as his lovers and had no desire for others. They inspired him to write and he wrote to please them.

3.

The next day, Jake sent the edits back to New York.

4.

A week after approving the final cover art for *Shared Heart*, Jake sat in his office at the back of his home, the Dell notebook computer humming contentedly in front of him. The cursor blinked in anticipation on a blank page of a Word document; Jake cracked his knuckles, wiggled his fingers and leaned over the keyboard.

In the darkness of midnight

He hit the back space key.

Robert – back space – *John* – back space – *Rutherford* – back space.

Jake found that, for the first time in years he did not have a story waiting to pour out of him. He tried to think if he had formulated his previous books' plots prior to sitting down to write them and couldn't recall doing so. It always seemed to just come out. He thought that he must have had the basic story in mind before starting, but he couldn't say for sure. Jake decided to take a walk into town to clear his head; take some time to run some ideas through his brain and then come back and get to work.

It was mid-morning. The day was cool but promised to warm up nicely as the sun continued to rise. Jake stopped in at Mary's Diner for a light breakfast and some coffee, but mostly to sit and think.

Danielle, a flirty blonde waitress whom Jake suspected was eager to have him ask her out, though not entirely certain, took his order and filled his coffee cup.

"How's the game, Shakespeare?" she asked.

"Good, thanks," Jake said. "I just sent the latest down to New York; getting ready to start something new."

"You'll sign my copy when it comes out, right?"

"Don't I always?" Jake asked. "Besides, if I didn't, there's no telling what you would do to my food."

Danielle smiled and softly touched his shoulder as she turned to put his order in. Jake stared out at Main Street as it began to come to life. He tried, unsuccessfully, to formulate the first paragraph, even the first line, of a story. By the time Danielle returned with two over-medium eggs, a side of bacon and white toast, he could feel a headache beginning to bloom behind his left eye. He opted to put writing thoughts aside, busied himself with his breakfast and leafed through the four-page Warnbury Gazette, a complimentary copy of which he obtained from the wire stand by the front door of the diner.

Jake wandered over to Betty's Books. He thought, not for the first time, how quaint this small town was and how innocent even the names of the businesses were; Mary's Diner, Betty's Books, Joe's Auto Repair, Johnson's Hardware. The window display prominently featured all of the Jake Stowe novels, in paperback and hardcover, lording over the latest offerings from other authors. Somehow, even though his new releases were always displayed in a matter befitting a best-selling author in stores like Barnes and Noble and Borders, he felt a particular sense of pride and accomplishment in seeing such devotion from the local bookstore, despite the fact that they surely accounted for less than a percent of his actual sales.

The bells jingled above the door as he entered. Betty, the gray-haired, bespectacled proprietor who looked exactly like a small town book store owner should look like, cast a glance over her shoulder, smiled and returned to sorting books in the Children's section; both shelves.

"Something particular, Jake?" she asked.

"Just browsing today, thanks," Jake replied to the back of her head.

Jake made his way through the bookshelves, glancing at everything, registering nothing. Fifteen minutes later he was walking back home with nothing in his hand or in his mind.

He spent the afternoon and early evening finding small projects around the house to occupy his time. He was restless. Usually when he was restless, he wrote. Unable to write, he became even more restless. He lay in bed that night, anxious for sleep; so anxious that sleep wouldn't come. Somewhere in the middle of the Late, Late Movie (*The Bad News Bears Go to Japan*) he finally dozed off.

His muses came to him and, subconsciously he breathed a sigh of relief, but his breathe caught in his throat seconds later. They didn't float to him. They didn't embrace him. They hovered several feet away. There was something off. The gleam was gone from their eyes. Their hair had no sheen; it hung flat, looked dirty. Their normally porcelain skin had a gray pallor. For what seemed an eternity they glared at Jake. There was a flash of blinding light, images of flames licking up at the sky and sharp, hungry looking teeth.

"WRITE!"

It was a shriek of the word that Jake felt more than he heard. He awoke, bolting upright in his bed, the covers disheveled, pillows on the floor and a cold, thick sweat covering his body. He sat there panting for several moments as he willed his heart to stop racing.

5.

It was just after four in the morning when Jake awoke from his nightmare; the first nightmare he could remember in several years. He didn't bother trying to go back to sleep.

At 7:00 a.m. he found himself sitting at the kitchen table, staring out the window, halfway through his second pot of coffee, watching the first rays of sunlight peer over the horizon. Despite the massive amounts of caffeine he had been pumping into his bay, Jake was able to calm himself and had begun rationalizing the situation.

"Not a big deal," he said to himself. Talking to himself was a habit when he was working; a necessary evil of bachelorhood, as far as he was concerned. "So I've got a little Writer's Block. It was bound to happen sooner or later. Just relax. Let it happen."

The nightmare was bothersome, but surely just a manifestation of his stress, just like the dreams were a sign of his satisfaction of his life and work. He spent the morning swinging in the hammock in the backyard, working his way through the short stories of other authors; not feeling any inspiration but enjoying the book. After lunch he sat down in front of the computer, stuck a John Coltrane CD in the disc drive and waited for the words…and waited…and waited.

He opened his web browser and searched Writer's Block. He found plenty of examples of successful authors dealing with it. Cures for The Block included sitting down and writing (duh), examining deep seated issues behind The Block (okay) and not being too hard on yourself (right). Eventually, Jake came across some potentially useful suggestions like looking at pictures for inspiration (he spent two hours clicking through web images of everything from monsters to landscapes to paparazzi photos of celebrities) or using one line suggestions that could spur a story like *What's in your fridge?* And *Write a story around a song title* (although this felt very plagiaristic to him, Jake tried it anyway; without success). In the end, the cursor continued to blink on the empty page of the Word document; no longer appearing anticipatory but rather mocking.

Returning to the hammock in the early evening, a new book from his office in hand, Jake decided to try to make the best of the situation. He could take this opportunity to catch up on some reading. It wasn't as if he needed to write for the money, he could easily retire on what he'd made the last few years. He wasn't under any sort of deadline with the publisher. Maybe he'd take a vacation, he thought. He felt better as he tried to convince himself that if he had nothing to write about just now, he just wouldn't write. Still, deep inside he was concerned. Forty five minutes into *The Boy in the Striped Pajamas* (a good movie that he anticipated the book would surpass) he dozed off with a gentle breeze rocking him in the hammock like a baby in its mother's arms.

The images were immediate; fiery eyes, sallow skin, sunken cheeks, clotted, scaly hair. A flash of fangs, claws, a sulfuric odor. He felt a pressure in his chest, a push; hard, angry.

WRITE!

Shrieking, screaming tore through his mind. Heat burned his face. He felt a searing pain across his abdomen.

WRITE!

He felt himself falling and awoke to find the ground rushing at him; hitting it hard as he fell from the hammock and realizing the impact was real only after he lay on the cool grass for a few moments, the stars clearing from his mind and the blood from his nose wetting his cheek.

Jake stumbled into the house, staggered through the kitchen, leaving a trail of blood droplets in his wake, and leaned over the sink, cupping cool water to his face and wincing each time he touched his broken nose.

6.

With bits of paper towel stuffed into his nose and a dizzying headache, Jake made his way into the bathroom thinking a shower would help him clear his mind. He looked in the mirror, his eyes already blackening, and groaned at the blood soaking into his Rolling Stones Bigger Bang Tour t-shirt. He felt an ache across his stomach and then noticed the duller, soaking from the inside out blood stains toward the bottom of the shirt. Lifting the shirt he saw four, bright, enflamed scratches running east to west across his belly.

"Looks like I was mauled by a fuckin' Puma," he said aloud as he tried to think what part of the hammock he could've scraped to leave the marks and then remembered the pain from the nightmare.

Stripping out of his clothes, he soaked under the steaming jets of water from the showerhead. He considered whether or not to go to the hospital, an hour's drive away, for his nose, felt it gingerly and decided it was essentially straight and he'd wait for the swelling to go down before making the decision.

He spent the rest of the night searching the computer about dreams and ghosts and poltergeists. Nothing seemed right and, at 2:30 in the morning, leaning back in his chair and smoking a cigarette (smell be damned) he found himself thinking of things to do that weren't going to sleep. His gaze fell over the shelf that supported the hardcover copies of his novels, the name STOWE glinting golden in the light from the desk lamp. He pulled one down at random, opened to the dedication page and read:

For My Muses

He set the book aside and typed *muses* into the web browser. He read a number of entries and was only slightly surprised to find that, although it was typically noted that there were nine muses, more ancient texts reported only three. He found nothing to suggest that the muses were evil in any way until he came across a comment, hardly more than a footnote, that suggested the earliest sources of information on the Muses, suggested that they were one and the same with the Furies, each being aspects of the same goddess in her creative or destructive phases.

Jake typed *furies* into the browser. Also known as the Erinyes (literally "the angry ones"), the Furies were the avengers of the ancient world. Clicking from entry to entry, he found that it was believed that once the Furies had decided to take vengeance on someone, there was no stopping them. They would continue until they were satisfied that the punishment was meted out, which usually meant the death or insanity of their prey.

As Jake read on he noted that the Furies were considered fearful but just. They punished crimes. The Furies took particular umbrage with the biggies like murder and rape and they weren't especially fond of adulterers. They also exacted punishment for crimes against the rules of society. They would protect beggars and dogs and even punish those who stole the young of birds.

Jake considered what crime he could have committed, momentarily cursed himself for falling into such a ridiculous superstition, and then went back to reviewing his offenses; just in case. He had certainly never killed anyone, not outside of his stories anyway. He'd never been married so he had no opportunity to be an adulterer and, although he may have taken advantage of a girl or two that had a bit too much to drink, he'd never done anything that would qualify him as a rapist.

Further research, back and forth between Muses and Furies, only slightly clarified anything. The Muses, apparently, didn't take very kindly to anyone claiming superiority over them, having punished the singer Thamyris, who claimed he could sing better than the Muses, by maiming him, taking away his voice and his memory.

Idly, Jake reached for his coffee cup and was surprised to find it cold. He noted the soft, morning light beginning to fill his study and realized he'd spent the entire night in front of the computer. While this wasn't exactly a rarity, he'd never done it before without writing something.

Tired, but still unwilling to sleep, Jake opted to walk back down to Mary's for breakfast. He also wanted to check in at Betty's and see if she might have something on Greek Mythology on her shelves.

7.

"Jesus H. Christ, Shakespeare!" said Danielle when she saw Jake's face. "Get a little fresh with one of your groupies?"

Jake forced a smile, though it hurt clear through his head, "You know I only have eyes for you."

"Yeah," she said, "a couple of black ones. What happened?"

"You'd hardly believe it, but I fell out of the hammock in the yard and broke my fall with my face."

Danielle half stifled a giggle, "Tell ya what, free dessert when you're up for it."

Jake smiled, it still hurt, and gave the waitress his order; the usual. When they arrived, he picked a bit at his eggs, nibbled a piece of bacon and decided his stomach wasn't ready for food. He finished his coffee, left his money on the table and walked over to the bookstore when he saw Betty arrived and unlock the door.

Betty was still placing her things behind the counter when the bells rang over the door.

"Well, you're here early…" she stopped mid-sentence. "Jake, honey, what happened?"

Jake shrugged, not really feeling like relating the story again.

"Those critics are getting rough," Betty said.

Jake smiled his painful smile, "Just a stupid accident."

"You look awful, boy." Betty walked around the counter and gave him a once over. "I mean, besides the nose, you look like you haven't been eating or sleeping. You're too thin to skip a meal, boy. Not like these farm boys around here."

"I'm good," said Jake. "Really."

He glanced around the bookstore and then hurried to change the subject.

"I was wondering if you might have some books on Mythology around?"

Betty smiled and said she was sure she could dig something up. She shuffled off to the back of the store and returned a few minutes later with three books.

"I've got two on Greek gods and what not, and one here on Native American myths."

"I'll take the Greeks," said Jake.

"Research for the next best-seller?"

"Yeah," he replied.

"Well, as always, bring 'em back in good shape and there's no charge, but if you dog ear a page or spill your coffee on it, you bought it."

"Fair enough. Thanks, Betty."

"You get some sleep and some food in you, young man," Betty called as Jake made for the exit. "And slow down on the coffee and cancer sticks. Gonna give yourself a stroke."

Jake waved over his shoulder as the bells jingled above him and headed home. He sat on one of the deck chairs in the yard, no more hammocks for him for awhile, and flipped through the mythology books. The first only had a passing reference to Muses and Furies, the second a bit more information. Along with the story of Thamyris, which he learned was from the Iliad, he read about nine daughters that the Muses turned into magpies.

He found nothing he hadn't already found online about the Furies and certainly no information on how to deal with either them or Muses, should they have it in for you. As he sat in the yard, the books resting closed in his lap, he wondered if he wasn't going a bit nutty.

"Of course," he laughed at himself, "that's what they do to you, right?"

Retrieving some aspirin from the bathroom medicine cabinet, he chased them down with a beer and returned to the deck chair.

"Writer's Block and a bad dream or two and I start getting all freaked out," he said to a squirrel, scrambling across the yard. "I should just write about this stuff. Whatcha think, Rocky?"

The squirrel stared.

"Yeah, your right. Deal with the headache first. Maybe a quick nap and then some work."

8.

In his dream, they came to him. They were lovely again; bright eyes, flowing dresses, shining hair. He embraced them, he felt their skin against his, felt the warmth of their breath. His hands ran across their bodies, caressing the crevices and curves. He stroked their hair. He felt something thick in his hand, felt it squirm.

Jake opened his eyes and saw the snake wriggled through his hand. The Muses pinned him down and hovered over him only they weren't his Muses anymore. They were thin, skeletal, and their skin was dark as coal. Their eyes burned with fire and blood leaked from them and down their cheeks. Fangs dripped saliva and it burned like acid where it fell, searing his chest. Snakes writhed in their hair.

Jake opened his mouth to scream and a serpentine tongue darted into his mouth, stifling him. He could feel it, them, it felt like a hundred snakes, slithering down his throat, coiling in his chest, biting and constricting around his heart.

Outside of his dream his body convulsed. He grunted and flopped from the chair onto the deck. The squirrel that had been investigating the yard for left over acorns, scurried up a nearby tree.

9.

Jenna Shelley sat at her large, mahogany desk reviewing the press release.

Jake Stowe, was found dead of an apparent heart attack at his home in Warnbury, Connecticut on Friday. The author had recently completed his latest novel, Shared Heart, and was beginning work on a new book.

Mr. Stowe, born Jacob Stowinczak, was 47 years old. His body of work included several New York Times Best Sellers, three of which had been adapted into successful movies.

She set the paper aside on her desk and hit the intercom button on her phone. Her assistant picked up.

"Yes, Ms. Shelley?"

"Caroline, can you come to my office please. I'd like you to get this press release down to marketing."

A few moments later, Caroline, entered the office, knocking courteously as she did so. Jenna handed her the press release.

"Have this sent over to the Times. Let them know we'll be issuing more information later."

"Yes, ma'am," said Caroline as she took the paper.

Jenna picked up a pile of papers from the corner of the desk. "You can get these in, as well," she said, looking over the edits Caroline had brought her the other day, for Jake's latest, "last" she corrected herself, book. "You know, it's funny," she went on. "After all these years, that he should make this change and it end up being the last thing he wrote."

Jenna was looking at the last sheet of the edits. In her handwriting she read: *What about the dedication?* Next to that, in large, block printing, as always, Jake had written *STAYS!* and underlined it several times. Except this time, that had been crossed out and underneath he had written, in the chicken-scratch printing she had become so used to:

For my fans; without whom none of this would be possible.

P.S. This time only, Jenna. ☺

Author's Notes:

I have never (knock on wood) experienced what I would consider writer's block. Certainly, I've struggled with a plot or a character or just where a story is going but, to date, I have never been at a loss for something to write about. Personally, I think "Writer's Block" and "Muses" are crutches writers use to excuse themselves from being lazy.

This story grew out of one word, "Muse," and then applying the simple "what if" technique; as in: What if my Muse was a real bitch?

A BUTTERFLY'S WINGS

It came across the ocean like a tsunami. It was a great wave of pestilence born in a far off place; the product, perhaps, of the proverbial butterfly flapping its wings and altering the destiny of places that sat peacefully on the other side of the globe.

A cruise ship lay in its path and, if anyone had been paying attention to witness it, they would have seen its lights flicker briefly before winking out entirely. The glow of the ship snuffed out along with the lives of those aboard.

Like a swarm of locust, it moved without sympathy or concern for what lay ahead of it. It reached the shores of the east coast of Florida in the late hours of the evening as most were surrendering themselves to sleep. In the hour when the clubs were just beginning to reach their crescendo of the evening; young women in tight, short dresses feeling the effects of the alcohol, allowing young men in baggy shorts, sports jerseys and studded, shimmering ball caps to press up against them in a dance of simulated sex.

It crept upon the sand and turned the grains dark, as if a large cloud had stolen across the moon and cast its shadow across the beach. It wafted over the lapping waves which fell silent as they were overtaken. The palms, which stood like sentinels along the shore of the ocean, withered, turned brown and drooped toward the earth. As if succumbing to a changing of seasons, which was foreign to the temperate, southern climate, the fronds fell to their death and the bark turned black as the disease washed over them.

Concrete and asphalt cracked and crumbled as the shadow rolled over the sidewalk and roadway that ran parallel along the ocean. The wrought iron railings on the hotel balconies overlooking the Atlantic pitted and rusted as if one hundred years of neglect had befallen them in only a few moments of time. They sagged, crumpled and fell away from the stucco façade of the building.

Tourists, enjoying the late evening breeze, sipping late night margaritas while lounging in the deck chairs outside their rooms, had only a few seconds to ponder the curiosity of the events. Their flowered shirts fell away from their skin only a heartbeat before the flesh itself began to sear and turn to dust.

The tendrils of the storm, the disease, the death that crept across the ocean silent and unforgiving reached only a few hundred yards across the mainland before losing the power to continue; a power given to it by the tide, the waves or the ocean breeze. A space two miles wide and creeping the length of a few football fields from the shoreline died in the span of a few seconds. Decimated. Unexplainable. Unprecedented. Unheard of.

Several hundred lives and years of development destroyed. They would search for answers but find none. A confluence of just the right ingredients, at just the right time, hundreds of miles away destroyed a small, vibrant Oceanside community.

The place would remain desolate for many years. Eventually it would be rebuilt, grander than before, and it would thrive. It would remain, however, only as long as God or nature allowed it. In a far off place, the seeds of death would be released again, perhaps to float harmlessly skyward to dissipate in the atmosphere but possibly to be pushed out to sea by the soft flapping of a butterfly's wings as it emerged from its cocoon.

Author's Notes:
This story came to me as I sat on a balcony in Boca Raton, Florida, enjoying a glass of wine and an absolutely gorgeous evening with a view of the ocean only yards away from me. That, in such a beautiful setting and under such lovely circumstances, my mind wandered to something horrific probably speaks volumes about my mental state, in general.

HAVE TO

1

BEEP!BEEP!BEEP!BEEP!

Jeremy Robbins opened one eyed and glared at the alarm clock on the nightstand. He fumbled his arm out from under the comforter and felt for the snooze button.

"Ten more minutes," he mumbled under his breath. "Ten more minutes before I *have* to get up."

He rolled over and pulled the comforter over his head. He could feel the soft, slow breathing of his wife asleep next to him. The warmth from her body radiated beneath the heavy cover. He tried to drift back to the dream that the alarm clock had wrenched him from but could only think of how the seconds were ticking by and how, with each breath, he moved closer to the moment of having to get out of his warm, comfortable bed and begin his day.

Although the alarm clock was electric, with a digital display, he swore he could hear the seconds ticking off, one by one. Unable to drift back to sleep, Jeremy pushed off the comforter and swung his feet to the floor. He turned the alarm clock off with four minutes remaining before the snooze period expired.

By the time Jeremy got out of the shower, his wife was up and preparing the kids for school. He stared at himself through the dissipating steam on the mirror. He wondered, not for the first time, what happened to the young man he had been only yesterday. Who was this person staring back at him now with crow's feet spreading around the corners of his eyes, gray hairs invading the area above his ears – Good Lord, even *in* his ears - and a second chin that currently needed a shave.

"You have to drop the kids at school on your way to work," his wife informed him as he adjusted his tie. "I'm waiting for the cable guy to get here. They said between eight and noon."

Jeremy quietly nodded his assent as he trundled to the kitchen to make a cup of coffee to go. He stared at the empty coffee pot.

"Oh, we're out of coffee," his wife called from the living room, "you'll have to pick some up on your way home. Try to remember to grab some milk and eggs, as well, would you, dear?"

Jeremy loaded his son and daughter into the car, thinking about having to do this and having to do that, and began his day without a drop of caffeine.

2

"Dad?" his son began as he hopped from the car in front of James Madison Elementary, "There's a scout meeting tonight. You have to have me to the rec center by six o'clock."

As he drove to Franklin High School his daughter informed him that she had made the cheerleading squad.

"Congratulations," said Jeremy Robbins.

"Thanks," his fifteen year old replied, "you have to write a check for $150.00. It's to cover the uniforms and stuff. I need to turn it in on Monday."

Again, Jeremy nodded silently.

"Love ya, bye," she said as she scampered toward the school doors. No kisses; not even on the cheek anymore. Not even a hug.

Jeremy checked the time on the radio clock. If he hurried he could stop by 7-Eleven or McDonald's and grab a coffee without being late to work.

"I *have* to get a coffee."

Jeremy Robbins got his coffee - extra sugar, extra cream – and arrived three minutes late to work. His boss glanced at the clock on the wall as Jeremy walked passed his office.

3

"That's fifteen minutes, Robbins!"

Jeremy rolled his eyes at his boss's comment, as he settled into his small cubicle. He wanted to tell his boss to go fuck himself. A minute or two late and now his already meager check was going to be docked fifteen minutes. How many times had he stayed late because he *had* to wrap up some pressing contract? Too many too count and not once was he paid an additional amount on his salary for it. Come in a few minutes late or have to leave a little early...well, that was something altogether different.

Of course, Jeremy couldn't tell his boss to fuck off and he didn't dare complain about his pay or the unfair treatment. He had to have his job.

He looked at the gray walls of his cubicle, the piles of paperwork on the desk, the small clock next to his computer that seemed to be under entirely different laws of time and space since it moved so incredible slow each day. Jeremy knew he had to just shut up and take it. He could feel the weight of the thought, a thought he had most every day, bearing down on his shoulders and he knew that by the time his little clock told him it was time to leave the office he would feel like Atlas with the weight of the world on his back.

"Have to work. Have to pay the mortgage. Have to buy the groceries. Have to keep the lights on. Have to, have to, *have to…*"

Jeremy had heard that there were people who loved their jobs. It seemed a very foreign idea; perhaps athletes or actors, maybe doctors. As he waited for his computer to boot up, he was certain nobody, none of the other prairie dogs who popped their heads up from the surrounding cubicles from time to time, could love this job.

"Robbins," his boss's voice snapped him back to the moment. The big man stood leaning at the cubicle opening that served as the door to Jeremy's work space. "I need that Johnson folder completed today, whatever it takes. You'll have to stay late if necessary."

"I have something scheduled with my son this evening."

"Well, if you don't get it done by the end of the day, I guess you'll need to be in here tomorrow. I need it on my desk Monday morning."

Another Saturday working for free was not an appealing idea. As the boss lumbered back to his office, a real office with a window and actual working door, Jeremy thought, "That fucker probably loves *his* job."

4

At 8:00 o'clock that evening, Jeremy warmed up the plate of dinner that he hadn't had time to eat between getting off work and taking his son to the scout meeting. He ate slowly, staring at the television but not really watching it, already dreading the beep, beep, beep of the alarm clock that would wake him tomorrow morning.

"I have to work tomorrow," he told his wife, who was seated across the living room, hand sewing a new merit badge onto his son's scout sash.

She looked at him, released a sigh of contempt and let her face fall in that disappointed way that faces do when the person behind that face wants to let you know just how disgusted they are with you.

"What?" Jeremy shrugged. "I have to get some work done."

After a pause, and although he didn't really believe it, he added, "It's important."

His wife turned her attention back to her sewing, as if ashamed to even look at him, "I thought you were going to get the outside work done this weekend. It's going to be snowing before you know it. The gutters need to be cleaned out, the last of the leaves need to be cleared. I thought you were going to cut the lawn and fertilize one last time."

"I'll have to do it when I get home...or Sunday."

Have to...

"I don't suppose you're getting paid for it."

"You know I don't get overtime," he said, thinking it was pretty low of her to bring it up.

"Yeah, I know" she said. "You should tell them you can't do it and if they really need you they will pay you. You should just not go in tomorrow."

Jeremy looked at her, sighed his own sigh and let his own face drop, though not in the "I'm disgusted" way but rather in the "I'm defeated" way, "Honey, I have to…"

She didn't say anymore. She didn't need to. The small shake of her head, the raise of the eyebrows as she focused on the needle and thread, the last, soft sigh; those things said all that was left to be said.

Jeremy knew she appreciated him. He knew that she was glad he was a responsible man who got up each morning and went to work; who paid the bills and was involved with the children. He knew she loved him, but he also knew that she could never understand him.

She couldn't understand the pressure of his job, the pure effort involved just to make it through each day. She didn't understand his constant worry about money and bills, especially since they lived comfortably and had a nice nest egg growing in the bank. She wouldn't understand, and he was incapable of explaining, the weight of it all. There just always seemed to be more work, more costs, something around the house needing attention. Always someone, something, saying "you have to, you have to…"

Jeremy knew she wasn't mad, just frustrated, but she didn't even acknowledge him when he said he was going to take a bath.

He let the tub fill nearly to the top before stepping in. The water was not just warm, it was hot. So hot that Jeremy had to ease himself slowly into it, an inch at a time, letting just slivers of his body become accustomed to it before easing in a little more.

Steam rose from the tub, the water lapped at his chest as it rolled softly back and forth, propelled originally by his entry into the water and maintained by the slow, steady rise and fall of his breathing. Jeremy lay in the tub for a long while, not unusual for him as he would often relax in the tub and read to unwind. If he were reading a particularly engrossing story he might remain there until the water cooled and he had to drain it and refill it with fresh, warm water to do his actual bathing.

This time, however, he didn't read. A collection of stories by Ray Bradbury lay atop the folded towel, on the floor next to the tub. Jeremy just soaked, breathing slowly, methodically, staring at the tiled space of wall between the faucet handles and the shower head mounted above. He wasn't seeing the tile, wasn't paying attention to the blue flecks within the white squares; he was looking through them. He thought about all the "have to's" that had been weighing on him throughout the day, the weeks, months, years. Jeremy lay there waiting for the water to relax him; waiting for his worries to seep out through his pores and be diluted among the hydrogen and oxygen atoms so he could release the drain and let them swirl away.

But instead of feeling better, Jeremy felt worse. As the sweat beaded on his forehead, he thought of even more "have to's" and more responsibilities and he felt less and less capable and he thought what a struggle it was going to be to get through the next day, and the next, and the next after that.

Jeremy took a deep breath. The water, which had nearly stilled, began its slow roll down the length of the tub, then back. He exhaled and slid beneath the water. The small ripples and eddys caused by his submersion settled and the water was still. The tip of his nose lay only millimeters below the surface. Jeremy stared at the white, slightly moldy bathroom ceiling. He thought, "That needs to be painted...but not by me. I have to do *this*."

A weak hum reached his ears; the sound of the house through the water. Moments later his mind began to scream that it wanted oxygen. The most basic instinct within him, survival, instructed him to lean up and out and suck in the air that waited just above the clear, liquid surface. "No," he commanded himself, "stay. Only a bit longer."

He felt his lungs begin to burn, his body twitched, yet he stayed beneath the water. He realized, ironically, the strength, the sheer power of will it took to remain less than an inch away from what his brain and body longed for. It was the strength that had so recently abandoned him, the will beyond that which he needed to face the trivial trials that life had, and would continue, to task him with. Surely, if he had this strength within him, he could face another day, another week, even years. He could once again find the pleasures in everyday that he knew were there and that easily outweighed the troubles and concerns and made life so very worth living.

As Jeremy came to this understanding his body reacted in self-defense to the lack of oxygen and he passed out beneath the water. Unconscious, his body gasped for air but found only water to fill its lungs. He thrashed, splashing the floor of the bathroom, his feet smacking against the white tiles with the blue flecks. There was a brief moment of awareness, as the danger shocked him back to consciousness, and Jeremy knew he was drowning, yet he was unable to find the clarity of mind needed to save himself.

By the time his wife jimmied open the locked bathroom door, alerted by the sounds of his struggle to save himself, Jeremy Robbins lay dead in ten inches of water. His last desperate thought…

"I have to live."

Author's Notes:

Sometimes life can seem very overwhelming and we just want to get away from it all. I can't say that everybody has felt that way, but I know I have. In the end though, most people's problems are pretty petty in the grand scheme of things and life is too big of a gift to waste. I suppose the moral of this story would be to think before you act…and wear a life preserver when bathing.

(FEELING) DOWN ON THE FARM

1.

Two hours before the sun would begin creeping up over the horizon and the rooster would call the farm to life, Stanley cracked the second egg into the pan for his breakfast. On the rear burner, bacon simmered and popped.

He ate alone at the kitchen table, as he had every morning for the past three months; since his father went to bed one July night and didn't wake up. His mother had been in the grave for over five years and Stanley had no siblings.

At forty two years old, Stanley had all but given up hope of finding someone to share his life with. As a farmer, he didn't meet many women, hadn't been on a date in over three years, since he parted ways with Loretta Browning. Loretta was a member of the Presbyterian Church over in Fayville, where Stanley served every Sunday as an usher. They'd dated for several months but, eventually, Loretta started making excuses for not being able to see him and had stopped returning his calls. They were still cordial when they saw each other, but Stanley had stopped asking her out. Loretta was the last woman Stanley had had sex with and only the third sexual partner in his life.

Stanley washed the plate and pans in the sink, stacked them on the counter to use later for dinner – which would also most likely consist of bacon and eggs – and prepared to face the day. The mid-October air was crisp but it was a short walk to the barn for the first of his daily chores so Stanley left his heavier coat hanging on the peg by the door, zipped his coveralls up over his thermal underwear and shoved his feet into the rubber boots that stunk of cow piss and manure.

His breath trailed behind him in small, white clouds as he plodded across the yard. He could hear the low, sleepy mooing of the cows as he entered the milk house and began gathering the equipment. Fifty seven cows didn't make for a large dairy farm but, between the milk and the soy bean and corn crops, it remained a going enterprise, if just.

Of course, every year was a bit more of a struggle. If crop prices went up, so did the price of seed and fertilizer; the equipment kept getting older and more costly to maintain. A small farm was not the way to get rich, but Stanley didn't require much to get by. With no children, he only needed to keep things afloat until he died, then…well, then it didn't much matter. The bank could take it all, as they sometimes threatened to do during a particular rough year. It would be nice to have someone to pass things on to, he thought, if there was anything left to pass on, and it wouldn't hurt to have some help around the place, particularly now that his father, as limited as he had been in helping out the last few years, had passed. He shrugged a "what can I do it about it" shrug as he walked into the barn.

"Good morning, ladies," Stanley said, out of habit, as he made his way along the line of cows. Their heads were stuck through stanchions – two rows of cows facing each other across a center aisle

– and their wide asses faced the outer aisles, hovering over the waste conveyor. Stanley nudged the first cow so that he could get in beside her, threw the strap over her back, hooked the hose to the airline running along the top of the stanchions and settled in to hook up the milking machine. The cow scooted sideways away from him as Stanley began to wipe her udder with the warm cloth.

"Come on, Betsy, let's not start the day off difficult."

Stupid names the cows had, Stanley thought, most of them anyway. Betsy, Mabel, Myrtle, Elvira…common he supposed. Then there were the ones the old man had thought clever; Oreo (a typical black and white Holstein), Chocolate (the almost all black girl), Bruce (one of the Jersey's on the other side of the barn). Stanley smiled a little though at the silliness of it. He had liked the names of the two bulls they'd kept, Willie and Waylon. It was a shame they'd had to sell Waylon off last year.

"Come on, Betsy, God damn it!"

The cow was fidgety, bumped Stanley in the nose, caused a jolt of pain to run up between his eyes, as he tried to secure the teat cups.

"Son of a…" Stanley lifted his hands to his nose.

"Sorry," said the cow. "I'm sore today."

2.

Stanley straightened his back, his hands still on his nose. "What?" he asked, his voice nasally.

"I said I'm sore," replied Betsy.

"Um…okay," Stanley said. "I'll try to be more careful."

"Thank you," said Betsy.

Stanley assumed he was going crazy but then… if he was crazy would he know it? An age old question, he imagined, thinking he had heard something to that effect on television once. Crazy or not it was nice to have someone, or some<u>thing</u>, to talk to.

"I wasn't aware you could speak," he said to the cow.

"I didn't know you could listen," the cow retorted.

Stanley found, in short order, that all the cows could converse with him. Chocolate informed him that the cows, in general, would prefer a bit more alfalfa mixed into their feed. Spot, one of the Holsteins, said that she much preferred the north pasture for grazing in the summer as there were more shade trees while the south pasture got better sun and was warmer during colder months. Bruce complained about having a boy's name.

The morning milking passed in reasonably quick fashion, time seeming to go by much faster as it does when one is enjoying conversation rather than stewing in one's own thoughts. Stanley found that he had a fair bit to talk about with the cows, which said something for the intelligence of the cows and, perhaps, something about Stanley's lack thereof.

The cows informed him that the chickens and the four hogs could speak as well, always had been able to. Stanley considered wandering over to the hog pen to see if he could talk to them but figured he had time for that and he wasn't sure if he wanted to know what the pigs had to say, anyway. He'd always heard that pigs were very intelligent, though he had seen nothing in their behavior to suggest they were any more intelligent than any other animal. Still, some part of him was reluctant to be proven intellectually inferior to a walking slab of bacon; at least for the time being.

Had Stanley been better read, he may have thought of Orwell's *Animal Farm*. As it was, he simply considered the morning's events as something miraculous or proof that he was going insane. For now, he had other chores which needed to be attended to and as he left the barn, to the murmur of conversation behind him, he figured he would wait to see what the rest of the day brought before drawing any conclusions.

3.

With thoughts wandering, Stanley pulled the combine through the thirty acre corn field at the west end of the farm. It was the first field of six, and the smallest, that he needed to tend to. Usually, while sitting high atop the John Deere tractor harvesting the corn fields, Stanley would be cursing the local deer population for the damage they had done to the crops. He was fortunate to be getting the corn off fairly early this year, so damage was slight. Still, the cursing would have been there had his mind not be turning over his morning experience.

Halfway through the field, Stanley thought he heard someone yelling over the sound of the machinery. Glancing around, he could spot no one and saw no vehicles on the dirt road that ran along the field's north edge. On his pass back across the field, he thought he heard it again. He powered down the tractor and listened.

"Over here! Behind you."

Stanley wheeled about in the seat of the Deere knocking his knee against the steering wheel and wincing. The half of the field he had cleared was deserted, save for a few crows picking through the corn stubble and the occasional missed stalk. Observing nearly a whole row of standing corn thirty paces back the way he had come, Stanley realized just how much his mind had been preoccupied.

"Just hearing things," he said aloud without recognizing the irony of the statement.

"You're hearing me," a voice said.

Stanley tracked the sound to the scarecrow hanging on a pole in the center of the field. The scarecrow was made up of an old pair of jeans – his or his father's he couldn't recall – and a red and black flannel shirt stuffed with straw and burlap bags. Its head was a burlap sack, filled out with more burlap sacks, with a crudely drawn, magic marker set of eyes and mouth and was topped with a University of Iowa ball cap. Pieces of straw and burlap poked through weathered holes in the jeans, shirt and face.

"You've got to be kidding," Stanley said as clambered off the tractor, his knee sore but nearly forgotten.

The scarecrow had been out in the field for longer than Stanley could say for sure. Several years ago, a couple of his young cousins had been visiting the farm and had insisted that the field needed a scarecrow. Despite knowing the ineffectiveness of scarecrows,

Stanley's father had agreed whole heartedly – for the amusement of the children, of course – and had even helped them create the decoration.

"He looks like an 'Orville'," Stanley's father had said, when they got the straw man in place, and the children had laughed their agreement. From that time on, this particular field had ceased being referred to as 'the west end' and had been called "Orville's Field" by Stanley's father and, eventually by Stanley and most everyone else who referenced it.

Stanley stood six feet in front of Orville, looking up at the burlap face four feet or so above him. The scarecrow was silent.

"You say something?" Stanley asked, feeling only slightly ridiculous given today's occurrences thus far.

"I asked, as I do every year, if you might help me down from here?" The scarecrow's magic marker mouth did not move and the eyes bore no expression, which was some solace to Stanley, but the voice clearly emanated from the burlap head.

"I've never heard you before."

"That doesn't make it any less true."

"I suppose not," said Stanley.

"Well now that you *are* hearing me, allow me to state my position," said the burlap sack.

"Please do," said Stanley, quite certain now that he had gone mad.

"I recognize that I am employed for a purpose. That purpose, frightening birds away from seeds and young plants, having been fulfilled with the harvest, I feel I am entitled to a reprieve. What is the sense in being left to the elements to watch over an empty field?"

"I guess you have a point," said Stanley. "Is there somewhere you want to go?"

"I hardly think I should care to travel but "inside" would be a nice start."

Stanley moved behind the scarecrow and worked at the knotted ropes that secured him in place. He was surprised when the straw man fell to the ground, stayed righted on its own legs and stretched as if just rising from bed.

"If you can climb up in the tractor, I'll give you a ride to the house," Stanley said.

"I'll walk, I think. It's a pleasant day and I would like to get these neglected limbs in order."

4.

Stanley left the field half harvested and pulled the tractor and combine into the equipment shed. By the time he had finished, the scarecrow was waiting by the door of the house. Stanley let him in and told him to make himself at home. He went out to feed the pigs, who he thankfully found to be non-conversational, and decided to spend the rest of the day chopping wood. It was good, physical labor that he found allowed him to get his mind off of other concerns. Later, in the barn for the evening milking, he recounted his experience with Orville to the cows.

"It sounds a bit odd," said Betsy, whom he found to be the most outspoken bovine. "Are you sure you didn't imagine it?"

"I don't think so," he said, "although I haven't been back to the house since this morning."

As if on cue, the door to the milk house opened and the straw man entered the barn.

"I was taking the tour," Orville said. "I thought I'd come see what you were up to."

Stanley nodded and continued about his work. He didn't say anymore to the cows, feeling embarrassed at the idea of the scarecrow seeing him talking with animals.

"So it's just you here on the farm? No wife? No kids?" Orville asked.

"Just me."

"Any prospects?"

"Pardon?"

Had the scarecrow been able, he would have rolled his eyes. "Do you have a girlfriend?"

"No."

"You're not a young man, Stanley. You may want to get a move on it. After all, a man should leave a legacy."

"He's right, you know." It was the Jersey, Bruce. Though she said she would like to be referred to as Barbara from now on. "Someone needs to keep the farm going when you...well, when you're gone."

"It would be a shame to see it out of the family," Betsy chimed in. "It's been the Fosten farm for over a hundred years now."

"There are not a lot of opportunities to meet women around here," said Stanley.

"What about that nice woman from the church? The one you used to bring around?" asked Bruce/Barbara.

"Things didn't work out."

"Maybe you should try again," said Orville, as he pushed open the door to the milk house and started through it. "Who knows? She may find that you're infinitely more interesting than you were."

That night, lying in bed, Stanley considered the advice of the cows and the scarecrow. He wasn't too old for children yet, although he was getting there. Tomorrow was Sunday. He would see Loretta at church. Maybe he would strike up a conversation; see how things went.

And he *was* more interesting now than he had been; Orville was right about that. He had a farm with talking animals and a living scarecrow, for Pete's sake. Perhaps she'd like to come by and see how things had changed?

5.

After Sunday services, Stanley – in his gray checkered sport coat, light blue shirt, black tie and gray slacks that he wore every week – cornered Loretta outside. His palms were sweaty and he buried his hands into the pockets of his trousers, giving him the look of a bashful school boy as he began speaking with her.

"I thought maybe you would like to join me for breakfast," he said. "We haven't see much of each other and it would be nice to catch up…just as friends, of course."

Loretta hemmed and hawed a bit, looked sheepishly at the ground to avoid eye contact and made excuses about errands that she needed to run and the fact that the diner was always so busy after services.

"Lunch or dinner, then," said Stanley. He smiled and forced a little laugh, "Come on, don't make me beg. I'll even cook."

She finally agreed to dinner that evening. Stanley had the sense that she did so to end the conversation and be on her way rather than out of any actual desire to spend time with him. Little victories though, he thought. Take what you can get.

Back at the farm, he hurried through the afternoon chores with a spring in his step. He joked with the cows and even had a short conversation with the hogs, which did make him feel slightly ignorant as they enjoyed using large words that he didn't always know the meaning of. He maintained his sense of superiority by reminding himself that they rooted in mud and their own feces while he showered regularly and slept on clean sheets.

Orville tagged along for most of the day and they discussed the impending dinner date – what to serve, what to talk about, how to show Loretta he still had feelings for her without coming on too strong and scaring her. On occasion, Stanley would turn from his work to find that Orville had wandered off, silently disappearing on his straw feet while Stanley was in mid-sentence.

When Loretta's car pulled into the dirt drive, Stanley was in the kitchen, just putting a pot of potatoes on to boil. He had a small roast in the oven and a few ears of sweet corn ready to be heated. Loretta presented a bottle of wine which made him think that perhaps she had warmed to the idea of spending the evening with him.

After pouring the wine, Stanley invited Loretta to join him on the living room couch. She sat at the end, the space between them a glaring indication of the feelings they no longer shared. Give it a little time, Stanley thought.

He tried a bit of small talk but found that he struggled to keep the conversation flowing. There was uneasiness in their banter; forced laughter, polite but contrived smiles.

"I've missed you," he said and regretted it almost as soon as the words were out of his mouth.

"Stanley…" she said and stared into the bottom of her glass.

"I'm just saying that I think we should give it another chance. I can really see us together.
Maybe even getting married; having kids."

He hadn't planned on spilling his feelings out but found it difficult to suppress them now that he had opened the flood gates.

"Marriage? Kids?" Loretta set her glass on the coffee table. "I think I should leave."

"No!" Stanley shouted, and then quickly composed himself. "I mean, no. I didn't mean to scare you. I just…well, with my dad dying and being alone here…Look, just forget I said anything. Dinner's almost ready. Let me check the potatoes."

He was up and out of the living room before she could protest, but he didn't go to the kitchen. Instead, he slipped quietly down the hallway to the back bedroom – his father's room – where Orville had been hiding out. They had both agreed that the shock of a living scarecrow might be a bit much to spring on Loretta right away.

"I'm blowing it!" Stanley gasped.

Orville, appearing somehow roused from slumber though devoid of facial expressions, took in Stanley's accounting of the events thus far. If Stanley didn't know that the scarecrow's face was nothing more that drawn on, he would have sworn it was frowning.

"Just get back to your date and try to keep it light," Orville said.

Stanley snuck back to the kitchen, checked the corn and potatoes and called out to Loretta to see if she wanted a refill on her wine.

"I'm fine, thanks," she said. Stanley presumed she was wary of drinking too much alcohol now that he had broached the subject of them getting back together.

He went to move the potatoes from the burner, heard a commotion in the other room and nearly dropped the pot; boiling water splashed on to his forearms and he hissed in pain. Moving quickly to the living room he found Loretta lying face down on the carpet, her purse and jacket on the floor next to her. There was a red liquid staining the carpet by her head, and it took a moment for Stanley to realize it was blood and not her spilled glass of wine, which lay a few feet away from her by the coffee table that had been pushed askew. Orville stood of to one side of the room, the bottle of wine on the floor beside him creating another red stain in the carpet. The straw man turned to Stanley.

"She was leaving. We can't have that just yet. She didn't even give us a chance."

6.

"What the fuck, Orville!?"

Stanley stood frozen in place, his gaze shifting back and forth from the scarecrow's expressionless, burlap sack face to Loretta's prone body; the red stain around her head growing wider and darker; her dressed hitched up slightly to reveal a shapely, though awkwardly twisted, leg.

"We need a bit of time with her; time to convince her."

"Well, I don't think bonking her with a bottle of wine is going to do much to make her anymore attracted to me."

Orville seemed to consider this; shifted his burlap face to look at the woman, then back at Stanley, "Yeah, I suppose I didn't think that through very well. What can I say? I'm a fuckin' scarecrow, not a marriage counselor."

Stanley knelt down and felt Loretta's neck, then her wrist. The color ran out of him. "I don't feel a pulse."

"Hmmm. That certainly puts a damper on any shred of hope that may have remained for a future relationship."

Had he not been so shocked, been working so hard to control the rising panic, Stanley may have allowed himself to act on the impulse to tear the scarecrow apart and strew his burlap and straw innards about the living room for the flippancy of his attitude. Instead, his hands went to his face, dragged slowly downward, pulling his eyes long, his mouth into a comic frown.

"Okay, new plan," said Orville. "We need to dispose of the body. Hide the evidence."

He was right, Stanley knew. People had seen him and Loretta talking at church earlier, folks knew about their previous relationship. It was a small town and sooner or later someone would miss Loretta, sooner most likely, and they'd be looking for her. They'd definitely want to ask him some questions and she probably mentioned to someone, a friend, her sister, her parents, that she was coming over to Stanley's for dinner.

Stanley needed to talk to the pigs.

7.

"So you can really eat a body?"

Stanley stood leaning against the side of the pig pen, the largest of the four hogs looking up at him, two others paying attention to the conversation but at a respectable distance behind the larger hog, and one lying in the back corner, seemingly uninterested.

"Mind you, I've never done it; none of us have, seeing as we've been raised here and fed regularly, but it's true that pigs, omnivores that we are, will eat pretty well anything edible. It's all about protein and nutrients. Now some of the bigger bones; the femur, the skull…well, they'd take a bit more time; hard to break down, not to mention the gastronomical consequences."

Omnivore? Gastronomical? Damn big words, Stanley thought. But whatever…the gist of it he understood.

Running back to the house, Stanley felt a bit more relaxed; confident even. Even if the pigs left a bit, he could hide some, or run it through the grinder and mix it with the feed. He could probably get the carpet cleaned easily enough, maybe he'd put Orville on that job, he'd gotten him in this mess in the first place. Loretta's car? He wasn't quite sure about that just yet, but he could probably just drive it back toward town, leave it on one dirt road or another. If anybody came asking questions he'd say she never showed up for dinner; could even show them the uneaten food gone cold.

He hefted Loretta's body and stumbled back toward the pigs.

"Are they going to do it?" Orville asked.

"Don't talk to me."

Nudging the latch on the gate of the pen with his knee, Stanley stepped into the muck, mud and straw of the sty. The hogs, whom for no reason he could think of they had never bothered to name, pressed against him; even the one that had seemed disinterested only moments ago.

"Back, pig! Git, hog!" Stanley growled at them. He lifted a foot to kick at the largest hog, slipped in the filth, went down hard, banged his head on the side of the pen, and laid unconscious under Loretta's weight.

The pigs moved in to feast.

8.

By morning, the county sheriff, both full time deputies, all three part timers and the whole volunteer fire department had converged on the Fosten farm. Deputy Brewen had come out first thing to ask Stanley a few questions, saw Loretta's car and found the house unlocked and empty other than a weathered scarecrow lying on a bed in one of the back bedrooms.

After calling for back up, which would take a full thirty minutes to arrive, the deputy began investigating the out buildings and, eventually, came across the gruesome scene of a couple of partially devoured bodies in the pig sty. He had to kick and push the hogs repeatedly to get them off the victims and manage to pull the corpses out into the barn yard.

Both Loretta and Stanley were easily identifiable; the pigs had not yet gotten to their faces. Stanley's throat was more or less gone and his stomach had been burrowed into; parts of what remained of his intestines were spread about the pig pen. The woman's body was largely untouched, barring a few bite marks on the legs; shapely for her age, the young officer thought, and he noted a large gash on the back of her head.

Eventually, with the help of some perhaps not well trained but at least somewhat trained, crime scene investigators from neighboring Port Hope, the police pieced together the murder of Loretta Browning, obviously bludgeoned by Stanley Fosten with the wine bottle found in the farm house living room. They surmised, accurately enough, that Mr. Fosten had an accident while trying to dispose of the body in the pig pen; justice served as far as they were concerned.

They did not hazard to guess why Mr. Fosten had pieces of burlap and handfuls of straw stuffed inside his clothing, why his eyes were outlined with black, magic marker nor why a comical, clown-like smile had been drawn on his face. The marker was found lying uncapped in the back bedroom, determined to be his deceased father's room, on the floor, where the curious scarecrow had been found on the bed.

"Think he just cracked, Chief?" the deputy asked when Sheriff Hartland first arrived on the scene.

"Who knows? Looks enough like he did."

The sheriff scratched the stubble of his beard, gray to match his hair if he were to let it grow in, and walked in a slow circle in the yard, taking in the barn, the house, the chicken coop, the equipment shed and finally, again, the pig pen.

"Out here all alone. Nobody to talk to…gets lonely on a farm."

Author's Notes:

I get a little antsy and stir crazy when left to myself. It can be pleasant for a short while, a bit of a respite from it all, but I am generally fond of the people that I surround myself with on a regular basis and tend to get sad if I don't see them for a while. I also have a tendency to talk to myself, and my dog, and the television, and inanimate objects like silverware and writing utensils. I spend a lot of time on a farm and I talk to the cows and the pigs and the sheep. So far, nobody's talked back.

TRAVELING MUSIC

1.

"Come on, honey, get the lead out!" Tim yelled up the stairs.
Shaking his head as he hefted the cooler, he wondered for the
umpteenth time what could possibly take her so long to get ready for
a weekend trip.

He rearranged the suitcase, sleeping bags and cases of beer and
soda in the trunk of the car so he could squeeze in the cooler full of
cold cuts, cheese, bread and wine. This was their contribution to the
potluck food supply for the weekend at Matty and Barb's cabin. He
thought about pulling a few of the beers out and trying to squeeze
them in among the bologna, salami and swiss so they would be cold
when they got to their destination. Considering Matty or Bill would
surely have some on ice already, he decided against it. He could bum
one or two from them while his got cold.

"My God, Timmy, why are you in such a rush?"

Tim looked up over the open trunk to see Katie standing on the
porch. Normally, he hated to be called Timmy, but he always like
the way it sounded coming from her. She wore sandals and a pair of
khaki shorts that hugged her hips and left a great deal of her taut
jogger's thighs exposed. Her white, spaghetti strap top stopped only
inches beneath her breasts, revealing her firm belly. Too large
sunglasses, the type that was in vogue these days, sat perched atop
her head holding her blonde hair out of her face. Whatever she had
been doing to get ready was worth waiting for, Tim decided.

"It's a three hour drive and it's already pushing nine o'clock," Tim said. "I want to get there before everybody's hitting the sack."

"You know they're going to be drinking, and with Bill and Matty that means until they pass out, not until they go to bed," she countered.

Of course, she was right. Still, even though it was a three day weekend and there was plenty of party time, Tim wanted to be a part of as much fun as possible.

Twenty minutes later they were on the expressway heading out of the congested city and looking forward to a weekend away from the hustle and bustle. Forty minutes after that, Tim eased the seat back a notch as they cleared the outskirts of Port John's and settled in to the two lane highway they would follow the rest of the way to Matt and Barb's place.

Traffic thinned quickly as they left civilization behind them. A few small towns dotted the map every twenty miles or so over the next hundred miles they would travel. In between there were rolling fields—some cultivated, some not—and stands of woods so dense that, as they pressed against the road, one could imagine any number of things hidden just a few feet within.

Often there was no sign of life other than the neat lines of one crop or another; crops that must have belonged to some unseen farmer in some unseen farmhouse hidden beyond the tree line.

Tree branches stretched overhead and across the road as if reaching to their kin on the other side, trying to pull themselves together to reclaim the space between them that man had carved out.

Tim switched on the high beams and scanned the roadside, expecting a deer to jump out at any minute. They'd been to the cabin several times in the last few years, and Tim preferred to make the drive during the day. The road was so dark and deserted it felt alien, but he was anxious to be away from the city and to join the fun. Matty, Barb, Bill and Jenny had all taken personal days from work to increase the length of their holiday weekend. Tim had used his vacation time up early in the year, as usual, and had been one of the few suffering through today at the nearly deserted office, dreaming of escape.

The speakers of the Pontiac Grand Prix crackled and spit as they began to lose the radio station they had tuned into. Katie hit the SEEK button and watched as the digital readout sped through the extent of its display twice before coming to rest at 95.4. Something sounding vaguely country emanated momentarily from the speakers before it was overtaken by the static.

"Shit! Maybe something on AM..." Katie mumbled.

Tim reached into the storage area of his door and held his prize up to Katie, shaking it slightly with a "lookie what I got" grin on his face. Katie smiled and grabbed the iPod from his hand.

"Well, somebody had a plan it seems," she said as she plugged the adaptor cable into the port next to the car radio, syncing the two. It was a feature Tim found absolutely brilliant. He rarely bothered to listen to the radio anymore and had yet to use the Grand Prix's disc player.

"After listening to static for two hours last time we made this trip, I thought it'd be a good idea," Tim replied.

"You don't care for my conversation?" she asked.

Tim only smiled, knowing the question was rhetorical and there was no good answer for it anyway.

"I hope this isn't just a bunch of jazz on here." Katie thumbed the control on the device to search the library of music.

"It's my entire catalogue," Tim smiled, "everything from Bird to Bon Jovi. Just hit the shuffle button."

Katie found the shuffle command and pressed the center of the control. Twangy guitar filled the cabin of the car and she shot a questioning glace at Tim.

"Loudon Wainwright. Dead Skunk," he said, a childish smile spreading across his face as he began to bob his head back and forth.

Tim sang along to the tune about a roadkill skunk as Katie laughed and shook her head, watching him. As the chorus of the song flowed from the speakers, Tim's eyes and smile widened. He pointed out the windshield into the glow cast by the headlights, "Hey! Look at that!"

On cue, Katie saw the black and white carcass straddling the center divider line on the blacktop. She grimaced and put her hand to her nose as the odor seeped into the car. Tim ignored the smell, laughing and singing along with the song even louder.

"How funny is that?" he asked. "I mean, it could have been a raccoon or an opossum. It probably should have been on the shoulder, that's where you usually see 'em, as if they just managed to crawl there with their last breath... but nope. A dead skunk right in the middle of the fucking road." He bellowed laughter and Katie laughed with him.

"You're a goof," she said, patting his hand.

He smiled at her and joined back in with the song.

2.

They traveled on, the headlights slicing through the darkness, their faces illuminated by the green glow of the dashboard control panel. A squiggly arrow warned Tim of an upcoming series of bends in the road and he eased his foot off the gas. The car didn't slow and Tim pushed the OFF button on the cruise control, trying to remember when he'd turned it on. Still the car continued at speed. Tim looked at the speedometer. Sixty miles an hour. He pushed lightly on the brake but felt no reaction in the car. The car entered into the first bend and Tim's knuckles whitened as he gripped the wheel tighter and eased it into the left hand lane, taking the turn tight. Katie dug her hands into the sides of her seat.

"What are you doing?" she asked.

Tim didn't have to look at her to see the fright in her face; he was too busy concentrating on the turns.

"I don't know. Something's wrong with the brake or the gas…or both."

He slid into the next curve, letting the car drift to the right side of the road and cutting as much out of the turn as possible, using the opposite lane to reduce the severity of the bend as he came out of it.

Sammy Hagar screamed from the radio.

The road straightened back out. Tim exhaled, only now realizing he had been holding his breath. He tapped the brake, tapped the gas. The car continued to hum along at sixty, oblivious to his actions. Tim pulled both feet back against the seat and pressed the cruise control button several times. Katie watched, not yet panicking, but clearly on the brink. Sammy continued to sing about his inability to drive within the confines of the speed limit.

Tim reached for the emergency brake. The Red Rocker faded to silence, and before he pulled the lever the car began to slow. He eased the Grand Prix to the side of the road. The brakes responded as they were supposed to and he put the car in park, killing the ignition.

"What was that all about?" Katie asked.

Tim drew his forearm across this brow, wiping the sweat that had beaded there.

"Well…?"

"I don't know. How the fuck should I know? I'm not a mechanic," he snapped.

"You don't have to be a dick about it," she retorted.

"I'm sorry. I'm just a little shook up. Let's just sit a second."

Katie reached for her purse and fumbled through it for her cell phone. "Damn! No signal."

"Who were you going to call?"

"I don't know. AAA or Barb or…somebody."

Tim started the car and eased it back on to the blacktop. He accelerated to fifteen miles per hour and hit the brakes, coming to a stop. He pushed the car to forty and stopped again.

"It seems alright now. Maybe I hit the cruise somehow and it got stuck or something. We'll just keep it around fifty five and take our time getting there, eh?"

"Yeah…okay." Katie sounded less than confident in the plan.

3.

Journey serenaded them as they made their way through a small town. The streets were empty, the shops closed. The lone streetlight blinked yellow, imploring them to slow down for just a second and have a look around, but not to worry about stopping. Steve Perry hardly had time to complete a verse before the town dropped away and the dark night gathered back in around them. Katie leaned her head on Tim's shoulder and he patted her thigh. He was a bit more comfortable now, having passed through the town with the car responding accordingly to his depressions of the brakes and gas.

He pushed the car back up to fifty five as the Divinyls shuffled in place on the iPod. The sexy song about pleasuring one's self, that most people were only familiar with from the Austin Powers movie, slithered sexily from the speakers.

Katie pulled herself away from him and leaned against her door. He looked over to her. She smiled in a sly, sexy way that instantly made him stir. She reclined her seat back several inches and spread her legs.

"Um…what's all this about?" he asked, honestly confused. Katie was no prude in bed but she wasn't the type to start messing around in the car either, and certainly not the type to do what it appeared she was about to do now.

She only smiled, her eyes closing as her hand slid across her stomach and flirted with the top of her khaki shorts. Her pinky finger slipped beneath the waistband for a moment before she popped the button and tugged down the zipper, revealing the red triangle of her panties.

Tim swallowed hard, trying to focus on the road but barely able to pull his eyes away from her. He glanced back and forth from the blacktop to his fiancée's erotic display. He could feel himself straining against his jeans.

As the Aussie lead singer crooned about wanting no one else, Katie arched her back and moaned as her hand slid beneath the panties and down between her legs. She ground her groin against her hand, her breathing coming in shallow grunts and moans. Her feet braced against the dashboard, the muscles standing out in her tan legs, the sandals forgotten on the floor.

Tim felt the car pull as the tire fell off the blacktop and into the soft shoulder of the road. He jerked it back quickly, at once concerned for their safety and afraid that he would disturb her performance. Katie never hesitated, lost in her own ecstasy, her arm moving quickly as she rubbed herself. The pitch of her moans became higher and she started to yelp, reaching her orgasm.

"Jesus Christ," Tim whispered, unaware the words had escaped his mouth.

As the sultry voice spoke the words of the chorus, Katie matched the oohs and aahs. The song faded, and she collapsed into the seat, her breathing long and slow now, recovering.

"Holy Shit!" Tim said, stunned at the whole scene.

Katie looked at him and he thought she looked a bit dazed, a little embarrassed possibly, although there was certainly another reason for the flush in her face.

"I…I just…," she started.

Hard guitar chords filled the space and Katie stopped, the sly, sexy smile returning to her face. Chad Kroeger's gravelly voice picked up as the guitar halted and the bass drum kept time for him…

The song belonged in a dark and smoky bar filled with lingerie-clad, single mothers gyrating on brass poles. The lead singer was telling a girl how good she looked with her mouth full.

Katie pulled her knees up on the seat and twisted her body so that she was leaning against Tim's shoulder, her breath hot on his ear and neck. He could smell her perfume, her sweat…her sex. The hand that had so recently been between her own legs slid between his and she pulled at his jeans. Her tongue danced on his earlobe, then his neck, and he thought that he was going to explode before he even cleared his pants. She pulled him out and gripped his shaft tight, her head dropping to his lap, her beautiful ass up in the air as she kneeled in the passenger seat.

"Oh God…"

Her mouth was wet and warm, the music was pounding through his head and Katie was keeping time to the beat. The words were foggy in Tim's head, barely registering as Kroeger encouraged Katie to never pull it out.

Tim reached down and reclined his seat as far as he dared without losing his grip on the steering wheel. Steering now with his left, he let his right hand caress her thigh, her ass. Her still loose shorts accepted his groping fingers and he squeezed the flesh of her buttocks before sliding his hand through the sweat in the small of her back, across the butterfly tattoo there, around and under her shirt to cup her breast, her nipple hard and coarse against his fingertips. He wound his fingers into her hair, pulling it away from her face so he could see her working on him. He let his hand fall and rise, fall and rise with the motion of her head. He leaned his head back, barely managing to focus on the road and thanking God that this particular stretch was fairly straight.

He could feel his own orgasm building, and even as he wondered if he should pull her away, she began to stroke him, her mouth still on him.

"I want it," she breathed heavily.

She had never let him finish in her mouth before and the thought of it practically made him explode at that instant. Almost absentmindedly he recognized the song was ending. He hoped something equally erotic would come on next. He considered reaching for the MP3 player and hitting the repeat button, but wasn't exactly sure where it was and didn't want to disrupt Katie's rhythm.

The song ended abruptly; mid-sentence. Ridiculously, he recalled that he thought the recording was messed up the first time he heard it before realizing the ending was by design. Katie's pace faltered for a moment, as if the beat of the music had kept her going. Please God, something fast, Tim thought.

The strum of a harp? A short trumpet refrain. Repeating.

Katie paused, her head motionless, Tim's cock throbbing in her mouth. Almost there, he thought. He put a bit of pressure on the back of her head with his hand, hoping to spur her back into action, as Roy Orbison began to warble the lyrics of a song that Nazareth would later go on to make exponentially more popular. A sorrowful rock ballad about the pain of love.

So close, just another few seconds. Then he felt her teeth tear into him and the pain brought instant tears to his eyes as Katie's mouth flooded with blood rather than semen.

4.

Tim pulled at Katie's hair yanking her back across the car, her heading banging sharply against the passenger side window.

"Jesus Christ! Holy Fuck!" He clutch at his groin feeling the hot, sticky wetness spreading across his jeans, flooding his seat and oozing through his fingers.

Katie sat stunned, absently rubbing her temple as blood trickled from the corners of her mouth, down her chin and left little, red polka dots on her white top.

"I don't know what happened! Timmy! Oh, Christ! What happened?!"

"You fuckin' bit me! What do you mean what happened? You bit my fucking dick!"

Katie cried, salty tears running down her face to mix with Tim's blood.

Tim turned the steering wheel toward the side of the road, one hand still trying to stem the flow of blood from his crotch. The car did not respond. In fact, it turned in the opposite direction following a slight curve in the road.

"What the fuck?"

"What's...wrong?" Katie asked. Her words were stunted in sharp, quick breaths and Tim thought she might be on the verge of hyperventilating. Fucking bitch...let her. Hope she fucking dies, Tim thought.

"The car's fucked up! Turn the damn music off!"

Katie pulled the adaptor cord from the dashboard but Roy Orbison continued to croon about how love will make you blue. Katie pushed the power button on the radio and still Roy sang.

"I can't stop it!"

"What the fuck is going on?" Tim was feeling a little light headed, but it seemed as though most of the bleeding had stopped. He looked down. God, it looked like a lot of blood.

Roy's voice faded out and for a moment there was silence. Then the sound of maracas and bongo drums burst from the speakers. The volume was intense. Katie covered her ears, and Tim cringed, his shoulders rising up as he compressed his neck downward.

Mick Jagger asked the listener to let him introduce himself.

"It's like I was in a trance…I was…I don't remember…"

Katie was losing it. Tim thought she must be in some kind of shock. It was him who should be in shock. He was the one who nearly had his dick severed.

"What is this?!" Tim yelled.

The music stopped.

A heart beat.

Then AC/DC nearly blew their eardrums out as the chorus of Highway to Hell filled the interior of the car.

Tim pulled the emergency brake. It came up easily in his hand and had absolutely no effect on the car whatsoever. They drove on, or something did, through the black night. The headlights flashed on and off, creating a strobe effect beyond the windshield. Tim's hands were no longer on the wheel, yet the car held true to the road. He looked stupidly at the wheel as it turned slightly left, then right.

Katie began to scream, the lower portion of her face a mix of blood and tears. She looked like a vampire from a B horror movie.

Tim pounded on the steering wheel, "Stop this! Stop this! Oh, God, please!"

Silence. Until…

Kid Rock thumped through the interior and screamed that he was their Rock and Roll Jesus. The bass penetrated through the seats and into Tim's thighs. He began talking to the car directly, hoping he was talking to whatever was controlling the Pontiac. "Please, for God's sake, please stop."

The Grand Prix went completely dark. The headlights, the interior lights, everything. There was silence except for Katie's sobbing and the wheels thrumming against the road. Tim could feel the car move left and right, following the blacktop. Ahead, he could see the glow of a town; a halo of light beckoning amidst the utter blackness of the surrounding countryside.

Suddenly, Brad Paisley's voice picked up where Kid Rock had left off and told them they had to get some mud on the tires.

The Grand Prix lurched hard to the right. Katie fell into Tim as he banged against his door. Then they were off the road. The lights came on to illuminate a tree only a few feet in front of them, then went off as they awaited the crash that never came. The car felt as though it went airborne, perhaps running through a ditch. Katie had never put her seat belt back on since freeing herself for her earlier performance. She bounced out of her seat and Tim heard her neck crack as she hit the roof of the car. She moaned in pain as she fell back to the seat, then lurched forward as the car jostled, and bounced her head off the windshield, opening a gash.

The back of the rear seat popped open and the trunk spilled its contents into the passenger compartment. The cooler tipped and opened, sending ice and packaged meat throughout the back seat; a case of beer expelled cans that become frightful projectiles as they bounded about. Several cans burst, spraying Tim and Katie with suds and amber liquid.

The car swerved hard left and found the road again. The headlights sparked back to life and Tim saw the REDUCED SPEED AHEAD sign as they flew past it, letting them know they were reaching the town limits.

Tim leaned forward and reached under the steering column, his hands searching for wires or something, anything he could pull to kill the vehicle.

The country song fell away and an unmistakable guitar riff took its place. Tim's seatbelt tightened and jerked him back hard. He felt the material tear into the flesh under his chin as it lifted him slightly. Nugent slid into the lengthy solo of Stranglehold.

The car sped into the small town. Tim saw a police car ahead, idling in the parking lot of a bank. The tires of the Pontiac locked up and the car came to a screeching halt in front of the cruiser. The seatbelt seared into Tim's chest as his weight tried to continue the momentum the car had so quickly given up. Katie was thrown forward into the dashboard, her arm making a sickening noise on impact. She groaned and collapsed to the floor, the top half of her body lying limply on the seat.

The flashers on the police cruiser spun to life and Tim's Pontiac accelerated away.

5.

The headlights went dead again but the interior lights flared to life; the green backlit glow disturbingly eerie. Tim watch as the needle on the speedometer slid past sixty, seventy and then eighty. He saw the rolling blue and red lights of the cruiser fading back in the mirror, the officers with more common sense, or care, than whatever had control of the Pontiac.

Tim leaned back in the seat, feeling defeated and resigned. Beer, blood, sweat, tears and the smell of sex filled the interior of the car. He rolled his head and glanced at Katie's crumbled body next to him as the Bobby Fuller Four roared from the speakers and bemoaned their lost battle with the law.

The Grand Prix continued to gain speed. The wheels screeched angrily as they tried to hold the car to the road through each turn. Tim's head rolled left and right as the car swerved through the darkness. He braced himself against the centrifugal force with his arms. Katie's body was rocked relentlessly. He was unsure if she was alive or dead.

The interior lights went off and all was dark. The night sky made brief appearances through the branches above. Gray clouds, illuminated by the crescent moon, floated lazily above the terror on the road. Then total darkness again as the trees overtook the road.

The car slowed, then sped up. It slowed again, sped up again. Tom Petty's nasally voice took over where Bobby Fuller stopped. It was the waiting, Petty sang, that was the hardest part.

Tim began to sob; heavy, unembarrassed sobs. He cried for Katie; he cried for himself.

The headlights flared to life and Tim saw a giant oak swell up in front of the Pontiac. He didn't even have time to scream. His mind barely registered Frank Sinatra beginning to croon My Way. The end was near, Frank's sultry tenor announced.

6.

The cruiser pulled up to the wreckage, stopping several yards back. The tire marks in the soft shoulder led to a great oak, which now had a large, fresh gash in its ancient hide. The car had rolled several times and lay in the center of the road on its crushed roof, hissing and smoking.

Clothes, beer cans and packaged meats were strewn about the twisted metal and broken glass leading from the initial site of impact to the resting place of the crumpled vehicle.

Officer Telly looked at his partner, "That fucker was plain crazy."

Officer Gallard nodded his affirmation, "Another drunk driver from the city, no doubt."

They approached the car cautiously, guns drawn despite the unlikelihood of any kind of encounter. As they rounded the rear of the vehicle they saw a man in a seated position, leaning against the steaming vehicle. A woman lay with her head in his lap. It was unclear if either of them were breathing.

Remarkably, they heard music.

Tim was just barely conscious. He wasn't sure how he was alive. He didn't remember dragging Katie's corpse from the car; didn't remember pulling himself from the wreckage.

Bleeding and broken, he felt his life slipping away from him. He was in so much pain that he had become numb to it; in shock most likely. He couldn't hear the voices of the police officers yelling to him; couldn't hear them radioing for the ambulance that would arrive too late.

Tim only heard the music. It was Eddie Vedder singing. He had always preferred this remake to the original. Vedder's voice sounded more soulful; more sorrowful.

With a great effort he brought his hand to Katie's head and pushed the hair, mottled with blood and beer, sweat and tears, away from her face. He fell to his side and painfully positioned himself so that he was lying next to her. Katie's eyes were open but lifeless. They stared through him. He rolled himself toward her lips. The street was filled with the lover's lament of a last kiss on the lips of his girlfriend following a terrible car crash.

Tim closed his eyes. The music, and his life, faded to black.

Author's Notes:

This story began as a submission call with a theme. The task was to write a story that involved transportation; taking a trip, riding a train, etc. I pretty quickly dismissed writing anything for this submission because, at the time, my thought was that I just don't work that way. I write whatever it is that comes to me and then see if it fits somewhere. But the seed had been planted and it rolled around in that reasonably empty, but oddly fertile, place between my ears.

Obviously, I'm a big music fan and it's safe to assume I was spending a fair amount of time listening to my MP3 player as this story gestated.

It was also one of the first stories I wrote that I had some concerns about people reading because it's, well, a little graphic. But I think it was Joe Hill (although he could have been quoting someone else) that said writer's block is when you won't allow yourself to write what it is you want to write, probably because you're afraid of what your mom will think of it...or something like that).

This story remains one of my favorites and one of the best received by readers (you're all a bunch of perverts).

- *This story has been revised and altered from its originally published form.*

A VAMPIRE'S PRAYER

I creep and skulk and prowl the night,
Forced outside by appetite
I'd be content if I could repose
'neath native soil, head and toes
But cursed I rise with end of light

I search for soft and supple flesh
For my teeth are not the best
I'm growing old, as I am able
Though never will I leave the table
As I can't pass that final test

A younger soul longed life eternal
No heed given to the infernal
For youth sees but only shortly
The promise once seemed courtly
Oh to be forever vernal

Now age, age beyond comprehension
Has shown my lack of apprehension
And had I been but older, wiser
No wish for lengthened, fanged incisor
But simple, holy ascension

Having drunk my fill and sated
A vile creature, loathed and hated
I return with hope so slight
To be found before next bite
Sent forth to death belated

Perhaps they'll tear my box asunder
Yells rain down the sound of thunder
Raise stake high and curse the beast
Pierce my heart and end the feast
At my final smile wonder

Author's Notes:
This little poem is my first and, thus far, only venture into the immensely popular world of the vampire. While my vampire may be a bit regretful, he (or she, I suppose) is still a monster; a cursed soul that has no choice but to search out its prey. My vampire IS NOT sparkly, attending high school or having stupid crushes with humans.

THE HIT

1.

Ted stood in front of the full length mirror, adjusting the bow tie.
He was never very good at tying the damn things; always had to do it
three or four times before getting it to look right. He swept up the
monogrammed, gold cuff links off the nightstand, the ones Maria
had given him for their 1st anniversary. He thought back to the days
when their marriage was new as he fumbled to put them in. Just over
six years now they had been married.

He'd had known Maria since she was just a kid. When he first
started working for Paul Morendino, better known as Big Paulie
around the greater New York area, he was eighteen years old and
Maria was Big Paulie's ten year old daughter. Ted had worked his
way up from running numbers and strong arming local business
owners to being Big Paulie's number one clean up guy, by the time
Maria entered high school. A stint in the Marines had made him an
efficient killer.

When Maria came home from Brown University, a year shy of
graduation, Teddy the Polack, his real surname nearly forgotten to
even him, had made quite a reputation for himself. On occasion, Ted
would even get a call from another family to take care of some mess.
Of course, he'd never do anything detrimental to Big Paulie's
interests, but he wasn't above a little moonlighting.

As Ted shrugged on his jacket, he thought about Jackie Silvia's
place, The Beat. Jackie's club was what you might call "friendly" to

the family. Although Ted would always be kept slightly outside the most inner circle, by virtue of the "ski" at the end of his last name, everyone knew how tight he was with Big Paulie and he was treated by everyone as if he were a made man. At Jackie's he was treated first class. He walked right past the line waiting for the bouncer to nod them in, had a VIP table reserved at all times and never paid for a drink.

Ted spent a lot of time at Jackie's. His profession wasn't one that lent itself to relationships and Jackie's was a good place to pick up disposable pussy. Drunk college girls, thirty-something housewives on a girl's night out and even the occasional b-list starlet were all prime candidates for a one-nighter if you hit them at the right time of the night. Ted was handsome, well-built and had a lot of money to throw around. He rarely went to bed alone if he didn't feel like it.

The night he'd run into Maria, for the first time since her high school graduation party, he had just arrived at Jackie's and saw Little Tony B entertaining a crowd by the bar. Little Tony was a hell of a storyteller. Granted there wasn't much truth in most of the stories, but they were well told. Tony had a habit of taking stories he'd heard and turning them into his own. More than once he had told Ted about some tight spot he gotten into or some yarn about a crazy broad he'd hooked up with and Ted would recognize it as something he had once told Tony about. Funny thing was though, Little Tony had such a way with a story, you'd just sit and listen to see how it turned out; and most of the time his version was a lot funnier and more interesting than the original.

As he weaved his way through the pulsating crowd, and neared the group taking in Little Tony's story, Ted spied a beautiful pair of stocking clad legs working their way up from a pair of three inch, stiletto heels and disappearing under a tight, white, leather skirt just before they made, what he imagined to be, a perfect ass out of themselves. A smiley face tattoo peeked out of the top of the skirt. Straight, jet black hair reflected the lights of the club and fell down to tickle the top of the tattoo.

Little Tony saw him approaching and managed a smile and nod in his direction without breaking stride in whatever story he was regaling the masses with. Ted sidled up next to the brunette and casually placed the palm of his hand over the smiley face, letting its weight rest on the top of her behind. It was a move that was subtle enough to be explained away by the close quarters of the club, but daring enough to open up an invitation if the girl was looking for some fun.

He kept his eyes focused on Little Tony, making like he was pulled in by the story and not acknowledging the brunette. Through his peripheral vision, he knew she was looking at him and he waited for her reaction. He didn't expect the excited shriek that came.

"Uncle Teddy!"

Ted turned to see that cute, little Maria had turned into a beautiful young woman. The dumbstruck look on his face didn't waver as Maria threw her arms around his neck.

"Oh my God, Uncle Teddy, it's so good to see you!"

Ted stammered out something about it being good to see her too, her perfume intoxicating him with a soft, vanilla scent. His eyes found Little Tony, who shot back a look simultaneously warning Ted he had better watch his step and concurring with the thoughts in Ted's own mind that Big Paulie's little girl had turned into one fine piece of ass.

Maria accompanied Ted to his VIP booth and he feigned interest in her stories about being away at school, why she'd come back home and what she planned to do next. All the while he tried to chase away the erotic images his mind continued to conjure up. The Grey Goose and O.J., "Goose and juice" he liked to call it, did nothing to drown the fantasies but he kept knocking them back.

As the night went on, Maria started calling him Ted, instead of Uncle Teddy. He wasn't really her uncle and she wasn't a child anymore, she said. Ted had to agree on both points. He noticed that she kept moving slightly closer as she talked, speaking lower as if to necessitate the movement. Soon her thigh was pressed against his and when Little Tony B stopped by to shoot the shit for a few minutes, he couldn't help feeling a bit embarrassed about it. He could see the look in Tony's eyes and when Tony excused himself several stories later, he leaned on Ted's shoulder and whispered in his ear, "Best be careful, Polack. Paulie'll have your balls you make his little girl cry."

Ted knew Tony's advice was solid but Maria had him in a trance. Maybe it was one or two or five too many drinks, but he was getting lost in those dark, Italian eyes and that olive skin. The scent of her, so close to him, and the heat he could feel through his slacks where her leg pressed against him were making it hard for him to concentrate on the recollections they were sharing about innocent times spent together. He was heading for trouble. And wouldn't you know it, just as he was getting ready to tell Maria he needed to get going…he had every intention too; straight home and into a cold shower…just as he was about to say it she leaned in close, put her hand on his thigh and whispered in his ear.

"Did you get enough of a feel of my ass back at the bar, or would you like to do some more exploring?"

The rest of the night was like an out of body experience, reminding him of the one time he had taken LSD. The vodka surely didn't improve the situation, but Ted was high on pheromones and testosterone as well. Hardly aware of leaving the bar or hailing the cab, Ted recalled, as he made his way down the central staircase of his elaborate home, how he and Maria had been all over each other as soon as the cab pulled away from the curb at The Beat. He remembered thinking what an idiot he was, but not caring enough to stop.

Checking himself again in the hall mirror, still not happy about the bow tie, Ted looked at his watch. The show would start in two and a half hours. He recalled looking at the alarm clock on his nightstand that first night…morning really…with Maria. They'd left the club somewhere around 1:00 a.m. The alarm clock told him it was 4:50 in the morning and this was the first pause they'd had in the action since exiting the cab and making their way to his apartment. As he lay there, sweat cooling his body as the ceiling fan above the bed whisked it away and Maria panting next to him, he felt a little pride in his ability, at 30 years old, to keep up with the much younger girl. She rolled so that she was looking up at him; her arms crossed over his chest and her chin resting on them. Her face was flushed, her hair damp and sticking to her skin, one bead of sweat resting adorably in the little cleft between her nose and full lips.

"I think I'm in love with you," she said, and Ted knew he was well and truly fucked.

2.

Ted walked through the great room to the kitchen and grabbed the car keys that were hanging on the hook by the door to the garage. He spun them on his finger, catching them in his palm; spun them again. *Swish-chink. Swish-chink.*

He looked around the kitchen; took in the stainless steel appliances, the sub-zero refrigerator, the ridiculously expensive, granite countertops. The kitchen was bigger than the whole loft apartment he had taken Maria back to that first night. This house did not fit him. It was too big. There were lots of places somebody could hide; get a jump on you. It would have been suicide for somebody to try that in his old apartment. He wasn't comfortable here.

The truth, he thought as he made his way back to the staircase, was that the hazards of a large house to a guy in his line of business, or at least the business he had been in, were just a small part of what made him uneasy in this house. It had been a wedding gift from Big

Paulie and every time he pulled up in front of it he could feel the weight of the larger than life mobster crushing his very soul. The house was a reminder of the fact that he was married to the daughter of one of the most powerful and dangerous men on the east coast. As he called up the stairs for Maria, trying to hurry her along so they wouldn't be late, he remembered when Paulie had first confronted him about the relationship.

It was a couple weeks after he had first hooked up with Maria at the club. They had gone out a few times, meeting at places where they were unlikely to be noticed by anybody connected with the family. They had tried to be careful about being tailed but Ted knew it was just a matter of time before they'd be found out, if they kept things going. The only daughter of a mob boss doesn't get out very often without somebody keeping tabs on her. Truth was, she'd probably end up telling her Daddy about it sooner or later; when the excitement of sneaky around wasn't fun for her anymore and she was ready to make Ted an honest man.

They would almost always end up back at Ted's loft and it was the morning after one of their rendezvous, as Ted was sleeping off the late night, that he heard someone fiddling with the door lock. Maria had gone home that night, early that morning to be more exact, and there was no reason for her to be returning as the sun crept above the horizon and pale light began to penetrate the cheap blinds hanging in the windows.

Ted was on the floor, the Glock 9mm from under his mattress in his hand and pointed at the door, before he was even aware he was awake. He vaguely noticed that his cock was poking through the flap in his boxers as he tried to figure who might be breaking into his place. There was always the chance it was somebody looking to rub him out for taking down one wiseguy or another. It was no secret, among the underworld crowd, that he was an assassin. When you were as good as Teddy the Polack, word got around. Maybe one of the other families had decided he was more of a liability than a potential asset.

He didn't want to have to take someone down at the doorway of his apartment. It would alert the other tenants and bring the police. With police came questions. Ted hated questions. He could probably pass it off as self-defense during a break in but they would want to know about the unregistered gun. Worse case, he'd have to go through a dog and pony show trial and Big Paulie would have to grease some palms to keep him from doing time. Unless…

"You got two seconds before I make coming to that door the worst fuckin' mistake you ever made," Ted shouted. He rolled across the wood floor, silent as a church mouse, and came up on one knee several feet from where he had been.

No sound at the door; no movement of the door knob or jiggling of the lock.

Ted concentrated on keeping his breathing slow, remaining calm, and aimed at what would be chest level of someone outside the door. One shot there and then a couple lower to compensate for them ducking, he thought.

"It's Vito."

Vito Cironni was one of Big Paulie's captain's. He was a squat, overweight Sicilian who was known for his penchant for violence. Thing was, Vito never carried out the violence himself; he had boys for that kind of thing. Ted lower the gun a little to compensate for Vito's stature.

"Is Jimmy with you?" Ted asked. Jimmy Mac was Vito's right hand man. Jimmy had no aversions to performing violent acts. In fact, Ted would say that Jimmy took a perverse pleasure in them.

"Yeah, he's here." There was a slight pause and Ted contemplated the shit storm he would be in if he was forced to take out the Capo and his thug. He'd have to get one of those Rosetta Stone CDs and learn some Spanish...pronto. "Let us in," Vito finally continued, "Paulie wants to talk to you."

"The place is a mess," Ted replied, already moving out of sight of the door and out of range of anything that might come through it, "I'm not prepared to entertain." He didn't try to hide the sarcasm in his voice. "Tell Paulie I'll be down to Gino's directly."

There was silence from the other side of the door and Ted imagined that Vito was considering his options. Vito was no dummy and, with or without Jimmy by his side, he knew he didn't stand a chance of rushing the room. If he had come with the intention of roughing Ted up, or worse, that ship had sailed. Funny thing though, if he had knocked, Ted would have let him right in without a second thought.

"Be there in an hour," Vito said, and Ted heard their footfalls as they made their way back down the hall. No doubt Vito was already calling Big Paulie on his cell to give him an update.

3.

Ted checked himself again in the mirror. He was restless, waiting for his wife to join him so they could be on their way. It gave him too much time to think; too much time to remember.

When he had arrived at Gino's Deli, on Lexington near 37th, a short walk from his apartment, Vito and Jimmy were sitting at one of the three tables that served the "eat in" customers. The other two tables were empty. One had bread crumbs and crumpled napkins still resting on the red and white checkered tablecloth, as though diners had just left. The other was as clean as could be. It may not have been used all morning.

There was nobody at the counter and Ted wondered if Gino was doing real work in back or if Vito had told him to make himself scarce. Ted concentrated on the weight of the Glock in the waistband at the small of his back. He let his mind draw on the feeling the small holster, with the snub nosed .45 in it, made against his shin. Knowing that he had those weapons; weapons that he was so adept at using, that he made a living with; made him feel calmer and more secure.

Jimmy sat facing Ted as he walked in, a coffee cup steaming in front of him, his hands out of view in his lap. Vito sat in profile, clearly enjoying one of Gino's sandwiches. He turned slightly to look up as Ted walked in, pastrami hanging from the corner of his mouth as he pulled his fat face away from the meal.

"Have a seat, Polack. Paulie should be here anytime."

Ted kept his eyes on Jimmy, "I'm good. I prefer to stand."

Vito shrugged and turned his concentration back to the pastrami on rye. The bell over the entrance door jingled and Paulie strolled into the deli. He nodded to Vito and Jimmy, met Ted's eye and motioned with a cock of his head for Ted to sit at the farthest, unoccupied table; the clean one.

Ted positioned himself so that he could keep an eye on Vito and Jimmy, over Big Paulie's shoulder, while they talked. Paulie leaned back in the plastic chair, crossed his large hands over his stomach and sighed deeply. The chair creaked with protest at supporting the man's weight.

"So, Polack, how ya been?"

Ted noticed that there was no smile on the big man's face, "I've been good, Boss."

"You know me, Polack. I don't like to bullshit around, so let's get right to it, okay?"

Ted nodded once and waited. Paulie leaned forward and rested his beefy forearms on the table, his hands clasped together. The table tipped slightly toward him.

"Maria's my little girl, Polack. I love you like a son, but I gotta tell ya, I'm not too thrilled about her going around with someone who ain't Italian."

Ted glanced over Paulie's shoulder to see Vito finishing up his sandwich and Jimmy staring out the window, trying to look like he wasn't paying attention to the conversation.

"Sending a couple guys over to take me out, especially after all the work I've done for you, all our history; seems a little extreme."

The big mobster cocked an eyebrow and then allowed a smile to spread across his full, fleshy face. "Well," he laughed, "sometimes I get a little carried away and hot headed."

"Did you really think it would be that easy? They come over to my place and just walk in and plug me?" Even as he said it, he realized that if Paulie had really wanted him dead, Ted would have never known it was coming. If anybody knew the way Paulie operated when he wanted someone taken care of, it was Ted. So this had been a warning.

"Well," Paulie smiled, "if it had been that easy, you wouldn't be worthy of marrying my princess, would ya?"

The idea of marriage stabbed at Ted's gut but he didn't say a thing and tried to keep his poker face while he waited for Paulie to go on.

"Look, I talked to Maria and she says you two are really in love. Course, she's just a girl. So I need to hear it from you. Do you love her, Polack?"

Ted thought back to their first time together and remembered Maria's declaration of love and the sinking feeling he'd had then. Well and truly fucked. He liked Maria, and she was a fucking wildcat in bed, but he wasn't in love with her. Of course, if he were planning on telling as much to the hulking man sitting across the red and white checkered table from him, he would be just as far ahead to pull the Glock from his waistband and swallow a bullet here and now.

"Yeah, Paulie, I love her. I really do."

4.

It had been a whirlwind after that meeting at Gino's. A big, Catholic wedding; the reception at the Morendino compound; the money…God, the money…they received from relatives and friends and people just trying to show how much they *wanted* to be family and friends.

Ted had hardly any family to speak of, only a younger brother, John, he rarely spoke to. He loved his brother, loved him with all his heart, but didn't want him to be anywhere close to the madness that was his own life. He'd sent him money over the years, was closer to him at times; had seen him through medical school. His brother was a successful doctor now, with a beautiful young family. For John's sake, although he knew his brother didn't understand, Ted had cut all ties with him.

Ted looked at the keys in his hand, fingering the one for the house they lived in now that overlooked the 10th hole of the Lake Success Village Golf Course; the gift from Paulie. He heard Maria's heels clicking down the main staircase. She did look beautiful still, but he felt no more love for her now than he did when he lied about it to the Boss. In fact, he liked her even less having come to know what a spoiled brat she was, how she expected to have everyone kissing her ass and for the way she had robbed him of his manhood.

When they got married, Big Paulie quit giving him contracts. He still gave them money, found bullshit jobs for Ted to do, but no more hired gun work. When Ted complained, Paulie told him that he didn't want to risk him getting pinched or killed because it would devastate Maria, she had told him as much. Ted tried to explain that being an assassin was not just his job, it's what he was, but Paulie wouldn't have it. The Boss had Vito spread the word that the Polack was out of the game, so the other families didn't call on him for service either. Jimmy Mac became the go to guy for clean-up work.

Six years, Ted thought as he opened the door for Maria. The Escalade waited outside in the drive. Six years in this house, under her thumb, with my own thumb up my ass. It's almost over.

As they passed Flushing Meadows, taking the Long Island into the city, Ted thought about his meeting with Jimmy at the shitty, hillbilly restaurant out in the sticks. It had been three weeks since they last talked.

"You know the kind of trouble I'm looking at for this," Jimmy said. It wasn't a question.

"The gun will be waiting there for you. The room has a perfect view. I got the last of the money in the truck outside," Ted replied.

"I still think you should just do it yourself."

"I would if I could. Look, it's not that I'm afraid of what will happen to me, but there are other people…" Ted thought of his brother, his young wife and their children. "If Paulie ever found out I had a hand in it…"

"Yeah, well what if he finds out I'm involved?" Jimmy asked.

"He won't. The money is my own, from before the marriage, so it won't show up if they look at Maria's or my accounts. The gun, if they ever find it, will trace back to Jackie Smiles."

Jimmy's eyes went wide, "Johnny Saturo's boy? Are you fucking crazy? That'll start a fucking war!"

"Would you rather they end up looking at you?"

Jimmy said nothing.

"If it gets that far, Big Paulie will figure it was a retribution hit for one thing or another. There's no love lost between those families. They'll go to war sooner or later, anyway."

Jimmy ran a hand through his greasy, black hair, "Man, Polack, this is some serious shit you're asking."

"And I'm paying some serious money. You know, as well as I do, there is no retirement in our line of business. The only guys that get to enjoy the last years of their lives are the ones who get through it alive and manage to sock away enough cash to disappear. The money I'm paying you is enough to live a long time somewhere warm, when you get to that point."

"One more time…" Jimmy leaned in close.

"We'll be coming from the Manhattan Club, up 52nd to the August Wilson. Curtain for the Jersey Boys is 8:00 p.m. 7:30 we'll be on the street. From the room in the Ellington you'll have a clear shot. I'll do what I can to have some open space around us."

"Alright. Let's get the rest of the cash," Jimmy conceded.

Ted beat Jimmy to his feet and put his hand down hard on the younger man's shoulder, holding him in his seat. Jimmy looked up as Ted leaned in close to his ear.

"If you fuck me on this, I will find you."

Jimmy nodded and Ted could tell Jimmy believed him.

"And Jimmy?" Ted continued, "Don't miss."

5.

Ted checked his watch as they strolled on 52nd toward the theatre. 7:32. Maria reached for his hand as they walked.

"Are you okay, Ted?" she asked. "Your hand's all sweaty."

He smiled at her, "You know how I get with these shows and getting all dressed up."

She squeezed his hand slightly, "Well, thank you for bringing me. I've wanted to see this since Ann told him how good it was."

Ted offered her a weak smile. It was just like her to take this moment to be sweet and appreciative. He had to admit that she had her good points, every now and again. She was still killer in the bedroom, although those sessions were fewer and farther between all the time. Maybe if he was able to do the work he was meant to do, it would be different. Maybe if Big Paulie didn't give her everything she asked for, undermining Ted's ability to be the head of the household and spoiling her like a child. He could still direct her down an alley or a side street; explain it away somehow later...

Ted shook the doubts from his mind, reminding himself of the years he'd spent hearing "my Daddy this" and "my Daddy that" anytime he asserted himself. He thought of the way he felt like a kept man, the forced marriage, the reality of his inability to do anything about it without suffering the direst of consequences.

It had been a huge risk approaching Jimmy about this job, but he knew Jimmy was a practical man and that he would go for the cash. Besides, Jimmy was an outsider, like Ted. He wasn't part of the family, not even Italian. In fact, as a Mick, he was probably even farther removed than Ted had been prior to marrying in.

Ted slowed his pace, allowing a young couple to get a few steps ahead of them on the sidewalk. He glanced over his shoulder to see that there was nobody directly behind them as they walked. A pause here to look at a window display, a quick step to beat the light at the corner and they had several feet clear in front of them and even more room behind.

"Hold on a sec, babe," Ted said as he bent and made like he was tying his shoe, untying it quickly before Maria noticed.

She stood waiting for him, gazing idly about, her body quartered slightly away from the third floor window that Ted looked up to. The room was dark, but Ted could sense the presence in the shadows beyond the window. He smiled, knowing that any second the deed would be done. He smiled at Jimmy, hidden in the darkness, trying to convey to him that now was the time.

His fingers worked at the lace on his shoe while his eyes stayed focused on the dark room on the third floor of the Ellington Hotel. Only another moment or two and the light behind them would change, people would walk on and overtake them, the older couple shuffling toward them from the opposite direction would move into the line of sight from the window.

The moment was now, it had to be now. Ted worried that Jimmy was pussying out on him. Then he saw it; a flash of light from the muzzle of the rifle. There was no sound beyond the street noise, the silencer would have muffled it anyway, just the flash.

Ted had a moment to think about the sweet freedom; out from under Maria's thumb; no longer stuck under the weight of Big Paulie's enormous shadow. The thoughts coming all at one time, the way the brain can do that, before you can even comprehend them. Sweet freedom. He thanked Jimmy for going through with it, despite the possible consequences. Sweet freedom, he thought once more as the bullet struck him between the eyes and splattered bits of his brain and skull on the sidewalk of 52nd street.

Author's Notes:

I don't really remember what inspired this story. You know, with some stories I can pretty much narrow them down to the little thought nugget that got 'em rolling and, usually, how they developed into whatever they became. Maybe I had watched Goodfellas for the hundredth time or maybe there was a Sopranos marathon on or perhaps I was enjoying Johnny Dangerously or re-reading something of Mario Puzo's.

I wanted to deal with that feeling of hopelessness that can seep into people and kind of linger there, and fester. And also, I suppose, I wanted to touch a bit on how rash, stupid decisions can lead to major problems. Mostly though, the obvious driving force behind this tale was that I wanted to be able to write about guys with names like Teddy the Polack, Little Tony B and Jackie Smiles.

MUNSTER HOUSE

Samantha stood in the chill of the September afternoon, the old house looming up in front of her. Her friends at school had always said the old place was haunted, information they'd received from the older children, and she had never questioned that fact. Like most children her age, seven just last month, she rarely doubted such information from her peers or seniors. Besides, the house definitely looked haunted.

It was a Victorian era mansion, built in the Gothic Revival style popular in the late 1800's. In its heyday it had been a lavish home that spoke to the wealth and power of the timber baron that had built it. The home had originally been a Robin's Egg blue with white trim, but now its paint and charm had faded to gray. Of course, the history of the home was unknown and inconsequential to Samantha, as she stood shivering in the cool, autumn air. To her, it was simply a place that was said to have ghosts.

The house sat high on a hill, overlooking the small town below. Most days, Samantha would not even dare to look up at it. On the short walk home from school with her friends, all of them so proud that their mothers would let them walk the block and a half like big kids to the corner where they were met, Samantha preferred to walk on the side of the street farthest from the house, even though this meant crossing the street upon coming out of school and then crossing back when she got to the corner where all the mothers were waiting. Although the house itself was a few hundred yards up a long drive from the street, she just felt better putting as much distance between her and it, as possible.

Samantha had often thought that the house looked very much like the one that was on the cover of one of her *Goosebump* books. She had heard some adults call it the Munster house (that was how they said it; m-uh-nster, not m-ah-nster like she first thought) so she guessed that was the name of the family that once lived there and who, presumably, haunted it now. The broken and crooked wooden steps, overgrown bushes, black, gaping maw of a doorway (from her current distance, Samantha was unsure whether the door was missing or simply open), and dusty, cob-web filled interior that could just be made out in the late afternoon sun, beyond the missing window glass and last remnants of tattered curtains, all combined to suggest the house's paranormal reputation was well deserved.

Leaves blew across the yard, whispering in the autumn breeze. They twirled in small whirlwinds and gathered in drifts against the house. The nearly bare trees added to the general spookiness of the home itself, but the *piece de resistance* lay presently to Samantha's right and slightly behind her. Surrounded by a leaning, peeling, weather worn picket fence was the family graveyard. Several headstones - most of them cracked and chipped and hard to read, a few of them losing the battle against the reclamation powers of the rich, loamy Michigan soil - stood in testament to the family which had once lived and died here. Leaves tumbled and gathered against the grave markers and what remained of the fence.

Purposefully, Samantha had avoided looking at the graveyard as she neared the house. Had she bothered, she would have been able to discern from some of the markers which could still be read that the family name had been Rowley, not Munster. It was a name mostly lost to time. Being only seven, she may not have noticed that the six headstones with the most recent dates (recent being a relative term) were all from the same year. Had old Mrs. Handaway not been killed earlier in the day, she would have been able to relate the history of those gravestones to Samantha, though it was a story better left untold to small children.

Mrs. Handaway was the town librarian and the head of the local historic society. She could have told Samantha about the 1918 Spanish Flu epidemic and how two Rowley children, a boy aged thirteen and a three year old girl, were taken by the illness before the first robin of spring had shown its red breast in the northern state. She may have been inclined to tell her that all six deaths were caused by influenza, in consideration of Samantha's tender age. She would probably not have informed her that the children's mother was struck by a severe case of depression, not entirely unexpected given the circumstances, and that she went quite mad. The mother Rowley had killed her two remaining children, a boy of eleven and a girl of six. In the note that her husband found pinned to her cotton night dress, she explained that she felt it best to deliver them to God in a less painful manner than that which the other children experienced. She had smothered them in their sleep. Unable to bear the thought of life without her children, she opted to hang herself from the stately oak in the front yard. Mr. Rowley had tried gamely to continue with life, but succumbed to his own depression and joined his family by shooting himself in his study two months later.

It seemed unbelievable that Samantha had found herself at the footpath that led from the beginnings of the grounds, back at the town's main street, through the small pear orchard which, despite years of neglect, still bore some excellent fruit, and finally along the edge of the graveyard. That she had walked that path, kept worn by teenagers beating back the weeds and crabgrass with the soles of their tennis shoes as they came up the hill from town to dare each other to face the terrors of the house or to find a place to drink beer they had pilfered from their parents' refrigerators, seemed inconceivable. The idea that Samantha stood here now, in front of the house and screwing up her courage to walk up those rickety steps, was craziest of all. The whole day had been crazy though and Samantha was still not sure she wasn't actually lying in her bed at home, tossing and turning, only moments away from waking in her bed with the tendrils of this nightmare clinging to her but fading as such wispy fears will do in even the weakest of morning light. She was, after all, wearing her light blue, footy pajamas at a time of day when she should be just considering getting into them, the sun drooping toward the horizon, and she had been in them all day. She could feel the wind against her cheeks and the cool, damp air growing cooler still. Her teddy hung from her left hand, and she spoke to him now, even though she was old enough to know he wasn't going to answer.

"I *wish* this was just a bad dream."

It was the horrors of the day that had forced Samantha up the hill. It was the terror that the house invoked that had drawn her to it.

She had awoken to the sound of screams. She knew immediately that it was her mother and she had a momentary thought that it seemed so ridiculously out of place; what with her cozy in the warmth or her bed, the early morning sunlight streaming through her window with the promise of a beautiful Saturday awaiting her. Samantha jumped from her bed, squeezing her teddy bear to her chest as she ran down the stairs towards the sound of her mother's yells. Maybe her mom had seen a mouse or a spider; she was really afraid of spiders. When she reached the kitchen she saw her father fighting with some men; her mother was backed into the corner where the counter met the refrigerator. She was clutching a knife from the butcher block in her hands but was making no effort to assist Samantha's dad, only screaming and shaking. Samantha stood wide eyed in the doorway trying to figure out what was going on. She thought that, maybe, these men were trying to rob them.

Steven, Samantha's fourteen year old brother, rushed into the kitchen. He didn't seem to notice her, his attention given completely to the commotion going on, and knocked her into the jamb of the door between the kitchen and the dining room.

"Holy shit!" Steven yelled, and Samantha waited to hear her mother scold him for his bad language. "Zombies! Just like they said on T.V.!" He turned to Samantha, screamed at her to run and, in a brave but foolish bit of heroism, ran to help their father.

It took a few seconds for Samantha to understand what her brother meant. Then she saw it. The tattered clothes, rotting flesh, vacant faces, muddy footprints on the linoleum floor; her father, and now her brother, were fighting zombies; dead people; monsters. Suddenly the smell of decay filled her nostrils; the hungry grunts reached her ears. Her father had been struggling with two of the things when Samantha had first reached the kitchen. Two more had lurched through the back door as Steven had joined the fray and now more were crowding together at the back door as they tried to get in, bumping into each other as they jostled through the doorway. Even Samantha could tell that her father and brother would soon be overrun; her mother lent nothing to the defense. For a moment she thought she should help somehow and then her father turned his face toward her. He was sweating and his face was red. She saw, for the first time she could ever think of, fear in her father's eyes.

"Run, baby!" he screamed at her. She thought he might be crying as he repeated, softly, almost begging, "Run."

She saw her father fall to the kitchen floor and one of the creatures land on him and sink what was left of its teeth into his neck. Steven was lost in the midst of three or four others and it seemed that there were dozens more filling the room and moving toward her mother. Samantha, with her teddy gripped tightly in her hand, ran through the front door and out into the street.

Once outside she could hear screams from other homes and see more of the zombies shuffling through the neighborhood and into homes. Gunshots rang out and Samantha crouched instinctively as

she ran. She ran north, toward her school and in the opposite
direction of the St. Bartholomew church and the town's largest
cemetery. It was not a calculated move. She had taken the path of
least resistance; she ran away from the large crowd of slow, but
steadily moving, gray shapes at the south end of her street. The
plastic bottoms of her footed pajamas slapped against the concrete
and she felt stones and pebbles stabbing the soles of her feet. For
half the day she sought refuge in the town library, but fled when she
heard bumps and grunts among the bookcases. She spent a few
chilly hours between a dumpster and the rear wall of the Kroger
supermarket, until she could no longer bear the thought of being
discovered or the sounds of terror around her. She ran toward her
school because it was one of the few places she knew; a place that
felt like it belonged to her; a place that had always been safe. On her
way there, she stopped as she past the Munster house.

The house scared her; the ghosts scared her, but she thought that
maybe it would scare the zombies, too. Maybe they wouldn't look
for anyone there. Maybe they would be too scared to go up the hill.
Certainly they would be afraid to go in the house. If only she could
overcome her own fear.

That was how Samantha had ended up staring at the house, afraid
to go forward and afraid to go back.

The breeze rustled some more leaves across the unkempt yard and
blew Samantha's thin, blonde hair across her face. As it died down
she heard another sound, similar at first to that of the scampering
leaves but somehow heavier and more solid. It came from behind

her, slightly right of her position…in the graveyard. The idea that zombies, if that's what these monsters really were, came from graves had not crossed her mind until now.

She did not realize that she had lost her grip on her teddy and allowed him to fall to the ground beside her. She considered running to the house but was unable to command her legs to do so. Although Samantha wanted desperately not to, she felt her body slowly turning.

An arm was sticking up from the earth in front of one of the larger tombstones. A swell of earth surrounded the extruding limb. As she watched, the ground heaved and another hand appeared, then the top of a head. Wisps of hair clung to a mostly fleshless skull, bits of moist earth stuck to the face as it pushed upward, the eye sockets were hollow but a surprising amount of skin remained on the face, albeit dried, gray and taut. The zombie seemed to have retained most of its teeth which, while dirty and dark, appeared locked in a mischievous grin as a result of flesh missing from the upper lip.

Samantha took two small steps backward, in the direction of the house, but was still unable to force her body to flee. Her teddy lay abandoned and forgotten on the ground.

The creature seemed to look around, as if getting its bearings, as its torso cleared the soil. It posed motionless, its body still interned in the earth from the waist down, as its gaze fell on the little girl. She wondered how it sensed her, as it had no eyes, but the thought was fleeting. It resumed its struggle to free itself from what should have been its final resting place and shortly stood in front of Samantha; its tattered clothes hanging limply, one shoe lost to the grave.

For a long moment neither girl nor monster moved. Samantha could feel her heart beating hard in her chest; could feel it throbbing in her head. The zombie stared at her with those dark, empty sockets. Samantha knew it could somehow see her.

"Mr. Munster?" she asked.

The creature's head tilted to the left, like a dog trying to understand a command it was unfamiliar with. It seemed to be pondering the inquiry; trying to make sense of the child that stood before it and, presumably, its own suddenly animated state of being. Samantha could hear the sounds of a battle floating up the hill from the town below; gunshots, screams and yelling, breaking glass and revving car engines.

"I don't want to die," she told the zombie, and a tear escaped her watery eyes and ran down her cheek. She stole a glance at the other grave sites and took small comfort in the fact that no movement was evident among them.

As it happened, the resurrected corpse that stood before the small girl was that of Jonathon Rowley, the patriarch of the Rowley family. Had a picture of Mr. Rowley's six year old daughter been held next to Samantha, the resemblance would have been striking. The corpse of Jonathon Rowley held out a bony, decayed hand toward Samantha, its head still listing left inquisitively. Somewhere deep within its rotted carcass, the zombie felt a twinge of something it could not define.

Samantha stared at the outstretched hand before her. She took a tentative step forward, then another. Her own small hand grasped two of the decayed fingers of the zombie in the soft, gentle way she would hold her father's hand when crossing a busy street or walking through a crowded parking lot. She looked up at the decrepit face of Jonathon Rowley's corpse with her big, bright blue eyes and smiled.

The zombie kneeled clumsily, nearly falling over, bringing its face, or what there was of it, level with the girl's. Again it tilted its head, in that questioning nature, to the left and then, slowly, to the right. The yearning that it felt grew stronger and, just as Samantha smiled wider and breathed a sigh of measured relief, the creature lunged forward and sunk its rotted teeth into the soft flesh of her neck. Her warm blood flooded the zombie's mouth, sprayed as her jugular vein tore open and dripped to the ground and onto her teddy, which lay blank faced as a silent witness to the events.

The creature stood after it had finished feeding, wobbling slightly on its unsteady legs. The hunger for flesh that it had felt had been sated, but already it felt driven to find more. Jonathon Rowley's corpse shuffled along the path that Samantha had followed, down toward the sounds of the town in search of another victim. Zombies will be zombies, after all.

A SIMPLE FLIGHT OF STAIRS

1.

The light from the kitchen illuminated the first few steps leading down the stairway to the basement. It could not, however, penetrate the darkness that waited below. Tommy silently cursed his father for not taking his advice and running a switch to the landing for the basement lights. After all, he had argued, it was a safety hazard to have to cross the basement to get to the light switch. Who in the world designed that?

Still clad in his varsity jacket, Tommy Renault stared down into the dank, damp underbelly of the house. Upon reaching the bottom of the steps, he would be in the finished area that his parents used for entertaining on occasion; carpeted floor, some cheap furniture, the oldest of the five televisions that were in the house that had come to reside here after making the rounds from the living room to his parent's bedroom and finally to the basement. It would take him exactly six strides to reach the light switch on the far wall; he had counted it, and three sprinting lopes to make the return trip to the stairs.

To the right of the bottom of the steps, a set of bi-fold doors led to the furnace room, which also served as a pantry, with makeshift shelves lining the walls. The shelves were stocked with several cans of various soups, boxes of macaroni and cheese, one or two extra bottles of ketchup and mustard, boxes of side pastas, and on and on. Cases of water and soda were stacked on the floor. Tommy's father was often teased about his "fallout shelter" in the basement but, in a pinch, you could always find something to eat or drink there.

To the left, across the carpeted floor, was another set of bi-fold doors. Behind these doors was the laundry room; Tommy's destination. He contemplated, for the fifth or sixth time since arriving home from school, ignoring his mother's request that he switch the clothes around. It would mean another speech about him not listening or being lazy, but that was infinitely more appealing at the moment than descending the steps.

Of course, he could only use the "I forgot" excuse so many times before it really bit him in the ass. She'd be sure to tell his dad not to give him his allowance for the week as punishment, even though he'd already cut the lawn and taken out the garbage this week, and he needed that twenty bucks to supplement the little cash he had in his pockets in order to keep gas in his car and have enough walking around money for his date tomorrow with Sue. There was always the chance his mom could ground him, as well, and totally blow up his plans. Tommy was pretty sure Sue was ready to go all the way, she'd already let him get to third base, and tomorrow after the football game, especially if he led his team over their city rival, would be a golden opportunity.

Tommy took in a deep breath and exhaled long and slow through his nose. He silently cursed his luck and took his first, tentative step downward. Tommy hated the basement.

2.

With each step, Tommy's heart began to beat a little harder. He could hear it thumping in his head. Cold beads of fear began to glisten on his forehead. Tommy could feel the dampness spreading under his arms. The darkness at the bottom of the steps enveloped him and he imagined he could feel it on his skin like an oily membrane.

He was on step seven, two more to go. He had counted them several times. He knew he could take them three at a time on the way back up. And the last three from the landing to the kitchen in one more side step kind of leap to account for the right turn.

Eight…

Tommy tried to open his eyes wider, hoping to suck any bits of available light into the rods and cones although he knew the futility of it from past experience.

Nine…

Tommy took purposeful strides across the carpeted floor, counting as he went. One, two…. He pushed his hands out in front; his eyes clenched shut now, waiting to feel something wet and slimy or filthy and furry. His heart was beating faster and he gasped as his leg brushed the back of the chair that it brushed every time he went through this routine. A brief moment of terror before his mind consoled him with memories of the layout of the furniture.

His hands found nothing alien in the darkness, only the hard, smooth surface of the paneled wall. Tommy slid his right hand down and over to locate the bank of three switches and flipped them on. The light penetrated his eyelids enough so that he knew they were on. Tommy opened his eyes slowly, holding his breath and knowing that this was the moment that something would jump out and grab him from behind, just when he felt a little safer.

Tommy turned and faced the basement. He felt reasonably secure for the moment, his back against the wall, the furniture visible, the doors and steps all within sight. Things in basements don't jump out in front of you if the lights are on. They only do that in the dark, when you can't see them coming. With the lights on they have to manage to sneak up behind you.

The smell of damp concrete behind musty carpet and paneling invaded his nostrils. Ten steps from here to the bi-fold doors of the laundry room. Tommy took another empowering breath and started counting.

3.

Three paces across the floor and a creak from above froze Tommy in his tracks. Feeling exposed in the middle of the basement, he listened for more sound above him, wondering if perhaps his mother or father had come home early.

This was another thing he didn't like about the basement. Besides what he knew to be unwarranted fears about what may or may not be lurking in the darkness or behind closed doors in the bowels of the house, he was a trapped rat should some unsavory character enter the house proper. It would be just his luck for some axe wielding lunatic, escaped from the asylum, to decide to search out his next victim in the Renault's tasteful Colonial. Tommy couldn't say where the closest psychiatric hospital might be - there probably wasn't one anywhere near their peaceful suburb - but it hardly seemed relevant at the moment.

After a few tense moments, without hearing any further creaking or croaking from above, Tommy let out the air he had trapped in his lungs and continued his trek toward the laundry. His imagination now conjured images of Jason and Michael Meyers upstairs along with thoughts of Freddy Kruger and other, more horrifying creatures, lurking in the basement.

Tommy reached the bi-fold doors and waited, his hand resting on the knob, prepared to pull it towards him. The light switch was on the inside wall, another terrible design flaw, but his immediate concern was of something leaping from the darkness within as he pulled the door open. Tommy glanced over his shoulder to survey the basement, making sure nothing had crept up behind him while his thoughts were otherwise occupied. He listened for any further movement above him.

Tommy knew his fears were irrational, but weren't most? People were scared of all kinds of things; crowds, tight spaces, spiders, elevators, germs. There was a whole psychoanalytical branch based on phobias. There was no Latin derived name for fear of basements; Tommy had checked the internet to see and couldn't find one. They probably didn't have a Latin word for basements. On the other hand, there were a number of forum posts and blogs from people with the same fear. Granted, many had referred to the fear in their youth and Tommy was seventeen not nine. Most likely, there was a whole cottage industry that cashed in on people's fear of basements; analysts and shrinks who paid for their fancy cars and lakeside, summer homes just by listening to people with Tommy's worries.

Maybe it wasn't so much the basement itself. Maybe it had to do with being alone. The fears, Tommy recognized, were significantly diminished when he wasn't alone in the house. Of course, that may just be because he was then free not to worry about the invading axe murder trapping him down here without hope of escape, at least not without some sort of forewarning as the psycho went through Tommy's mom and/or dad. It could be simply that, with someone else home, he at least had the hope of screaming for help if something did reach out from the shadows.

Another deep breath blown out through the nose in an audible sigh… Tommy pulled open the door for the laundry. As the door pulled out, folded on itself and slid to the right, Tommy closed his eyes and braced for the impact from whatever was lurking there.

4.

A moment or two was all it took to reassure him that the laundry room was safe. He quickly removed the clothes from the dryer, unceremoniously piling them into an empty hamper. He glanced back through the open door to verify the fact that he was still alone in the basement, at least as far as he could see. He supposed any ghouls or goblins wouldn't be standing right out there in the open. They would be creeping up using the furniture and shadows as camouflage. Maybe just waiting on the other side of that old chair, the one he would have to pass to turn the lights back off. Waiting there to grab him…

Tommy hurried the wet clothes from the washer into the dryer. Water from the clothes sprinkled the floor. He tore a fabric softener sheet from the box and turned the dryer cycle on, not bothering to clear the lint trap.

Dumping a pile of clothes into the washer, not separating them or worrying about balancing them, Tommy sloshed the detergent on top. His mother would likely give him the business for mixing colors and darks and he might even be sent back down here to rearrange the clothes if the washer starting thumping and trying to walk out of the laundry room because of the weight being too much off center…didn't matter right now. All that mattered was getting out of this basement.

He grabbed the hamper of clean clothes, exited the laundry room and surveyed the rest of the basement. Holding the hamper in front of him, prepared to use it like a lion tamer's chair, Tommy made his way back across the room.

Clearing the potential danger of the chair without any beastie grabbing his leg, Tommy stood with his back to the wall. He fixed his eyes on the top of the basement steps, the hamper on the floor in front of him, his hand hovering over the light switch. He simultaneously plotted his exit strategy – flip off switch, grab hamper, hightail it straight for the steps, take them two or three at a time, done in seconds – and cursed himself for his silly fears.

Tommy flipped the switch and plunged himself back into darkness, the light from the kitchen illuminating the top of the steps served as his beacon, his lighthouse, to guide him to safety. "Funny," he thought, "that I never considered a monster's ability to travel upstairs."

"Because you know they're not real," he replied to himself.

Bending for the hamper, his eyes staying focused on the light ahead, Tommy felt a warm, whisper of air steal across his neck. A breath? He screamed – only in his mind, of course, he was too terrified to actually make a sound.

Grasping the sides of the hamper, he bolted for the steps. In an instant, in that way the mind can think a hundred things at once, Tommy cursed himself for bothering to even turn the lights off. He could have left them on and went straight upstairs. How could something have snuck up on him? Where could it have been hiding? There wasn't even any room between him and the wall. There couldn't really be something there; it was just that silly fear, his mind playing tricks.

He couldn't see the bottom of the steps but he knew where they were and knew he could leap after the third running stride. Maybe only two steps at a time with the hamper in his hand.

His front foot had just found purchase on the second step, the trailing leg already coming forward to take another set, when he felt his shirt collar pull against his neck. Something had ahold of him! His feet tried desperately to continue the escape as the upper part of his body was pulled backward. He landed with a sickening snap of his neck and lay still in a warm pile of static free whites that gave off a pleasant, outdoor scent he was unable to smell.

Author's Notes:

Basements are scary. They are decidedly less scary with the lights on and when they are finished to serve as rec rooms and such, but they are still subterranean spaces that would seem to be the most appealing areas of refuge for ghouls and monsters and crazed serial killers.

There are exactly nine steps, from the landing to the basement, in my house.

ELEVEN

1

Emily crouched in the corner of the living room farthest from the door. From here she had a good vantage point to the main entrance and if anyone were to come in from some other part of the house, they wouldn't be able to sneak up on her.

She was tired, but certain she wouldn't doze off. Even though the sun was easing its way down behind the trees and roof tops and she wanted nothing more than to surrender herself to the embrace of her down comforter which was lying in wait, unused for weeks now, on her equally neglected queen size bed , just up the stairs and down the hall. She'd slept in only short, restless spurts since she'd had to shoot her father. She was constantly tense and on high alert. She showered with the curtain and bathroom door open, leaning her body out of the streaming water every moment or two to stare at the doorway and listen for strange sounds in the house, thinking she must look like some weird bird peeking out from behind a brush pile. Her father's 12 gauge pump shotgun had become her constant companion, always leaning within easy reach when not resting across her lap, as it was now, or actually in her hands.

She flinched involuntarily as the furnace belched to life, some loose piece of ductwork popping as the blower forced air throughout the house. She was thankful when the heat began blowing across her legs from the nearby wall register, the loose fabric of her pajama bottoms fluttering against her skin. She had thought that maybe the gas would be turned off, the electric as well. It had only been a month or so though, since the real craziness began. She supposed the utility companies probably didn't start cutting services until a person got a few months behind. She wouldn't know for sure, being only eighteen and having never lived on her own she was just assuming. Presumably, her father quit paying the household bills after he got sick. If the mail was still being delivered she was sure she would have seen a number of past due notices.

Of course, the army could have cut all the power if they had wanted to. They wouldn't care if you had just sent your current bill in ten days ahead of the due date. Apparently it hadn't come to that. They seemed to just be waiting this thing out, much the same as she was doing.

She had seen them just outside of town, the soldiers, looking very alien in their HAZMAT suits, holding machine guns, making sure that nobody left town and nobody came in. She had been turned back when she had tried to run over to the neighboring town for some aspirin for her father; Johnson's pharmacy having been depleted. The army had M-25 blocked off; a couple of Humvees across the road. When she stopped, one of the guys in a suit bellowed at her through a loudspeaker and told her to turn around and return to her home. When she got out of her car to explain that she just wanted to get some aspirin, he repeated the command much more forcefully and several of the other guys, their own white suits gleaming in the sunlight, leveled their guns at her. She had almost peed in her pants.

She had known the army was there. Her friend, Janice, had told her about how she had been walking through the woods with her boyfriend. They were just wandering really, drinking a few beers he had stolen from his dad's refrigerator, when they cleared the back few acres of the Thompson place and reached Ridgeline Road. As soon as they cleared the trees they had several guns pointed at them and a bunch of guys yelling at them to go back where they came from. She said that when she looked up and down the road she saw men in white suits spaced every 50 feet apart or so, for as far as she could see. There were also a number of camouflaged vehicles up and down the road. It seemed that the army had surrounded the town. Emily had thought they would surely let someone through to get some aspirin, especially if that someone intended to come right back. She'd been wrong, but she hadn't understood the whole of the situation at that time.

The "situation" at present was that she was cowering in her own home, waiting for… for what?

The shades were drawn, all the doors closed, but she could see through the half-round window in the front door that it was beginning to snow. Sparse, but large, flakes were being highlighted by the setting sun. Though she hadn't done it since she was a small child, she longed to run out the door and chase after the flakes; trying to gather them in on her tongue. The truth of it was that she just wanted to be outside, to no longer be a prisoner in her own home.

For a while they were able to follow the news on the television. It was very surreal seeing aerial views of your hometown on CNN. She knew that her little, nothing town was the center of the news universe right now. It was the epicenter for this new virus. Scientists had no explanation for what caused it. Some said it was a mutation of Mad Cow Disease, others said it was something entirely new. Other than a few isolated cases elsewhere, all of the infected were right here in Gentry, Michigan. The experts weren't sure how the disease was transferred but they had laid out the symptoms and stages of progression.

It started with pretty basic flu-like symptoms; head and joint aches, upset stomach. After your body purged itself of any food you tried to ingest and any bile that might be lingering, you started vomiting blood. The headache worsened and you started hallucinating. They said people exhibited traits like rabid animals. Emily thought they just went flat out crazy. She should know... she watched it happen to her father.

This was the only time in the last five years that she ever felt happy that her mother had died. She would have hated to see her get sick like that or even for her to have to deal with this madness. Emily was pretty certain she could never have shot her mother.

There was no news now. No signal reached either the television or the radio. Emily guessed this was by design; some part of the government's plan to deal with the situation. It made her nervous not to have any information. The last bits of information from CNN stated only that the town had been put under quarantine so the disease could be contained. Everyone outside of Gentry was advised to stay clear and to stay in their homes as much as possible. Schools and businesses across the country were closed out of fear that someone somewhere may be carrying the disease beyond this small town in the thumb of Michigan.

The citizens of Gentry were not given any advice or instructions. It seemed to Emily that the town had been left to die.

2

Throughout the early evening, Emily was able to nod off for a few minutes at a time. Whenever she awoke she would listen intently for any unusual noise in or around the house. She would stay perfectly still for minutes, not even bothering to brush aside the long, stray strands of her auburn hair which had escaped from the rubber band holding it back, until she was certain nothing was different. Then she would adjust her position, maybe get up and go to the bathroom, certain to take the shotgun with her and to leave the door open as she squatted on the toilet.

She was out of bottled water, never having had the opportunity to stock up, so she would drink water from the tap. At first, she always made sure to boil it, just in case the disease was spread through the water supply. Now she was pretty certain that she was immune to whatever this was and she didn't bother with such precautions. Frankly, she was getting to the point where she didn't much care.

There was always somebody with immunity it seemed. Ebola cases in Africa, Malaria in South America. Somebody always walked out unscathed. She supposed the army people would want to examine her in any number of ways to see if they could figure out what made her special. Of course, that supposition assumed she would get to them. She'd seen what the disease did to people before it killed them. It always killed them, too. 100% death rate if infected. The news had said as much a week or so ago before the signals quit coming through.

It was getting quieter outside each day. The crazed growls, howls and snarls of the sick seemed to be diminishing. The pleas and prayers of those being attacked by the most advanced of the infectoids, most in the early stages of the disease themselves, were lessening as well. Emily guessed another day or two and she would have a good chance of being able to walk out of here without too much trouble. She had plenty of shells for the shotgun.

Her car and all the others she could see were mangled wrecks. Some infectoid or another had smashed windows and slashed tires. Actually, it was probably a band of them. They seemed to gravitate into small groups as they reached a certain stage, sort of like wild dogs. Then they would attack whatever they came across until, one by one, they died off or were killed by some other crazy. The disease was, at least, fairly fast acting. It took about a week to go through the whole process from simple flu to rabid animal to rotting corpse. Emily realized she was basically waiting here for everyone else to die. It would have been tragically sad to her if she had not long passed the point of having any such emotions

As she settled back into her corner, having relieved herself and gotten a glass of water, she wondered if the army folks would even take her in if she made it to them. Certainly they would be able to see that she wasn't sick but they might fear that she was carrying the disease just the same. Maybe they would put her into some sort of quarantine for a while. Then again, maybe they would just shoot her and save themselves the trouble. Either way, she certainly couldn't stay in this house forever. If they killed her, she would see her mother again. For that matter, she would see her father also. Presumably, in Heaven, he would be his old self.

As she glanced at the clock, she couldn't help but smile. It was 11:11 pm. For as long as she could remember 11 had been her lucky number. It had started with the simple act she had just completed...checking the clock. It seemed it was always 11:11. Morning or evening, it was when she seemed to wonder about the time. Of course, she knew it was probably more a case of the number being so recognizable and just sticking in her mind. Chances were she'd checked the clock just as often at 12:54 or 3:17, but those numbers didn't mean anything. They weren't bold enough to take root in one's subconscious. 11:11 though...well, that was special.

As time went on, she had opted for 11 as her own special number. If she played on a sports team and had a numbered jersey, she always tried to get 11 or traded with another girl for it. When she got on her Facebook page and filled out some silly, mind numbing questionnaire that happened to ask her favorite number, she never hesitated. 11.

Emily got up from her corner and went to the kitchen. The calendar on the refrigerator, held by two, gaudy magnets they had gotten on one or another vacation, reminded her it was November, the 11th month of the year. Even more interesting was that tomorrow was the 11th of November. Certainly this left no doubt about what she should do. Tomorrow would be the day, November 11th, in the year of our Lord 2011; Emily would walk out of this hellhole. 11-11-11. Surely a great day, right?

It was curious as Emily was not an especially superstitious person. In fact, she often scoffed at those who put any sort of faith into things like horoscopes or psychics. She didn't worry about black cats or walking under ladders; she never threw salt over her shoulder and she didn't carry a lucky rabbit's foot or other talisman. Deep down, she supposed, she didn't really put any weight into the idea that 11 was any kind of special number, but these days, amongst all this insanity… well, one had to hold on to something.

3

Emily was trying to block the memories of her father; drool running down his chin, the maniacal grin on his face as he came toward her. She had brought the gun up, her arms shaking, tears streaming down her cheeks.

The banging against the front door snapped her back to the present. For a moment, she was unsure of what she had heard. It came again, someone knocking. She raised the shotgun to her shoulder and pointed it at the door. A cold sweat broke quickly on her forehead. Her heart was pounding so hard she felt it would burst through her chest.

Who could be knocking? It was after midnight, in a town that was dying or killing itself, depending on how you looked at things. An infectoid, from what she had seen, didn't have that sort of thought process. They might pound, in an effort to break the door down, or even hurl themselves at the door but they would not knock as if delivering a package or coming to borrow a cup of sugar. The knocking came again and Emily considered firing the shotgun through the door, but hesitated. Should she call out? Ask who it is? That would give away her presence. So far she had been happy to believe that nobody knew she was here; she wasn't in a hurry to change that.

Emily pushed with her legs, sliding her body up the wall, keeping the gun trained at the door. Should she try to peer out of one of the windows? It would put her uncomfortably close to whatever might be out there. Could it be the army? Maybe they were doing a sweep of houses, looking for survivors. But wouldn't they call out? Announce themselves? She took a tentative step forward, the gun steady though she felt as if every atom of her body were shaking itself loose of her.

"Hello?"

For a moment, Emily thought the word had escaped her own lips, and then she realized it had come from the other side of the door. It was low, barely audible, as if whoever had spoken it was trying to ensure that only someone in the house, close to the door, could hear it; daring to speak only so loudly.

Emily's bare feet took another soft step forward. She moved on her toes and the balls of her feet. Her manicured toenails, French manicured, the tips shiny white, peeked out from beneath the pink pajama bottoms, pictures of hearts and roses on them, the word "sassy" in red, cursive letters across her bottom.

"Hello? Are you there?"

The voice was male. She could hear the fear in it and it somehow eased her own terror. She stepped closer to the door. She began to speak and realized her throat, mouth and lips had dried beyond the ability to form words. Was it a symptom of her current fear or due to the fact that she hadn't spoken to anyone in days? She swallowed, forced saliva into her mouth and licked her lips. She was only a step or two away from the door now.

"Who is it?" Emily asked, the gun still aimed at the spot where she had last heard the voice, her finger twitching slightly on the trigger.

"Oh, thank God!" The voice from the other side of the door exhaled in relief. "It's me... Jimmy. Jimmy Felsher."

She knew him from school, unsurprising in such a small town. Jimmy had been a year ahead of Emily, graduating last June. They were casual acquaintances, although Emily had to admit she'd had a crush on him from afar, always afraid to be direct about her feelings when she chanced upon him at parties and such. His family lived on the outskirts of town, farming a hundred acres or so.

"Are you sick?" she asked.

"No!" He sounded upset at the accusation. "I don't even have a fever. I... I'm all alone."

Emily considered her options. She could tell Jimmy to go away, leave him out there with the infectoids, or she could let him in. It would certainly be nice to have some company. She wasn't worried about getting sick herself but she didn't want to let somebody in who might go all cuckoo crazy on her in the middle of the night.

"What are you doing here?" she asked.

"I was running. The... they... sick ones, they killed my family. Broke into our house and... I ran. I've been running. I saw you through the window, last night. I.."

It sounded as though he had begun to sob; heavy, painful sobs that touch at her and caused a bitter, salty taste to rise in the back of her throat.

"I'm going to unlock the door," Emily said, her hand, manicured to match her toes, already reaching toward the knob. "When I say "go" you count to ten, and then come in. Got it?"

"Got it."

Emily flipped the thumb latch on the knob. She reached up a few inches and switched over the deadbolt. She wished it hadn't made such an audible click. She backed away a couple steps, the gun still in position, and said "go." She backed into her corner and went down to one knee, silently counting in her mind.

She reached ten as the door knob began to turn and felt a comfort in that Jimmy had followed her instructions. Jimmy eased through the door, his face turned away from her, peering back into the street. He shut the door and quickly turned the locks, once again securing Emily's personal fortress. Then he turned to face her, his eyes widening and his hands reaching for the ceiling.

"Holy…! Hey, I'm not here to hurt you!"

Emily was surprised to feel the delight his reaction caused and she had to repress a smile.

"You just stay there a minute…" she considered her next words and knew she sounded like a television show cop as she said them, "…and keep your hands where I can see 'em."

Sidestepping her way to the hallway, keeping the barrel aimed at Jimmy, she reached an arm through the bathroom door and fumbled in the near cabinet. Pill bottles tumbled to the counter top and bounced to the floor as she searched blindly. Her left arm ached now supporting the weight of the shotgun on its own. Her fingers finally found purchase on the object of her search and she slid it across the floor to Jimmy's feet.

"Pick it up," she directed.

Jimmy bent down slowly, his hand searching for the item at his feet as he kept his eyes trained on the weapon pointed at him. He picked up the thermometer and stared at it a moment before looking back to the girl.

"If you're a hair over 98.6 you can just go right back out that door."

Jimmy placed the thermometer in his mouth and they stood silent for what seemed to both to be an interminable amount of time. She let her eyes wander about his body. His shoulders were broad and his arms defined from hours of labor on the farm. His dirty, white t-shirt seemed to labor at restraining his muscular torso. He was movie star tall, 6'2 at least. His hair was dark, almost solid black. It was disheveled and falling into his eyes. And those eyes... They nearly took her breath away and she could imagine herself getting lost in them. Seeming greener and brighter than possible, contrasting the dark locks on his head. She could nearly feel his calloused hand on her cheek, his breath whispering across her skin as their faces came together, his eyes penetrating her soul...

The thermometer beeped and Emily blinked herself back to reality. Jimmy checked the digital screen, afraid of what it might say; terrified to be forced back out to the loneliness of the streets of Gentry and the monsters that lurked in its shadows.

He slid the thermometer across the floor to Emily, who bent to retrieve it and allowed a small smile to finally grace her pretty face as she read 98.5 on the display. She lowered the gun, only slightly less grateful at the action than Jimmy was.

4

Emily and Jimmy shared their experiences of the last few weeks. She told him how her dad became ill, how she had hoped against hope that it was just a regular, old flu rather than this terrible virus and how she had stayed at his bedside as he worsened.

Jimmy told her about his ten year old brother becoming sick and running out of the house one afternoon in nothing but his Spiderman underwear. He hadn't seen him since.

She heaved and sobbed her way through a description of her father giving her the shotgun, anticipating his death and the potential loss of sanity that would precede it. Jimmy held her as she broke down while recounting the night he came at her and she had to use the gun.

All through the night they talked. After a band of the afflicted… that was what Jimmy called them and Emily took to using it so that the "infectoid" term wouldn't seem cruel given what happened to Jimmy's brother… after they broke into his house and he'd escaped, leaving his parents behind, he'd been making his way through town, breaking into vacant houses for food, shelter and a place to hide. He had been on his own for a week. Last night he broke into the Peterman's across the road and happened to catch a glimpse of her moving past one of the windows.

"I was afraid it was another of the afflicted just crashing through, but I knew after a few minutes that it must be someone healthy, or at least not too far gone. An afflicted one… a crazy one… would have been trashing the place."

After Jimmy had proved himself through the temperature test, Emily did the same. He hadn't asked her to but she felt he deserved it. From what they could tell, Jimmy having a little better grasp on the situation than herself, having been out in the town for days, it seemed they were likely the only two souls in Gentry that hadn't contracted the virus.

He came on the eve of November 11th. A boy she had always had a bit of a crush on. They were the only two survivors in this death trap. She felt as though it could be some fated experience. Maybe 11 really was lucky after all.

Their talk turned to reminiscing about friends, parties they had been to, teachers they liked or hated at the High School. Before long they were probing each other for information like new, young couples will do. Favorite songs, favorite colors, what they each looked for in a guy or a girl.

Emily was aloof, feeling silly at her shyness. Jimmy was more direct. He said he liked girls with a sense of humor, ones that were down to earth, and all the things boys always say. But as he described what attracted him physically, he may as well have just said, "you."

There was a pause in the conversation, an awkward silence. Jimmy stared into her dark, brown eyes; eyes so dark that the pupil was nearly lost in them. He wanted to pull her to him. His feelings rushed forward and he could feel the heat rising on his neck, sure his ears were reddening. He turned from her, unable to meet her gaze for fear of melting within it.

"So," he began, running his hand through his hair, feeling the dirt and oil and thinking how he must appear to her, how he must smell, "do you think I could take a shower? I mean, I haven't had one in a while. I must smell like a goat."

She laughed at his joke, harder than was merited, her own desires causing her awkwardness. She hoped she wasn't too obvious. He was glad that she was.

She sat on the couch as Jimmy showered, feeling more at ease than she had in weeks. She was comforted just by having his presence in the house and she opted not to cower in the familiar corner of the room, although she kept the shotgun at the ready by her side.

They had talked about her plan to walk out today. Jimmy had confirmed that he was seeing lees and less mobile bodies on the streets of Gentry the last couple of days. The sun was just now beginning to peek above the horizon and she envied its oblivion to the happenings on the planet that it gave light and life to. It had taken her a while to confess her superstition to Jimmy. She felt childish and naïve as she explained the significance of the date, but he didn't laugh at her or make fun even though she could tell that such things held little weight with him.

"Well, we might as well go for broke and leave around 11:00 am," he said, smiling but not sounding at all condescending. "In fact, let's step out the door right at 11:11."

Emily walked through the rooms of the house, peering out the windows looking for any sign of life. All was quiet. She thought if she could have ignored the battered remains of the town and the bodies lying still and stinking in the street, she could have convinced herself that things were normal outside her home.

The steam swirled around her and engulfed her as she opened the door to the bathroom. She leaned the shotgun against the wall. As she undressed, she had only the slightest concern to the inappropriateness of her actions. She couldn't say exactly why the feeling had come on so strong, but she knew that what she wanted more than anything at that moment was to join Jimmy under the streams of hot water.

His back was to her as she stepped quietly into the tub and his eyes were wide with surprise as he turned. As he grasped the moment he felt himself becoming erect and his face flushed with shame and desire. As their eyes met, Emily felt a brief moment of doubt and she smiled shyly. It was all he needed to act and he pulled her into his wet, glistening body. They made love in the shower, both of them realizing the carelessness and danger and neither of them willing to relinquish the moment.

She wanted to make breakfast for him, to sit at the table like a newlywed couple resplendent in white bathrobes with bacon and eggs steaming on their plates, orange juice and coffee next to a stack of buttered toast and the sun shining through windows. Instead they ate the last of the Pop-tarts, not bothering to heat them, washing them down with tap water as they sat on the couch listening to the silence outside.

Jimmy looked slightly comical in a pair of her father's sweatpants that were pulled up to just below his knees to disguise how short they were on him. Emily dressed in blue jeans and a University of Michigan sweatshirt; the first time in weeks she had worn anything but pajamas. They had coats lying over the arm of the recliner in the living room, waiting to be of use to them. Emily retrieved a 9mm pistol and bullets from her father's gun case for Jimmy. It sat in his lap and the shotgun lay next to her. The seconds crept by as they waited.

At 11 minutes after 11 o'clock on the 11th day of November in the year 2011 Emily and Jimmy stepped out into the world. They walked through the deserted streets, past the damaged and burned out storefronts and along M-25 toward the edge of town. They went without incident, seeing many bodies but none living. There were no army vehicles blocking the road. There were no soldiers wearing white suits and holding machine guns. They looked at each other when they reached the outskirts of Gentry, unsure of what do to next.

"I guess we just keep walking," said Jimmy.

"Do you think they moved farther back? Maybe they increased the area that was under quarantine?"

Jimmy shrugged, "At least we haven't run into any problems. I think you were right. Today is a lucky day."

She smiled up at him at let him wrap his arm around her, leaning into him. They walked on, both allowing a feeling of happiness and contentment to overtake them. Whatever the rest of their lives brought them, at least they had each other.

5

In a large room, far away from Gentry, Michigan, several very important men sat around a very large table. They were wearing crisp uniforms decorated with very important looking medals and ribbons. Several of them had stars along the shoulders of their jackets.

The man with the most stars picked up the solitary phone in the room as it rang the second time. He glanced at his companions briefly, searching their faces before raising the phone to his ear.

"Yes?" he asked.

He listened intently. Nodding as he received information from the other end of the cable. He hung up and looked solemnly around the room.

"It has been confirmed that the virus has spread beyond Gentry. Cases have been reported in several small towns in the surrounding area. Last night, the last of the troops pulled out. All military personnel in the state have relocated to Ohio."

"Their families?" one of the other important looking men asked.

"Collateral damage. We can't risk widespread panic. People would try to flee."

All the men nodded in understanding.

"A plane has just left Selfridge. The President has confirmed the order. Expected arrival at the drop site is 1200 hours."

A few of the men slumped back in their chairs; one cradled his forehead in his hands.

"Gentlemen, sometimes we must sacrifice the few for the many. November 11th, 2011 will be remembered throughout history as a day when tough decisions had to be made for the preservation of our great country and the world."

One of the important men, with less stars on his shoulder, sighed heavily, "Tell that to the southeastern portion of Michigan."

The man next to him turned, put a hand on his shoulder and said, "There won't be anyone left to tell."

Author's Notes:
Sometimes you work through all the trials and tribulations that lay in front of you and, in the end, you're still fucked. I'd like to believe in luck or in fate or in blessings or in karma. I'd like to but the world makes it hard.

ASLEEP IN BETHANY

A rumbling noise rouses him. He feels the vibrations, like a
thousand fingers tickling his back and legs. He is cramped, stiff. He
lays on something hard and cold; uncomfortable. He can't recall his
dreams.

His name is yelled; it seems from a great distance. "Come out!"
The words echo around him. The voice is hollow; far away but
authoritative. He must listen.

Trying to rise, he finds his hands are bound in front of him; his arms
are held tightly to his sides. With great difficulty he manages,
finally, to roll himself into a seated position, his legs dangling off the
stone surface where he has been laying. His feet, too, are bound and
as he stands he nearly topples forward. It's hard to balance.

There is a light before him. His view is hazy and he realizes he is
looking through a thin cloth that covers his face. He shakes his head
in an effort to dislodge the covering but it remains fast. His useless
arms and hands strain against their bindings momentarily, until he
remembers that he cannot move them.

He hops, staggers, waddles toward the light. Even through the
cloth, the sunshine assaults his eyes and he winces as he emerges
into the daylight. He sees, through the shroud, the forms of many
people. He hears their gasps.

"Loose him and let him go."

The voice is the same as the one that called him forward. It's
clearer outside the confines of the cave and he recognizes it as that

of the prophet; the one his sisters love so dearly; that he, himself, believes in.

Some of the ghostly, dark forms move toward him. They reach to free him of his burial cloths. It's slow work as they stop to gag, retch and vomit from the smell of him. It's the smell of decay and he is only now self-aware of it. It's the smell of death.

With the cloth removed, he can see his sisters among those that work to release his hands and feet. They are crying. He remembers them standing over him, in his sickness, telling him that the prophet will come and heal him. They believed he would stop death, not reverse its hold.

He looks to the prophet, surrounded by many. The prophet's eyes are sad. He has been crying, as well.

Free of the burial garments, his movements are still stiff and difficult. Those who have been loosening him move away, their hands covering their faces. The crowd moves off, surrounding the prophet. They praise him and his miracle. He stands alone, outside of his grave, wondering if he stands only as a symbol of the prophet's greatness. What other purpose might there be for the walking dead?

He turns and shambles back inside the cave and lays himself on the cold, hard, stone surface. He waits for life or death, unsure which he belongs to and which will claim him now. He groans within himself.

Author's Notes:

Truth be told, I have some issues with my religious beliefs and those issues sometimes creep into my stories. I had a parochial education and, during that time, I asked a lot of questions. Those questions were often answered with, "That's just one of those things you'll have to ask God when you get to heaven." That seems a bit of a cop out, no?

I'm still asking questions. I'm still not getting much by way of answers.

I suggest you read the Lazarus story in the Bible and then come back to this story again. You'll probably pick up on a couple of phrases and such that will add a bit to the whole thing for you. You know, I can't hold your hand through all of them.

USELESS

For years I had been stopping by my parents' house on Sundays. I guess it started to be a real ritual shortly after I had finished college, so that puts it going on something like 13 years.

Sunday was usually the only day of the week that I would see them, outside of a holiday or other special occasion, even though I live only a few miles from them and have no family of my own. Every Sunday, about 12:30, I would stop by their little, suburban bungalow. My mom would have spent the morning making her homemade, chicken soup. It was delicious soup. She boiled a chicken breast in with it, and while the soup didn't have much actual chicken in it, only what managed to fall away from the breast of its own volition, it seemed that she managed to squeeze an immense amount of flavor out of the breast and into the broth.

My father and I would sit at their small dining table and mom would serve the soup while chatting with me about the week's events. My father was always served the chicken breast, as well. Now, the soup was plenty, I wasn't really there for the food anyway, despite the fact that my mom's chicken soup is second to none. However, the fact that my father would greedily dig away at the breast, sucking on the bone as if he were trying to extract every last bit of marrow, without so much as once bothering to offer me some, just goes to exemplify the man's nature. I've long suspected that it was at his insistence that my mother didn't simply include a second piece of chicken. I am sure that he took pleasure in devouring the fowl in front of me while I slurped my nearly meatless soup across the small table from him. To mom's credit, I am pretty sure that she, on occasion, would fill my bowl with just a bit more soup than my father's.

I could say that I didn't go over more often because I am busy with work (true) and because I am still renovating my home (sort of true) and because I have an active dating life (unfortunately, not very true at all, of late). I could comment that seeing my parents once each week is more than most, if not all, 35 year old, single males could say. For that matter, I would propose that most children (man or woman, married or not, spanning a great breadth of age) do not visit their parents so often and certainly not with such regularity. The truth of it all, though, is that I felt obligated to visit my mother but really couldn't bear spending much more than a few hours each week with my father.

My father was a difficult man to be around if you were (a) his wife or (b) his son. Although my mother never said as much, I know that he beat her. I suspect that there was a time, during their courtship and perhaps early in their marriage, when he was a charming man. My mom was not an ignorant woman and I am certain that if Jack Salowicz had shown his true colors prior to their marriage, mom never would have gone through with it. Mom may not have left my father even if he had starting slapping her around as soon as the honeymoon, they were both from Old World Polish families, each of their parents straight off the boat and with a slew of siblings, but I am sure that my mother would have confided in her own mother or one of her sisters that her new husband was prone to violence. I am equally certain that the information would have gotten back to my grandfather or one of my uncles and that my father would have had to answer to them. Those sorts of families don't believe in divorce and they believe in a woman respecting, honoring and obeying her husband, but I know they would not have stood for their daughter or sister being beaten. My father would have been made to understand that any harm that came to my mom, to Jedrek Makolowski's little *kwiat* (his little flower), would have come back to him in spades.

No, I think there were years spent in love. Years when my father worked hard and proved his love by providing for my mom. I have seen flashes of my father's loving side toward my mom, certainly rare in my lifetime but I imagine they were more frequent early on. I have seen him amongst relatives and friends, charming and confident in himself. He could be the type of man who exuded a certain air of contentment with himself and his life that others would be envious of. He was not rich and not an especially educated man, but when he wanted to I believe he came across as a person very comfortable in his own skin. Privately, I know this to be untrue. I know that he was bitter and increasingly unhappy with his life. I can only guess when the physical and/or mental abuse began toward my mother. I would lay odds that it coincided very closely to the birth of their only child, yours truly, for I do not recall a time when abuse was not a prevalent theme in my own life.

My father made no secret of the fact that he did not want a child, or at least that I was not the child he wanted. Maybe my father wanted a daughter, maybe a more athletic and "manly" son would have pleased him. Then again, perhaps anybody or anything that took attention away from him would have been unacceptable; this is probably why we never had pets. A dog or cat would be one more thing in the house that required attention, robbing my father of even more of my mother's devotion. Quite simply, my father was a selfish and jealous man.

It is not without some calculation that I always refer to my father as such. I mean, I always call him "father" when speaking about him, never "dad" or "pop" or "the old man". The word "father" seems to me to be the one which conveys the least emotion. It seems the most biological title to use, acknowledging his part as the sire to my birth but not, necessarily, anything more. Speaking to him, I would go with "dad". This was only because I suspected that he would have felt that I was trying to sound uppity or above myself if I referred to him as "father". "Father, may I borrow the car?" Certainly, never something I would have asked, but had I done so, and in that fashion, even I must admit that it sounds like it should have either an English accent attached to it or the accent that seems to be specific to people from the upper, East coast states and only if their families have a net worth which makes things like 40 foot yachts, summer homes on one cape or another and dinner parties requiring formal dress and tables that set a minimum of 20, regular necessities rather than luxuries. I am sure if I ever called him father while speaking to him, he would have delivered one of those quick, sharp slaps with the back of his hand that stung so severely but rarely resulted in anything more than a slight, fleeting red mark and he would have said something like, "Who the hell do you think you are talking like that? We work for a living in this house and we aren't ashamed to talk like it", or some other similar comment that made little sense, if any. My father had a way of turning a phrase that seemed to convey that he was at once proud and ashamed of his blue collar position in life.

Now, mom… well, mom I loved. Sometimes I would call her mother, but it was out of respect. Mostly she was mom or mommy. Even later, when I was a grown man visiting for Sunday's soup, I might tease her a bit as she placed the steaming bowl in front of me, saying "Thank you, mommy" in a little, sing-song tone as if I were still just a small boy. It would always make her giggle and she would playfully wave the air as if she were somewhere between shooing me away and slapping at me, the way older women do when embarrassed, and say "Stop it" but not meaning it as her other hand would come up to her mouth to hide her smile. My father would grunt from across the table, maybe taking a moment to look up from his bowl, or from his newspaper if he hadn't already started eating, and glare at the two of us as if he were disgusted that we should have this playfulness between us. He was probably feeling jealous or slighted by the thought that we cared for each other; loved each other.

I suppose most boys believe their mothers to be saints or nearly so. My mom was a sweet woman who would go out of her way to help others. She was the type of woman who would take a casserole to a sick neighbor; spend hours upon hours crafting little drink coasters out of plastic canvass or crocheting dish towels so that her friends could use them as door prizes for a daughter's baby shower or some such. Mommy knew just the right way to blow on a skinned knee so that it would stop hurting and just the right speed with which to pull a band aid off so that it didn't come off too slow and cause a long, dull pain nor too fast and pull sensitive little peach fuzz hairs off a boy's leg or arm. Mom could make as many different voices as were required to bring a bedtime story to life and she could tuck the covers around me in just such a way that I felt both loved and secure. I loved my mother with all my heart. Some Freudian shrink would probably say it was too much so and that I have an Oedipus Complex which explains the reason I am still single. Personally, I think Freud was a quack.

When I was about 8 years old one of my Aunts passed away. I was still young enough to not quite understand death. My father decided that this time I would go to the funeral home instead of being left with a sitter and spared the trauma of the reality of death. My mother protested, arguing that I should be a couple years older, at least, before I was introduced to death up close and personal. Of course her pleas fell on deaf ears. He was "damn sick and tired" of my mother babying me all the time. She was turning me into a little momma's boy and he wasn't going to have that anymore. Of course, it was a foolish idea that exposing me to the workings of a funeral should do anything to increase my "manliness", but rarely did my father's arguments regarding my upbringing make sense.

I watched as all of my relatives, a large number of which I couldn't recall ever seeing before, marched past the casket where my Aunt Sylvia lay. All of the women were crying and most of the men appeared to be stoically comforting them, jaws set and seeming to stand straighter than normal, as if physically restraining their emotions caused them to stiffen right up. I don't remember a great deal about how I felt or even what I saw. I recall quite vividly that there were no children there my age and that I spent most of the time at my parents' sides. I remember my father escorting me to the coffin several times. At first, I was only to stand there and view the body. Then I was encouraged (forced really) to touch my Aunt's cold, stiff hand in a farewell gesture. My father explained quite coldly that Aunt Sylvia was gone and would never be back. She wasn't sleeping; the body was just an empty shell. He lifted me to the coffin and told me to kiss my Aunt goodbye, I was afraid and cried and pleaded with him not to make me, but he insisted that it be done and he leaned me toward her. I recall thinking that if I kissed her quickly that I could at least be away from her, otherwise he would likely hold me inches from her face, the smells of powder, make up and death assaulting my nostrils, for as long as it took for me to relent. It was traumatic and one of several moments in life that I never forgave him for.

I came away from that experience with a new, albeit premature, understanding of the finality of death. There followed a two or three year period when I was acutely aware of the fact that my mother was older than I was and most likely destined to die before I did. This terrified me for a couple of reasons. First and foremost, I loved my mom more than anyone in the world and I couldn't bear the idea of never seeing her again or at least not until I joined her in heaven, as they taught us in Sunday School. Secondly, I was afraid of the idea that I would be left alone with my father. Already, at that young age, I was convinced that my father didn't care much for me and I was sure that if my mother wasn't around to temper his hate, I would probably end up in an indentured servant sort of existence, if I was allowed to stick around at all. Being so young, I had no concept of foster care, or of the possibility of living with other relatives and the like.

Therefore, every night after mommy read me a story and tucked me into bed, I would make her promise that she wouldn't die and furthermore, that she would not die until I was ready to die and then we could die together. I realize now how difficult that must have been for her, how it must have just pulled at her heart that her little boy was so terrified that she was going to die. Yet every night she would smile at me, kiss me softly on the forehead and promise that she would wait.

A little over a year ago, at age 60, Helen Salowicz broke that promise.

My mom was diagnosed with breast cancer at age 58. Shortly after her diagnosis, she had a mastectomy. She had some chemo and what not, but only two months after the operation she was declared cancer free. About one year later, my father retired from his job at a plastics factory, at the age of 65. One month after that my mom passed away.

The doctors said that the cancer returned and that it was so aggressive that there was nothing they could do. By the time it was caught at one of her regular screenings, it had spread so much that it was inoperable. She died quickly and did not go through much of the suffering that I have seen in other cancer victims, for which I am grateful. However, I am of the opinion that my father's retirement and her death were connected. I think she just didn't want to live with the son of bitch home all the time.

 I always carried a little guilt about going away to college and then moving into my apartment and eventually my own home. I felt like I abandoned my mom. I know that she made her choice to marry the man, but I am sure my presence had at least some bearing on her staying with him. I always felt that with the two of us there he had to spread out his anger. Sometimes mom would take the brunt of it and sometimes it would be me. This guilt, illogical as it may have been, only increased upon her death. I believe this is why I continued to visit my father each Sunday. Perhaps, in part, it was because I felt some sort of duty as a son to check in on him. Mostly, though, I believe it was an act of penance.

 The coinciding of my father's retirement and my mother's passing led to an increase in my father's alcohol intake. He had always been a drinker and most of his physical, violent outbursts were short flashes of rage and generally occurred when he was drunk (regardless of his blood/alcohol level, he always seemed capable and prepared for the mental abuse). I cannot think of a single day that I did not see my father with at least one beer. On weekdays he would come home from work, sometimes having had a few on his lunch hour, and he would start drinking after dinner. Most times only a beer or two, but some days he would have things on his mind and he would go through a six pack or more in just a few hours. On weekends he would generally be out in the yard or the garage. On cold days he might be puttering around in the basement, where he would sometimes build model cars (cars that I was not allowed to touch) that to this day line the basement recreation room of their home. Saturdays and Sundays he would start drinking usually around noon, but sometimes as early as nine or ten in the morning. He would drink slowly at first, a beer every 45 minutes or so. After a few, his pace would increase. I am aware of this because if I was anywhere within earshot I would respond to his yelling for someone to get him a beer. Otherwise the task would fall to mom. I can't remember him leaving the garage or yard or even the basement work table (the "beer fridge" was in the basement) to get his own beer. Presumably he did, because there had to be days I was off playing and mom was shopping or something, and I don't imagine the inconvenience of stopping whatever critical task he was in the middle of to retrieve his own libation would have stopped him. Certainly it pissed him off, and I am sure one of us paid for it in the end.

Even when I was there to retrieve his beer for him, I was never quick enough about it or I would do it correctly. You wouldn't think the simple task of running to get a beer out of the fridge could be so demanding but, in my father's eyes, I was never able to complete the mission acceptably. If I ran my fastest I would invariably be scolded for shaking the beer and making it foam up. If I took pains to deliver it more carefully, I would be told how slow I was. God forbid I should drop one of the longnecks! It happened on one occasion and I was reprimanded with his thick leather belt. Not only had I wasted the beer, delayed his drinking and created a mess; I had also deprived him of the deposit on the bottle. Without fail, upon delivery of the beer and the accompanying dissertation on the folly of my attempt, my father would use his favorite line, "Boy, you are as useless as tits on a bull."

Useless as tits on a bull. It's a saying that was probably humorous the first few times it was used, a hundred odd years ago or so. I suppose it holds its humor for anybody who has never heard it before. My father, however, would use it on a pretty regular basis, like daily. There was never any variation, never any ingenuity in looking for a new way to describe my ineptitude as seen by him. At least that would have made it interesting. I can think of several similar turns of phrase that he could have substituted, if only occasionally, to break the monotony. How about as useless as a windshield wiper on a submarine or a pogo stick in quicksand, a men's bathroom at Lilith Fair or a condom machine in a convent? One of the funnier variations I once heard was "as useless as a hatful of busted assholes." Men like my father, I suppose, are not necessarily very creative.

Some people go through stages as they drink and reach different levels of inebriation. Usually, at some point, they are happy. It may be when they start drinking or a few drinks in when they reach that first buzz, or maybe when they are absolutely, shit-faced drunk that they become Goodtime Charlie. My father never seemed to be happy. He generally started off in a crabby mood which progressed to downright anger as he went along. I guess this is what people call a "mean drunk" but I am not sure that is applicable because he was mean to begin with. Being drunk just meant he had less restraint.

My father was always quick to point out mine or my mother's inadequacies. It may have been my struggles at sport, which never resulted in encouragement or time spent helping me practice but rather an oration on my inexplicable inabilities and my similarities to the female gender. It could have been a critique of my mom's cooking, which I always found excellent but which my father never seemed satisfied with. Perhaps he would fly into a tirade about the cleanliness of the house, another ridiculous complaint as my mom always kept a clean home, but a single dirty dish could be the culprit. Sometimes my mother, presumably hoping to forge a bond between my father and I, would suggest that I help him with some household project or another, which would lead only to some screaming and yelling about how I didn't know a Phillips head from a standard screwdriver and, eventually, the aforementioned comparison of my usefulness to that of the mammary glands of a bull.

Despite the fact that the mental torment was nearly constant, it was preferable to the physical abuse, which seemed only to occur if alcohol was involved. I can remember distinctly the first time he struck me. I was eight years old; it was only a short while after the funeral home incident. My mother suggested that my father let me help him work on one of his model cars. My father, apparently in a generous mood, agreed. This led to my subsequent banishment from all things model car related, as I believe I've mentioned. My father essential had me watch as he glued the small pieces together, the smell of the model glue making me light-headed. The model he was making, a replica of an open-wheeled Indy car, came with an assortment of decals which had to be soaked in water and applied. He told me to place the decal on the spoiler of the race car, after he had wetted it and shown me how to place it with tweezers. I placed it and looked to him for approval.

"No! Jesus! Are you stupid?" he yelled. "It's crooked as hell!"

I had thought I had done a good job. At eight years of age, I admit, my eye my have not have had the critical aptitude of an adult but I would swear today that it was straight. Having expected a "good job" and foolishly hoping for perhaps a pat on the back or a ruffle of my hair, I was taken aback by his outburst. I shrunk away from him, startled, and knocked over the small bowl of water that he was using for the decals. This sent water streaming across the work area and, in reaction, I threw my hands out across the table as if I could gather the water back in. I inadvertently hit the model and sent it to the floor. It was a classic, slow motion moment in which I saw the model cartwheeling downward toward the black and white tile of the basement, landing and splintering into several pieces. My father was already standing, having shot to his feet to avoid the spilling water, his chair tumbling forcefully backwards.

"Look what you've done! You ruined it!"

I was still staring at the shattered model on the floor and I looked up, fearfully, as he yelled. I had never seen him so angry, his face red and his eyes bulging and ominous. He lashed out his hand, snapping it quickly across my cheek. The force knocked me to the ground and I lay there, my body unsure how to react. I wanted to cry but I was in shock. I wanted to yell for my mom, but the pain surging through my jaw left me silent. Eventually, and it seemed a very long time, I rolled onto my back and looked up at my father. For a moment I saw regret and a bit of sorrow on his face, but it dissolved quickly back into anger and he yelled at me, "Get out of here!"

I suspect that he felt bad for hitting me. At that time I am sure he had already crossed the line between mental and physical abuse with my mother, but I think he surprised himself that he could cross the same line with me. Of course, after that incident, it seemed that he came to terms with his violent nature and with each passing year was more apt to resort to physicality when angry.

It wasn't as if my father beat me daily and I think any physical abuse against my mom was limited to maybe once every couple of months. It wasn't as if we were walking around covered in bruises. In fact, he rarely left any trace of the act. It may have been worse that I could not count on his reaction. If I knew his anger would always resort in a beating, at least I would have been prepared. Instead I would be tensed, trying to anticipate the strike in the midst of his yelling. Sometimes it would come, and I was rarely ready for it, but just as often it would not. He would simply stop yelling, shake his head in disgust and turn away.

The last Sunday that I visited my father was unremarkable from the weekly visits since my mom passed. I arrived around one thirty. I was less punctual since mom died as there was no need to be there for a prepared meal. My father was sitting at the dining room table, reading the paper, drinking a beer.

"Hi, Dad."

He grunted at me in response, not lifting his eyes from the paper in front of him. There was a plate on the dining table, the remnants of a sandwich on it.

"If you had gotten here earlier, you could have had lunch," he said.

Certainly I wasn't incapable of making myself a sandwich; he simply wished to point out that I was late. If I had arrived earlier he would have said he wasn't hungry. It was the same exchange we had every Sunday.

As with every other Sunday since mom had passed, I tried the usual small talk. How are you feeling? How about those Falcons (or Braves or Hawks, depending on the season)? Anything interesting in the paper? The only time he would take me up on a subject was if there was something he wanted to complain about. He might decide to talk about how stupid a trade one of the sports teams made was, or he might go off on a tangent about a particular politician. If I tried to offer a counterpoint, he would cut me off abruptly and tell me I didn't know what I was talking about. If I agreed with him, he would ask if I had any independent thoughts or simply agreed with what everyone else said. It was a lose/lose situation.

A few times I had tried to bring up mom. He would fix me with a cold gaze, "I don't want to talk about it."

I asked myself why I came here. Why did I put myself through this each week? What was the purpose of coming here?

I was trapped. I was trapped in the cycle of coming to this little bungalow every Sunday. If I stopped I would be a bad son, and that would disappoint my mom, dead or alive. If I stopped I would be admitting that he had a power over me. Certainly he did, I'm no fool. He had the power of fear over me, even now. But if I let him drive me away completely, not settling the issues between us, then it would be like…like he beat me.

All this time, despite the abuse, maybe even in some ways because of it, I continued on toward success. I excelled in school, I got my degree, I landed a successful job. I had good relationships, both romantic and casual, that were devoid of irrational anger or abuse. I was, all in all, a well-adjusted human being, despite my father. I owed it to the constant support of my mother. And yet she was the one that had died. That wasn't fair, but it seemed that was always how it worked. The ornery, mean, asshole bastards in life never seemed to get what they deserved. I should have been visiting with my mom; comforting her at the loss of her husband; not meaning it.

I would have to keep coming here until he died. Sometime before that I would have to try to talk to him about the years of abuse, about mom. I would have to get him to open up so that I could have what the experts called "closure" in my life.

I went to the refrigerator looking for something to drink, a soda or a water.

"There's stuff in the basement," said my father from behind me, "get me a beer while you're down there."

In the basement I went to the fridge and pulled out a Pepsi and a Budweiser long-neck. As I walked through the rec room I could feel the cars on the shelves around me, their headlights, like eyes, following me as I moved. I scanned the room and saw it there, on the second shelf of the far wall, the infamous Indy car. He had rebuilt it that same day that he first struck me, without my help of course.

I set the drinks on the table and walked across the room, plucking it from its place on the shelf, leaving a clear shape in the dust, like a capital I. I turned it in my hands, fingering the decals as I did. I took my thumb nail and scratched at the decal on the rear fin. It came off easier than I expected. I grabbed the little steering wheel between my thumb and forefinger and wiggled it off. I plucked one of the front tires off and let it drop to the floor. It wasn't really meant to be malicious; in fact I was barely conscious that I was doing it. I set the model on the table and picked the drinks back up.

As I reached the top of the stairs I saw my father finish his beer and set it back on the table. His back was to me and he hollered over his shoulder, "Come on, boy! I'll die of thirst by the time you get back up here! Did you get lost?"

Obviously he had not heard me come back up the stairs. I shook the beer slowly but steadily in my hand, letting the carbonation and pressure build up in the bottle. I began to walk toward him softly and as I did he said softly, under his breath, "I swear, that boy is useless as tits on a…"

It was all he got out before the bottle struck the back of his head. He listed to the left as the foam and caramel colored liquid sprayed across the kitchen and the small dining area. He froze there for a moment, on the verge of straightening back up. Then in slow motion, just like the tumbling Indy car, I watched him fall to the floor, spinning out of his chair and landing on his back. Blood began to pool around his head.

I remember thinking that this wasn't the kind of closure that Dr. Phil might recommend, but it was exactly the Old World type of closure that my Grandpa Jedrek would have wanted for his little flower.

My father lay there with the blood spreading out farther about him on the linoleum. I wasn't sure if he was dead or just unconscious. His eyes were closed and for some reason that seemed to me to indicate that he was still alive. I thought that his eyes should be wide open in a state of shocked disbelief, frozen at the moment of death; too much television maybe. I stood there with my Pepsi in one hand and the jagged long-neck in the other. I let the soda fall to the floor and straddled my father's body. I plunged the jagged glass into his throat and was startled by the skin, blood and tissue that exploded through the top of the bottle. It reminded me of a science experiment

I made in the fourth grade; a volcano with baking soda, vinegar and food dye; even more so as a few rivulets of blood began to run down the sides of the bottle.

I guess that is all I have to say in my defense, Your Honor. I admit that I killed him. I will not try to claim that I was temporarily insane. No, if anything the insanity has been there my whole life because it was insane to have to live with a man like that. I won't say it was self-defense because he wasn't hitting me at the time, he hadn't raised a hand to me since I first left home. Call it murder, or if you like, Patricide, that has an ominous ring to it. You can throw the book at me, put me away for the rest of my life, give me the death penalty. Does Georgia still have the death penalty? You'd think I would know. You can call it what you like, do with me what you like. I have found closure...and freedom. I feel like I have accomplished something necessary. I feel useful.

Author's Notes:

I was worried what my Dad would think about this story when he read it. I love my Dad, have had a great relationship with him my whole life and think he did a pretty good job of being "Dad." Writing this story was an exercise in putting myself in the mind set of someplace I've never been. Fortunately, I have a reasonable sense of empathy and, if my third grade teacher can be believed, a very active imagination.

I think a lot of fiction authors have a little concern in the back of their minds about people that they know recognizing parts of themselves in stories (we do draw from real life sometimes…okay, ALL the time) and thinking that whatever other attributes are given to that character are a reflection of what the author thinks of them. My experience is that it is rarely the case. I have, however, made frequent trips to the basement, over the years, to retrieve a beer for the old man. In fact, there is a humorous family story about how, when I was just a wee lad, I had a school assignment to tell how I showed my parents I loved them. My response was that I gave my Mom hugs and kisses and I went to the basement to get my Dad a cold beer. That's what kids are for, right?

DO YOU MAKE HOUSE CALLS?

1.

"I can't take it anymore, John. I'm at my wit's end and I just can't take…" Marjorie's words trailed off into a collection of sobs and sniffles. She buried her face in her hands, unable to meet her husband's eyes. John watched the tears leech around her fingers and felt his heart breaking.

He put his hand gently on her back and spoke softly, "I'm just scared. There are so many horror stories about these back alley operations. If we could just wait until it was legalized. I heard it was supposed to go back to a vote…"

"And how long, John?" she interrupted, snapping her face back toward him; her eyes rimmed red and snot trickling out of her nose to rest on the top of her upper lip. "How long until it's legal…if ever? How long can we live this way?"

Not long, he knew. She was right. Their marriage was strained to the point of breaking. Her mind had made her a prisoner in their bedroom; her bedroom, John spent most nights sleeping in the den. The anti-depressants did nothing but induce sleep, where she escaped the evils of her waking mind only to be devoured by the nightmares of her subconscious. They hadn't spent a night together – a real night like a husband and wife should – in over a year.

The abortion had been a decision made out of love and reason. How could they subject a child to a life like the doctors predicted? Deformation, brain damage, a life of constant care and monitoring; a life likely to last for only a brief time full of pain and suffering. Their decision was heart rending but, they thought, merciful. There was a danger to Marjorie in going through with birth as well and that had weighed into John's opinion though, he knew, Marjorie had not given any thought to her own well-being.

Her depression and nightmares were not unexpected the first couple of months; a perverse twist of the post-partum syndrome. John had taken it much easier but, to him, the baby was more of an abstract idea; something only vaguely real until he could see it and hold it in his arms. To Marjorie, as he assumed it would be to most women, it was a growing, living entity that had become as much a part of her as she was a part of herself. He had sat with her through the counseling they had tried, listening to her recounting visions of bloody, crawling fetuses and rotting baby corpses; cursing herself as a murderer and fearing damnation from a God that insisted on blind acceptance of any trial, tribulation or horror as His will.

If only they could go back to a time before the abortion; before the pregnancy. Though they didn't live in a world where time travel was possible they did have an option. Illegal, dangerous, expensive; they couldn't go back in time but they could erase the memory of it.

"Okay," John said, pulling his wife to him, feeling her tears soak through his shirt to his chest, her body heaving with each uncontrollable sob. "I'll make some calls; make the arrangements."

John laid there with her until the drugs began to kick in and she fell into a fitful sleep. He pulled the covers up over her, despite the heat in the room, and took note of the chewed nails, the oily, stringy hair and the pale, sickly complexion. He smiled softly at the thought of having "his Marjorie" back.

Back in the den, John called a friend who worked with someone that had an acquaintance who knew a guy and told him to set it up. He polished off half of a beer and fell asleep sitting up, with a cigarette burning in the ashtray and the weatherman on Channel 6 warning of thunderstorms. He dreamed of a bloody, deformed fetus clawing through his wife's skull and eating her brain.

2.

Two nights later, John sat in the living room wringing his hands over a stuffed envelope that lay on the coffee table. Marjorie, as usual, was in the upstairs bedroom. He found that her spirits had lifted dramatically just at the anticipation of the operation. For the longest time it had been Marjorie who bore the cross of anxiety based on their decision; John had felt pain too, but he was Simon the Cyrene to her Jesus.

The rain drummed out a beat on the awnings and the thunder crashed like accompanying cymbals. Flashes of lightning caused an occasional strobe effect through the windows and John thought it ominous that the storm that was supposed to have come through yesterday had waited to arrive like a precursor to their visitor.

The first knock was muffled by the sounds of the storm and John stared at the front door, unsure if he had heard it; hesitant, uneasy, hoping he had not. A heavy pounding a few moments later left no doubt and he went to greet the guest with a suddenly dry mouth; finding it difficult to swallow.

A tall, broad man in a long, black overcoat stood waiting for him. Rain dripped from the man's black fedora. His face, partially shadowed by the brim of the hat, was square-jawed and flat-nosed with a bit of gray stubble along his chin. John opened the prime door and cracked the storm door enough to stick his head out, not yet inviting full entry to the man. The man held a large black bag in his hand, similar to a medical bag of a house calling doctor, but larger, and when he spoke it was in broken, heavily accented English.

"I Doctor Smith," he said.

Sure, John thought, *Smith*. The man could have been Russian or from one of the other old Eastern Bloc countries based on his accent. The chances that the man was an actual doctor were probably only marginally better than the chance that his name was actually Smith. John wanted to tell the man that there was a mistake, that he was at the wrong place, but his thoughts of the last year with Marjorie stifled his tongue. He found it hard to work any saliva into his mouth so he held open the storm door and nodded to indicate the man should come in. John had to lean back into the door to give enough room for the large man to pass by.

The doctor turned back to him as John shut the storm back outside. He set his large bag on the floor but made no move to remove his coat or hat; just stood there dripping in the middle of the living room.

"You have money?" the doctor asked.

"Oh…yes, of course," John walked by him to retrieve the envelope from the coffee table and handed it over.

Doctor Smith spread the envelope with large, meaty thumbs and peered inside, "Is all here."

John couldn't tell if it was a statement or a question so he answered anyways. "Yes," he said, "fifteen thousand." It pained him to say it. It was practically all of their savings.

The doctor nodded, bounced the envelope in one hand, as if weighing it, and John watched it disappear inside the overcoat.

"Is for wife, yes?" asked the doctor, gesturing to the large, black bag.

"Um, yes. She's upstairs."

"We go."

"Yes, of course," John said, "but…well…how exactly does this work? I mean, what is…"

"Is for wife," The doctor interrupted. "I talk wife." He picked up the bag and stared at John, "We go."

The doctor's gaze was flat and soulless and, though he felt slighted and angry at being dismissed so handily after turning over fifteen thousand dollars, John said nothing and led the way to the stairs leading to the bedroom.

Marjorie lay in the bed with her hands clasped together over her stomach. She looked like a body laid out for viewing at a funeral; she bore an unusually peaceful expression which added to the effect. A dim bedside light was the only illumination in the room, save the occasional lightning flash from the ongoing storm.

"Marjorie," John said, "this is Doctor Smith."

The big man set the bag on the floor and moved to the bed, resting his bulk on the side of it, next to Marjorie. She turned and smiled softly at him.

"I'll give you some light," John said.

"Is fine," answered the doctor, and John stopped with his hand hovering over the wall switch. "I talk wife. You go."

"I'd really rather stay. I'm sure Marjorie's nervous and…"

"You go," the doctor commanded, turning to John. "Is important to talk patient only. Make sure right memories taken. Other person influence device."

"But you're another person," John retorted.

"I professional. I doctor."

"It's okay, John," Marjorie said. Her voice was soft and calm; the small smile still on her face. "It's fine. Do what he asks."

John hesitated a few moments longer then grudgingly walked out of the bedroom.

"Close door," the doctor called behind him and John did as he was told, gritting his teeth to suppress the anger.

John stood outside the door, listening. He could hear their murmurings but couldn't decipher the words. The deep, rumbling baritone of the doctor sounded like the thunder rolling off into the distance. He heard Marjorie's soprano whispers; could hear the hitch in her voice; knew she was sobbing. He leaned against the hallway wall, squeezing the bridge of his nose with his thumb and forefinger, trying to suppress a rising headache. His stomach was turning itself in knots and he felt ready to vomit. He slid down the wall to a seated position on the floor and stared out the window at the end of the hall, watching the rain slide down it in sheets, waiting for the lightning and counting the seconds to the thunder clap. Though it had been pouring for a while, it seemed the storm was moving closer still.

3

The thunder shook the house and John's eyes popped open. The last flashes of the lightning were flickering away as the thunder rolled. The storm was right on top of them. The hall light dimmed, fluttered, glowed back to life. John realized he had dozed off sitting on the floor.

He heard thumping from the bedroom, through the door; the sounds of a struggle. He jumped to his feet and burst into the room, his eyes wide, adjusting to the dimness; wide with fear.

Marjorie was convulsing in the bed as if she were being electrocuted. John saw two suction cups attached to her temples, they appeared to be smoking. Wires led from the suction cups to a box on the doctor's lap. It was the size of a bread box.

Irrationally, John thought of the game 20 Questions. *Nothing's the size of a bread box. Everything's either smaller or bigger than a bread box.*

The device had several knobs and switches and lights that were flashing at an alarming rate. The doctor still wore his coat but was hatless; John noticed it hanging on the post at the foot of the bed. The doctor's hair was gray, short; cut in a military crew. He turned to John, his dark, excited eyes catching the light spilling in from the hallway. Beads of sweat glistened on his forehead.

"What the fuck is happening!?" John screamed.

"Is normal. Don't worry."

"It doesn't look fucking normal! Get that God damned thing off her!"

The doctor turned back to the device on his lap; twisting knobs, flipping switches, "Is almost done."

Marjorie continued to flop on the bed. Her eyes were wide, staring off into nothing. Grunts and groans dragged out of her mouth; *unngh...uhhh...gah.* John grabbed the doctor's wide shoulders.

"Turn it off, you bastard! Just stop it! Turn it off!"

The doctor shrugged John off him like a child just as Marjorie quit convulsing and came to rest on the bed. The suddenness with which she stopped moving drew John's attention from the doctor; sure she was dead. Her eyes were closed, her body still, but she was breathing; shallow, labored breaths but breaths all the same.

"Take those things off her head!"

The doctor set the device to the side and reached for the suction cups attached to Marjorie's temples. They came away from her skin with audible pops and left two, red, glistening circles behind them. The doctor rose, grabbed the bag and began placing the device back inside of it. John pushed his way past the large man.

"You fried her! You fried her brain!" He held her face in his hands, tears welling up in his eyes. "God, Marjorie, I'm so sorry. I shouldn't have let this happen. We should have waited. We should have tried something else."

"Is normal," the doctor said behind him.

"Wh..what?" John turned to him.

"Is normal. Procedure is hard, but is normal." The doctor closed his bag, grabbed his hat and replaced it on his head, "Is done. She sleep for a while. Wake up, no bad memory."

The doctor walked from the room and John was torn between chasing after him or staying at Marjorie's side. As the doctor started down the stairs, John ran from the bedroom, "Where are you going?"

"Is done. I leave."

"But what about when she wakes up? Shouldn't you stay and make sure she's okay? What if something went wrong?" John stood, grasping the banister along the stairway, staring down at the doctor who had reached the bottom of the steps and turned to look back at him. His eyes were flat and cold again.

"I am doctor of device. If she feel bad, call real doctor," he said and turned; walking out of John's sight toward the living room.

"You son of a bitch!" John yelled and took the stairs three at a time after the doctor, nearly falling on his way down. The front door was closing as John entered the living room and he ran to it, throwing it open and bounding out onto the porch. The doctor was halfway down the walk, the rain pouring down on him. He paid no interest to it; didn't hunch over to protect himself, didn't pull the collar of his long, black coat up around his neck. He strode down the walk as if it was a gorgeous spring day and he didn't have a care in the world. He turned at the sidewalk and headed down the street. John went as far as the sidewalk and watched the man walk away, a shadow among the streetlights, reaching the end of the block and turning out of sight. John stood a few minutes longer, the rain soaking him through, wondering just what he had done.

4

John sat by Marjorie's side for two days. Her breathing had returned to normal and she lay there in a peaceful sleep, but a very long one. Occasionally he would talk to her, tell her everything would be fine. Sometimes he would gently shake her, asking her to wake up; to come back to him. He slept in the bed with her, wanting to feel immediately if she stirred. He woke up one morning to find her eyes open, staring at the ceiling.

"Marjorie!" he sprung to a seated position next to her. "Babe? Can you hear me?"

Marjorie didn't move, didn't make a sound, didn't so much as turn her eyes toward him. He wrestled her up to a seated position, propping her up with pillows. Her eyes stared into nothingness; a thin stream of drool ran out of the corner of her mouth and down her chin. John sat staring at her. He grabbed a tissue from the box on the nightstand and wiped her face. He used the same tissue to dry his own tears.

For two more days, a full week since they had made the decision to schedule an illegal appointment to use an outlawed device, John tried to get some sort of response from his wife. He tried feeding her soup only to watch the lukewarm liquid collect in her mouth until it spilled over her lips and onto her stained pajama top. He tried yelling in her ear. In frustration and desperation, he slapped her hard across the face, leaving a red palm print on her cheek and only managing to direct her gaze in a different direction.

He traced her features softly with his hand, lingering at the red scars on her temples. It was as if someone had removed a set of horns that had grown there or, perhaps, that a set of horns were preparing to sprout. Small wonder as he had practically invited the Devil into their home.

He knew the old saying, that two wrongs didn't make a right, but how did the math play out for three. He wondered as he laid her back in that peaceful, sleeping position; her hands crossed at her midsection; as he pressed the pillow down over her face in an act of mercy that was yet another outlawed procedure.

At least, he thought, *she doesn't have to live with those memories.* Perhaps this was the best that could have been hoped for in the end. She no longer had to live with the guilt of murdering an innocent. Now it was John's turn.

Author's Notes:

This was another one of those "here's a direction, write a story" things for an anthology. Although I wasn't too keen on working that way, the first time I did it, I've found that sometimes I enjoy the challenge. The idea here was to have some sort of memory erasing device in the story.

Since I don't see that sort of thing (erasing memories) as a very good idea, I decided it should be something illegal, so it became a "back alley" procedure in my story. That led me to think of abortion and then euthanasia. I mixed them altogether in a big bowl (that I think still had some brownie residue in it) and baked at 350 for about a week. This is what turned up.

INUIT MOON

1.

Anana knelt close to the fire and stirred the stew that hung in the pot. Bits of caribou meat rose to the surface then sank back into the brown liquid. Near the fire, Anana could feel the beads of sweat forming on her face; her skin was damp beneath her fur-lined clothing. She thought to remove a layer or two but knew that as soon as she was away from the flames, the heat they offered would be greedily absorbed by the cold of the land that crept into the small shack that was her home. She would only have to put the clothes back on to obtain a semblance of comfort.

The winters were always bitter in this land; too much darkness, the sun cresting the horizon for the briefest of periods each day. The snow gathered, it seemed, each day; the drifts piling high against the wood walls. She imagined the gods of the wind and snow conspiring to bury her alive but knew that the winter was no harsher; the snow drifts no higher, than they had been, in general, for the last sixteen years that she had been alive. She stirred the stew again, watched the pieces of meat and the sparse vegetables swirl, rise and fall. She should be used to the seasons but Anana yearned for the spring; for the warmth of the sun to chase away the endless white and expose the tender green seedlings of new life.

It was mid-winter, when the days were shortest, the winds were strongest and the cold was constant. It burrowed its way through the thin walls of the house, through the layers of clothing, the blankets, her skin; digging itself deep into her bones, curling up and sleeping there. This first winter after her father died, gone to join a mother she never knew, seemed colder for his absence. And it could be true, she thought, one less body to share its heat, but the reality was that the extra cold came from the inside and spread outward. It started in her heart and spread through her veins to mix with the cold that burrowed through her skin from the outside.

Tatkret, her brother, sat at the wooden table behind her. She imagined she could feel his eyes on her but when she stood and turned, he was staring at the window across the room. Anana followed his gaze. Outside, the sun had already completed its brief, low run through the sky and the darkness outside was complete. Anana walked to the window, looked past the glassy flames reflected there, and stared toward the village that she knew was there but was well out of sight.

The snowmobile tracks from her brother's trip to the village earlier in the day – a trip for the whiskey bottle that sat in front of him now under the guise of trading some of his seal skins for vegetables – had already been blown smooth and swallowed by the snow, though she could not see this either. Tatkret had returned from his trip with news that no new supplies had reached the village, that the couple small, withered, softening potatoes and sickly looking carrots were all he could manage. Anana had added them to the stew, thankful for what they could get, and was then saddened when the full bottle of whiskey appeared from beneath Tatkret's jacket. Some supplies, she thought, were always available.

"The stew will be ready soon," Anana said, half to herself and half to her brother. She watched as the words turned to fog and frosted the window pane. She received a grunt in reply.

"I wish the moon were out," she said, wanting to speak if only to cut the silence which seemed to make the cold even more bitter. "Even weak moonlight is better than nothing."

"Annigan is eating," Tatkret said. His voice was quiet and as cold as the snow.

Anana turned to her brother. His gaze had not shifted and he stared through her. She moved from the window, uncomfortable in front of his black eyes, dark like her own; so dark that she imagined they were pools of oil and she could almost see the rainbow colors rippling across them. He raised the bottle to his lips, wiped a trickle of whiskey from a chin speckled with coarse whiskers that refused to grow together.

"In the village they say he is about to catch her," he said.

Anana knew the old story of Annigan, the moon god, and his sister Malina, the sun. She had thought it a terrible story and wondered about the mentality of her ancestors, that they would create such a horrible tale to explain the movements in the heavens.

It was told that Malina was a beautiful young woman and that one night, while she was dancing in a great hut, with other young people, a wind came and blew out the torches. In the darkness, Malina was attacked and raped but she did not know by whom. The torches were re-lit but, again, a wind came and extinguished them and, again, Malina was raped. To determine who was doing this terrible thing,

Malina rubbed her hands in soot and when the torches were again blown out, and she was again attacked, she pressed her hands against the back of her attacker.

This time, when the torches were re-lit, Malina ran about the hut searching for the man with the hand prints on his back. To her terror, she found that it was her brother, Annigan, who had the sooty hand prints marking him as the rapist. She screamed at him that the thing he had done was wrong and unnatural. In her fury, she took a knife and cut off her own breasts, throwing them at her brother and telling him to have them if it was what he wanted so badly. She then grabbed a torch and ran from the hut.

Annigan grabbed a torch, as well, and ran after her but he stumbled and his torch fell into the snow so that it was glowing only with embers. As they ran, another great wind came and lifted them into the sky. Malina became the sun, her torch burning brightly, and Annigan became the moon, his light less because he had dropped his torch in the snow.

They can be seen in the sky now with Annigan continuing to chase after his sister, Malina. His lust is so great that he does not eat as he chases her and this is why the moon becomes less and less. For three days, the period of the New Moon, Annigan goes away to eat. He comes back and renews the chase, waxing full and then wasting away again.

It is said that when the moon eclipses the sun, Annigan has caught Malina. But this is a time for men to be afraid and to stay indoors as Malina releases her fury upon them during this event.

Thinking about it now, Anana wonders at the silliness of the myth. Why would Malina not cry out and tell others about the first attack? Why would she continue to stay and dance after being raped, not only once but twice, and then plan to find the attacker by allowing herself to be raped a third time? Why would she cut off her breasts? Why, most of all, would her ancestors create such a disturbing, incestuous tale to begin with?

Anana had heard variations of the story; most varied in telling the circumstances that brought Malina and Annigan together. Sometimes it was a copulation party, which Anana thought even more depraved. Sometimes the story was told that Annigan simple came to Malina in the night. Sometimes the story is told that the siblings simply had a fight and Malina darkened Annigan's face with lamp oil and then the chase began.

It was Anana's experience that, when given variations of a story or a myth, the worst was usually the true, original version. Over time, as sensibilities improved, the stories were often modified so that they were less abrasive.

2.

After dinner, Anana busied herself with mending clothes by the firelight. Tatkret sat at the table dividing his time between repairing one of their father's fishing nets – nets that now belonged to Tatkret, Anana supposed – and finishing the bottle of whiskey.

Before long, Anana saw that Tatkret had set the net aside and was concentrate all of his efforts on the bottle. He stared out the window with his black, oily eyes; his shaggy, dark hair matted and wild, in need of washing and cutting. From time to time, Tatkret's eyelids would grow heavy and begin to droop. His head would fall forward only to be snapped back as he started awake. Anana waited for the one time when he would wake too late and his head would strike the table. She giggled to herself at the thought, knew it was not very sisterly of her, silently reprimanded herself and apologized to the spirits of her parents, then waited for it to happen just the same.

As she shifted her eyes back and forth between her brother and her mending, Anana's focus fell away from Tatkret's drooping eyelids and settled on the lines surrounding them. When, she wondered, did he begin to look so old. Though the harsh life their people lived aged them far too quickly, Tatkret was only nineteen; three years her senior. It was the death of her father that aged him so, she thought. Of course, Anana had taken it hard but it seemed to her that it had affected Tatkret the most.

After the expected mourning and crying and cursing, Tatkret had grown very sullen and withdrawn. He had begun drinking heavily and spending more and more time away from home; hunting, fishing or fighting in the village barroom. His few friends, whom he never saw regularly – close friendships were rare in this frozen tundra – had quit visiting at all. The short days of the deep winter seemed to make him crawl deeper within himself. He could not occupy himself as much with hunting or fishing and rarely had the money to waste away the hours in the village. He sat, like he was tonight; silent, staring.

A sudden certainty overwhelmed her. Tatkret would die young; young even when compared to the shorter lifespan of the people in this hard place. She could see in those black, oily eyes that, inside, he was already dead. And what would she do? Find some young man in the village, with whiskey on his breath to take care of her? Learn to hunt and fish and hope to survive on her own? Leave this place and search for somewhere where the cold winds didn't split your skin and wrinkle your face with weathered age?

She felt a lump rising in her throat; felt the burning sting of tears pushing the lump upward. She put her mending aside and added more logs to the fire, hoping it would burn warm enough and long enough to see them through the night.

"Good night, brother," she said and started for the bedroom which was really just another part of the single, large room that was their house, separated by a half wall like the other bedroom that had been her father's and, once, her mother's.

"Mmmph," Tatkret grunted, raising the whiskey bottle to his lips.

Anana felt her heart hurt for him, placed her hands on his shoulders and lean down to kiss his cheek.

"I love you," she said.

Tatkret swallowed the mouthful of liquor. He turned, just slightly, as if her lips had pulled him toward her as they left his cheek, the gravity of her love gathering him to her. He smiled a weak, sad smile.

"I love you, too, Anana."

She listened to the sound of the wind singing across the snow and through the trees; pale, amber glow from the firelight danced across the walls and ceiling. She imagined the shadows dancing to the wind's song as she thought of her father and let sleep take her; hoping she might see him in her dreams.

Anana was awoken by a loud bang. For a moment she wondered if Tatkret had fallen. Then a smile spread softly across her lips and she imagined him dozing off and banging his head on the table. More bumps and crashes and she realized her brother was stumbling through the house. She heard his footfalls coming into their bedroom. They had always shared the room, his bed across from hers, but Tatkret had been sleeping in their father's bed for several months now. He's drunk, she thought, and falling back to old, natural habits.

She heard him shuffle to his bed and fall heavily on to it; heard him struggling out of his clothes. She didn't know how long she had been sleeping but she could tell from the darkness that the fire had died down considerably. She thought to tell Tatkret to put more logs on before he went to bed but judged by his noisy walk to the bedroom that he had drank too much of the whiskey bottle to manage any practical task. And she was warm beneath her covers, the fur blanket closest to her body retaining her own heat.

She heard the floor creak and his bed groan and she had thought he had dropped on to his bed, above the covers, and was considering if she really wanted to crawl out from her warm cocoon to throw his own blankets on to him so he didn't freeze in the night, when she felt his weight on her own bed. Her eyes went wide as she felt the covers lift and felt him slide his body up against her.

His arm fell over her waist and she tensed, pulling herself tightly together, curling her legs and tucking her arms to her chest. His breath, the fiery, bitter scent of whiskey, was in her ear. He moaned, shifted, pressed himself against her and she felt him – *Him! It!* – hard against her bottom. He moaned, softly. Anana closed her eyes, swallowed. He pressed harder against her. His hand was on her belly and she felt it moving, softly, down across her navel; his fingers brushed the top of her pajama bottoms.

Anana reached down and grabbed Tatkret's hand; halting its movement. She lifted his arm and eased herself away from the pressure behind her. She rolled herself from under the covers and off the opposite side of the bed. Tatkret made no noise; didn't acknowledge her flight. The floor was cold on her bare feet as she made her way back toward the main room.

"The fire's dying," she said, softly but loud enough that he could hear her; an excuse rather than an accusation.

"Everything's dying," he mumbled, just barely audible.

Anana added logs to the fire, poked at it much longer than necessary to get it burning well. She stayed there, hunched in front of the flames, until she heard Tatkret's drunken snores from the bedroom. She went to her father's room and cried herself to sleep, thinking of Malina and Annigan.

3.

The roar of Tatkret's snowmobile woke Anana. It took her a moment to realize she was in her father's bed…and then to remember why. Walking to the window, she followed the tracks of the snowmobile and saw Takret shrinking away from her. She wondered if he remembered what he had done; if that was at least part of the reason he was off so early.

The chair that Tatkret had been sitting in last night was overturned on the floor; the whiskey bottle lay empty on the table. Anana stood the chair up, disposed of the bottle and began washing the supper dishes she had ignored the night before. She cleaned ashes from the fireplace and returned to mending the clothes she had set aside.

Her mind wandered, as it was prone to do. The tasks of her day were repetitive and boring. When her father was alive, she would sometimes go with him to set traps or to fish; he would always take her to the village when they needed supplies. Since he died she rarely left the house. During the short, warm season she could busy herself outside; making minor repairs to the shack or tending their small garden. During the long, bleak, dark, cold winter she felt like a prisoner.

When Anana's mind wandered, she would usually think of her father or she would make up pretend stories of things she would have done with her mother had she lived through Anana's birth. Sometimes this made her feel guilty, as if her mother's death was a necessity for Anana's own existence. Today, however, she could only think of Tatkret and what had happened in her bed. He was just drunk, she rationalized, probably didn't know what he was doing; doesn't even remember it.

She thought about the few seconds that she had laid there while he pressed against her. What he had done – tried to do – was disgusting; sick. For a moment though, she had felt a stirring within her. She had never known a man that way, had only felt the pleasure of her own touch, and she wondered how different it would be. In the bed, with his hardness pulsing against her, she had felt her nipples hardening; felt that stirring between her legs. Even now, as she thought about it, she had a desire to address the growing dampness while, at the same time, her stomach turned at the depravity of it.

A shadow fell across her, graciously distracting her from the vision that was intent on overtaking her. Anana turned to the window, half expecting to see someone standing there despite the relative isolation of the house. There was nobody there but she noticed that the landscape appeared to have been washed over with a soft gray. She set the clothing aside and went to the window, expecting to see clouds gathering; wondering if they would appear dark and menacing and threatening to bring more cold and snow. Instead, Anana saw that a bite had been taken out of the sun.

It was the beginning of an eclipse. This is what the villagers must have meant when they had told Tatkret that the moon god would be successful in his quest across the sky. Was this cosmic event partly to blame for her brother's actions? Had the moon affected him as the ancestors had believed that it could; pushed him toward lunacy? Would it take much? She had already seen the changes in him since their father had died; thought him sullen, withdrawn, changed. Was he more fragile than she had imagined?

Anana's eyes wandered to the vast blanket of snow as these thoughts swam in her head. She saw the windswept, almost hidden foot steps leading from the house to the shed where her father's – her brother's – traps and fishing nets were kept and where Tatkret parked the snowmobile. She saw the tracks of the sled heading away. And she saw, crossing both the snowmobile tracks and the shallow imprints of her brothers boots, the soft imprints of snowshoes that seemed to lead to the door. No more had she registered this and given just a moment's thought to the idea that she had a visitor calling, than the door swung open and Tatkret stalked inside.

"Tatkret!" she exclaimed, her breath catching, "You frightened me."

He said nothing in return. Simply closed the door and bent to remove the snowshoes.

"Where is the snowmobile?" Anana asked, but again she was met with silence.

When he stood, she knew, that Tatkret – the Tatkret that she had known her whole life – was no longer behind those dark, oily eyes. He took a step forward and she instinctively backed away from him.

"What's wrong, sister?" he asked, but his voice was as cold as the wind she could hear growing and whispering outside.

He didn't move closer, only that single first step, but a grin – a frightening, maniacal grin – spread across his face. That grin seemed to stretch and grow along with the darkening of the room as the moon continued to eat away at the sun.

Through the clenched teeth of that fearful sneer Tatkret said, "I love you, too, sister." But there was no love in his words; they were thick and heavy and terrifying. Behind them she could hear the sound of the wind rising from a whisper to a howl, as if it was gathering strength from the growing darkness.

"Tatkret..." Anana started, but she had no other words to put with it.

"Annigan," he said.

"No, Tatkret..." tears were swelling in her eyes and through the blur of them his face took on an even more sinister appearance.

"Malina," he said, "we will be gods."

He pulled a bottle of whiskey from the pocket of his jacket. It was nearly empty and he swallowed down what was left of it and dropped the bottle to the floor, where it shattered. All the while his eyes were on Anana; all the while the world darkening.

The wind howled, gusted, screamed its anger. The door crashed open, drawing Anana's eyes away from her brother for the briefest of moments, and the cold air and snow barged into the room. The dying fire – Anana had not fed it as she had sat losing herself in thoughts arousing and disturbing – flared from the rush of oxygen, then dwindled to embers. Tatkret had her in his rough hands before she was aware that he had advanced.

Anana screamed, matching the howl of the wind, then lost her breath as Tatkret whirled her to the left, smoothly slipping his boot behind her leg, throwing her to the ground. Her head smacked against the hard, wooden floor and she saw stars. He was on top of her, clawing at her clothes with one hand while pinning her arms above her with the other, spreading and locking her legs with his own. His hot, whiskey breath was on her face, then her neck, and she felt his mouth greedily sucking and biting at her.

"No," she tried to cry out but it was weak, choked back by fear and tears.

The room continued to darken as he tore at her. She felt his fingernails scrape across her flesh and nipple as he ripped through her shirt. She could feel blood swell and trickle to the hollow in her chest between her breasts. She struggled but he was much heavier, much stronger. His mouth, breath like fire, was on her breast as his hand tore at her pants and at his own, trying to access her and free himself. She wondered if he tasted the blood, if he was sucking harder because of it.

The room fell to the dark of midnight as if a heavy curtain had been pulled slowly across the windows. How long, she wondered, until the sun would be free again. Somehow, if only there was sunlight, she knew Tatkret would stop this madness. If only he could see the fear in her face, the tears streaming down her cheeks leaving dark trails of terror behind them, he would come to his senses. Too long, she thought, even a few minutes would be too long.

The wind howled even louder. Anana didn't think it possible. She felt her eardrums would burst. She felt the cold wash over her face, her exposed belly. She felt pinpricks of snow stabbing and melting against her skin. In the light of the last, struggling embers of the fire she thought she saw movement over her brother's shoulder; a trick of the eclipse, of the snow, of the wind. She bucked and thrashed beneath him.

Then, suddenly, he rolled off of her, striking the side of her head with an elbow – she thought it was an elbow – as he did. She squeezed her eyes tight from the pain. Her head swam – still feeling the effects of striking the floor. The darkness was complete as she drifted into unconsciousness, perhaps her mind shutting itself down in self-preservation, and the moon swallowed the sun.

Slowly, from much farther away than she thought possible, the sounds of the wind, the cold breath of it across her breasts – a stark contrast to the hot, hungry breath of Tatkret – called her back. She swam up out of the darkness to find herself lying there on the cold floor. She slowly opened her eyes; sharp, searing pain on her chest. How long? Light was returning to the world. The moon was sliding past the sun. She let her hand slide down between her legs. Her pants were pulled loose but not off, there was no pain there.

The room continued to brighten and she cautiously rolled to look for her brother. Had he somehow sobered up? Had a change of heart? Realized what he was doing? She saw him lying near the table, face down on the floor. She thought to run but found herself crawling toward him, still concerned for him, still loving him.

She grabbed his shoulder, shook him, then rolled him toward her. His eyes were wide but unseeing. Across his neck was a ragged, bleeding gash that looked to her very much like the evil, demonic grin that had been on his face. A piece of the broken whiskey bottle lay near him, dripping blood.

Anana screamed and pushed him away from her. He rolled back to his chest, his head, arm, leg lolling like a rag doll. The light was nearly full now and she saw them on the back of his jacket; two sooty hand prints as if someone had grabbed him by the shoulders. She stared at them. Had someone pulled him off of her? Who? And where had they gone?

She glanced around the room – nobody – then back at the black prints. Something was wrong with them. She stared. The thumbs. The thumbs were wrong. She could see the prints clearly, each digit in stark, accusing contrast on Tatkret's light colored jacket. The thumb prints were not pointing inward toward each other, as they would if he had been grabbed from behind, but outward, on his shoulders, as if someone had hugged him.

Anana ran from the house, her clothes still loose and pulled away, the snow and wind biting at her exposed chest but not feeling it. She ran toward the sun, tears in her eyes, the wind whistling around her. She hoped it would gust strong and lift her up into the sky, away from this cold, lonely, often too dark world and into the sky. She ran pumping her arms and lifting her legs high to fight through the snow. She ran with dark, black, sooty ashes on her hands.

Author's Notes:

I'm often reading mythology and religious books, as I find it incredibly interesting to see how we humans try to explain the world around us, and I recalled something about this myth but not the exact details. An hour or two worth of Googling later and I had refreshed my memory and this story started to take shape.

I found some of this story hard to write but if I never wrote the things that were difficult, this would be a fairly short collection. And, while this is an extreme case, I think that we all have some desires, perhaps brief and fleeting but there none the less, that we wish we didn't have.

DANSE WITH ME

1.

He sits at the desk in his home office and rubs his temples where the gray is starting to show. The rest of the house is dark; everyone else is asleep. The desk lamp throws a soft glow over the papers in front of him, illuminating the letters seeking contributions to his campaign. Tomorrow, his family will leave for an extended stay at their summer home on the lake. He will remain behind; shaking hands, kissing babies, attending dinners that cost more for a single plate of food than many people make in a year.

He wishes he could be with his family, splashing around in the lake with his daughter, enjoying a glass of wine on the deck with his wife as the sun slips below the horizon and colors the sky red. He has a job to do, though; a duty.

He is signing yet another letter, one of dozens that his assistant has prepared for him, when he feels the numbness in his left arm. *Leaning on it wrong*, he thinks, *it's falling asleep*. He shakes it to clear the pins and needles and a sharp pain causes him to wince and clutch his chest. The pain fades.

A figure stands in front of his desk. A man, tall and thin; one might call him gaunt. His complexion is pale, his cheeks slightly sunken, yet he is not unattractive. He sports a pencil thin mustache and wears a dark, pinstriped suit with a matching fedora. The red band on his hat matches the bright carnation that decorates his lapel.

The figure glides around the desk to stand next to him and extends a skeletal hand. "Dance with me," he says. A question. A statement. A demand.

Obeying without willful decision, the man takes the figure's hand and stands. He hears music, slow and quiet. It reminds him of the last dance of his high school prom. One of the last moments he can remember of pure freedom, when the world was still wide open ahead of him. He had few concerns about issues past, present or future then, only optimism and the simple joy of having his girlfriend's head resting softly in the nook of his shoulder as they moved across the wooden floor of a rented hall amid a swirl of colored lights.

"I'm not ready," he says to the dark eyes staring back at him. "I'm just reaching a point in my career where I can make a *real* difference."

The words sink into the darkness at the edges of the room. They echo softly and ring hollow even to his own ears. They are the words that he used over and over again to explain his absences at dance recitals and baseball games, family reunions and weddings, the dinner table on countless nights and the marital bed on countless more.

He said them when he was first elected to city council, when he became mayor, when he was elected to the State Senate and when he served as Governor. He said them time and again as he worked for and won election to serve on Capitol Hill and as he prepared to run for the highest office in the land.

They sway slowly, like two awkward teenagers who have not yet learned the finer points of dancing or perhaps an old, married couple who have lost the ability to do more. The tall, dapper man stares at him but says nothing.

"I have my faults, I know," he says, contemplating his life and all the ways he feels he has been lacking; sensing suddenly that he is being judged. "I know that I have sometimes let my family down. Maybe I haven't been as good of a friend as I should have been. Maybe I allowed a thirst for power to cloud some of my decisions, my judgment, but I always intended to make this country a better place and to serve the people who chose me to govern or represent them. I've always *wanted* to be a good man."

A smile back at him from the sunken, pale face of his dancing partner and the man sighs, knowing that his life is over. If he is to be judged, that life will speak for itself and there is nothing he can do to change it; nothing now. He rests his head against the bony shoulder beneath the suit jacket and lets Death lead him slowly to the music and out of the room.

2.

She has her cell phone to her ear, held in place with her shoulder, and is scrolling through emails on her Blackberry. Her leather briefcase hangs on a strap, bouncing on her hip and slightly compressing the shoulder pad of her power suit; dark blue with light, slimming stripes on the jacket and a skirt of moderate length, reaching just below her knees. The hustle and bustle of the city crowds in upon her but she pushes it aside; to her, it is nothing more than an annoying fly to be swatted away with a wave of her hand.

She has worked her way up to the top of the food chain; the CEO of a large, powerful company. She makes a million dollar deal on her phone and another worth three or four times that amount through an email on her Blackberry. Acquisitions, mergers, buyouts; she strides across the street towards the coffee shop feeling every bit as rich and powerful as the company she heads.

She hears the screech of the braking tires and looks up in time to see the dinner plate-sized, dark chocolate eyes of the taxi driver. She has a moment in which to wonder if she had checked the light at the crosswalk and to note that the taxi driver is wearing a red turban, before the car hits her and she is propelled up and over the cab. Her briefcase, cell phone and Blackberry arc through the air. Her body thuds as it careens off the windshield, spider webbing the glass so the cab driver's view is as if he is looking through a kaleidoscope and her body makes another *thud* when it hits the pavement. Her belongings go clattering around the scene.

She sits on the curb while a crowd gathers in the street. A shadow falls over her and she looks up to see a tall man in a dark, pin stripped suit extending his thin, bony hand to her.

She thinks about the fact that she is unmarried; has not yet started a family; has been a slave to her career. She rarely stopped to enjoy life. Even on the rare vacation that she permitted herself, she would be anxious when she was in a cell phone dead zone or had spent more than an hour or two away from the hotel; away from her computer and emails.

She wishes now that she had taken more time to enjoy life. Maybe she pushed herself too hard to succeed; a full load of classes each semester to finish college early, internships along with those classes that robbed her of a social life, a hard-nosed, determined, singularly focused drive to advance. Always, she thought, there would be time. A tear trickles down her cheek.

She takes the skeletal hand and rises, letting the figure lead her in a waltz along the busy sidewalk. They turn and spin in and out of the people, some who have stopped to see the carnage on the street, others who walk hurriedly past at if nothing unusual has happened.

"I've saved companies," she says to her dancing partner, craning her neck to look into his face. "I've created jobs; made people's lives better."

He leads her back up the street. Everyone is oblivious to their dance except one man who is leaning against a building, next to a window display of the season's newest fashions. He is dressed sharply. He is well groomed and the gray creeping into his hair at the temples gives him a distinguished look. As they near him, he steps forward and cuts in. Death steps aside.

"My family is proud of me," she tells him, her eyes wet.

"Mine, too," he smiles back.

They continue their waltz away from the street, away from the sirens that are closing in on the scene. Death follows along behind them, his head softly rolling back and forth to the sound of the music.

3.

He leans against a wall of dirt and sand bags. His heart thuds heavily in his chest; the adrenaline makes him forget how tired he really is. The sound of machine gun fire fills the night. He hears it from the left and right of him, down the trench. He hears it popping in the distance across a non-descript, unimportant chunk of land that two, opposing ideologies have decided to use as a line drawn in the sand. Bullets whiz over his head, plunking into the sand bags and dirt that serve as his barricade. Mortars fall and shower him with earth.

He takes a deep breath and swings his rifle up and over the top of the barricade, firing blindly into the darkness, trusting the bullets to find a target. Something punches him in the neck and he swings back down for cover.

A tall man in a dark suit stands in the middle of the trench, smiling at him. The red band on the man's hat and the red carnation on his lapel provide the only color in a world washed in gray. His eyes drop to the man's feet and he sees the body of a soldier with an alarmingly large portion of his neck missing.

"Damn it," he says.

He thinks of his wife, an ocean away, and the baby, a little girl, that is due in only a few weeks; a daughter that he will never see. His eyes water and his throat burns as he holds back the sobs. He pictures the porcelain faced doll that is tucked away in his foot locker, the gift he was to give his precious child upon his return. He hopes it still finds its way to her. He mourns the kisses and hugs from his wife welcoming him home that he will never receive.

He looks at the soldier – himself – lying in the mud at the bottom of the trench, at the feet of the tall, thin man in the dark suit. He wonders, for only a moment, how the man's shoes are able to stay clean and shiny, highly polished, even as he stands in the filth of this war. *Because he's not a man*, he thinks.

The body – his body – is dressed in army fatigues. There are stripes on one of his sleeves. Dirty and worn but still proud and inspiring, he sees the flag that adorns the shoulder. It is a flag that nurtures dreams, promises freedom and is a beacon of hope, help and protection. His chest swells with pride.

He may not see his wife and new child in this life, perhaps he'll never see them again; he searches the tall man's drawn, yet handsome face for some indication of what awaits him and finds nothing. He knows, however, that he has done all in his power to ensure that others will have the opportunities, freedoms and precious moments that have been taken away from him by an unknown enemy's bullet. He knows that others like him will sacrifice themselves to ensure the safety and freedom of his own wife and child.

The sounds of the fire fight around him fade as music fills his ears. The sounds remind him, somehow, of South America; of flowing skirts, and dark skinned women and lusty, sweaty movements. They are sounds that are full of life and hope and pleasure.

The tall man opens his arms; smiling, inviting. "Dance with me," he says.

The two clasp hands, place their free hands on the other's hips and shoot determined stares down the length of the trench as their cheeks come together, the tall man hunching slightly to bring their faces level. Their feet slap through the mud and the blood and the filth of war as their tango leads them past the others of his company that continue the fight and over those for whom, like him, the fight has ended.

They approach a man and a woman. The man has a certain distinguished air about him; he is dressed in a conservative but stylish suit. The woman, dressed sharply as well, steps forward and the tall, thin man steps aside to allow her his place.

The soldier and the woman continue the dance in the other direction, turn sharply, smiling, and return to the men. The man with the graying hair cuts in for the soldier and he and the woman dance on. They think how fortunate they have been to have lived in a place that allowed them so many freedoms, so many luxuries, so many opportunities.

The three of them continue the exchange of partners; continue the dance as the music enlivens them. The tall, thin, skeletal man leads them through the trench, past the soldiers continuing their fight, around and over the fallen and into the darkness.

4.

He sits down heavily on the couch, a plate of cold chicken on his lap. His feet, his legs, his back and his mind are all sore and exhausted from yet another swing shift. He flips on the television to catch the score of today's game and spies the picture that rests above it on the entertainment center.

It's a picture they took last Christmas; a family portrait. He is seated in the picture, next to but slightly behind his wife. His daughter stands behind him, her hand on his shoulder and her husband to her side with an arm around her waist. Their son – his grandson – sits on grandpa's lap. Behind his wife, his son, fresh out of medical school, stands proud and handsome. The son's fiancé, a nurse that he met while interning, smiles the type of smile that says she knows the whole world is laid out before them.

It's a beautiful picture of a beautiful family and a smile of his own spreads across his face. *Some things*, he thinks, *make everything else worthwhile*.

He takes a bite of chicken, feels the small bone crunch between his teeth, tries to work it free of the meat and inadvertently swallows it. It lodges in his throat and he tries to cough it back up. He struggles to breathe, flails his way off of the couch and makes it halfway down the hall before he collapses.

He feels hands slip under his armpits. They are bony and they dig into his flesh as they lift him from the carpet. A tall, thin, sharply dressed man in a hat smiles at him and leads him back to the couch. He glances at the family portrait as he sits. His feet, legs and back make no protests of pain. For a moment, a shadow of remorse flickers over him.

"It's been a pretty good life, hasn't it?" he asks.

The thin, dark man continues to smile.

"I mean, I've been married to a great woman for a good, long while; I've helped to raise two great kids who have both gone through college and started their own lives; lives that promise to be more successful than mine."

He looks at the portrait and smiles. He hopes they won't be too sad for too long.

"It was a lot of hard work, a lot of long shifts, but there were a whole lot of good times in there; vacations, trips to the lake, football games and Daddy-daughter dances. Some give and take, work hard to play hard, but a good life, all in all."

The tall man takes his hand and lifts him from the couch. "Dance with me," the man says.

He hears music; a quick beat, horns. He's never danced a jig before, but he dances one now. As he spins and jumps around the living room two men, one in a suit and one in army fatigues, and a women dressed in a sharp business suit join him.

They move through the living room like guests at a wedding reception forming a conga line. They dance through the kitchen, each remembering the best of times with family and friends. Some have more to recall than others but they all find moments of love and happiness to reflect on. They pass into the dining room, circle the table and dance out through the front door, down the street and into the night.

5.

   She's lying in her bed, staring out the window at the sunshine, trying not to dwell on the sounds of the other kids playing. It seems to her like she's been sick for a long time, at least according to the doctors and her parents and all the hospital visits and tests that they've done.

   But it's only in the last few weeks has she *felt* sick. Only since the headaches got real bad and since it got hard to walk because her legs just wouldn't do what she wanted them to do anymore.

   It's hard to eat and it's hard to drink and sometimes it's even hard to breathe but, most of all, it's hard to look at her mother and father as they sit at her bedside trying not to cry and pretending that their eyes aren't rimmed red.

   Her father is at work and her mother is downstairs in the kitchen making her a bowl of soup that she won't be able to eat. The sun is shining brightly through her window, beaming across the patchwork comforter that she lies under. She watches the dust motes dance in the sunbeam for a few moments and then closes her eyes. She is so very, very tired.

   When she opens her eyes again, there is a tall man standing by her bed. He is much taller than her father and very thin. He reminds her of something between a scarecrow and a skeleton but she feels no fear of him. His is holding his hat in his hands. He smiles at her and she thinks his smile is a little sad.

"It's okay," she says, as she swings her legs out from under the covers and stands, barefooted, on her bedroom floor. "You've made my headache go away. I feel much better."

The tall, thin man's eyes look watery. He replaces his hat as she takes his hand. She's knows that look. It's a look she has seen it many times. He is trying not to cry.

There are four grown-ups standing off in the corner of her room. They look like they might cry, as well.

"Are you dead too?" she asks them. They all nod silently.

"Are you sad that you're dead?" she asks. They look at each other. They seem confused.

"I'm not sad," she says, looking back at the tall man's bony face. "I'm not sad because I can hear the music. Can't you hear it?"

The tall man cocks his head, listening. The others do the same. They *can* hear it. It's music full of nursery rhymes and fairy tales, tinny xylophones and great, bellowing tubas, clapping hands and stomping feet and the trumpeting of elephants. It's a child's music and it is the happiest, most delightful music they've ever heard.

The little girl spins around the tall man, she jumps on her bed and bounces to touch the ceiling. She jumps to the floor, rolls in a somersault and skips through the room waving her arms in the air. Hesitantly, at first, the others join in.

The girl stops and looks up into the tall man's eyes. "Dance with me," she says, smiling, and he does, moving like a marionette as he swings his lanky arms and legs about.

They dance a dance of pure joy and unrepentant, unrelenting fun. They dance a dance that celebrates all that is right in the world, all which is joyful in living no matter how long or short that life may be. They dance the dance of innocence out of the bedroom, down the stairs and into the sunshine.

They dance towards whatever awaits them, celebrating all that they leave behind.

Author's Notes:

A modern spin on the Danse Macabre theme (look it up). I don't know what waits beyond this life; maybe nothing. I hope, though, that I can live this life to the fullest and limit my regrets when it's all said and done.

ABOVE THE CLOUDS

CHAPTER ONE

I'm alive.

I can't tell you how many times that I've been told how lucky I am; how thankful I should be for that. But when I am lying in bed, staring up into the darkness and my mind is free from the distractions of the day and I am unable to stop the black bits from rising to the surface, I am not so sure of my luck. And when sleep finally takes me and those black bits start merging together, and I have lost any last semblance of control for my conscience mind to rein them in, and the horror and the memories come to life for the thousandth time…at that time I am certain that I am not lucky at all and I am thankful for nothing.

I am a writer and it was my success, as humble as it may have been, that led me to this place I am now. My therapist…well, let's be honest shall we, that's kind of the point of all of this…"therapist" is a word that they use to make you feel better. When you are in "therapy" you're just working through some stuff; everybody has little things to work through now and then, right? You're not crazy, just confused. A bit of "therapy" will help you come to terms with it all.

Well, anyway, my therapist, my shrink, my fucking head doctor suggested that I use my writing as an outlet. That I put to paper all the things that I am unable to articulate verbally. Dr. Rocher may be the only one that ever reads this, and I don't care really. I guess, good doctor, you are entitled to this story if for no other reason than you have been able to keep me from going absolutely bat-shit crazy over the last year. Not that I necessarily think you have any great medical ability or that the endless hours I have spent lying in your office have helped, but I am pretty certain that your liberal use of the prescription pad has kept me from killing myself or anyone else so far.

This is not a story like the dozen or so that I was able to get published in various magazines and which led to an agent contacting me and suggesting a compilation of them to publish as a real, live book; like a real, live author. It was that book which led to a comfortable sum of money and a limited amount of critical acclaim. That, of course, led to a little more money and even a little fame, which stepped lively toward a few public appearances, radio interviews and book signings.

Then, in a surprise twist, like something right out of one of those stories, just as I was reaching such incredible heights, I was dropped straight into hell.

Maybe, the good doctor is on to something, and I will work this all out in my head if only I work through it using my trusty Toshiba. Maybe I can find some reason behind it all, maybe some reasoning if only I replay the whole thing for the millionth time but this time I punch it all into this stupid keyboard. Maybe I can wrap it all up in a pretty, little bow and type "The End" after my final sentence.

This is the first time I have tried to string words together in some semblance of a coherent thought, since the time I now think of as the end of my normal life. And, honestly, I find it incredibly laborious and difficult. There is no joy in it. There is no excitement. There is only pain that I can feel rushing through my body, seeming to begin in my mind and run through my hands into the keyboard of my once beloved laptop. I use to feel such a charge as the stories took shape in my mind and on the simulated page of the computer screen. The excitement that I felt as the story came to life was the greatest feeling I ever had. I don't know if other authors know how their stories will end when they begin them, but I rarely have even a clue. I am as surprised at the twists and turns that turn up in them as I am when I read someone else's work.

I look at this computer now with loathing. It was here that those first stories came to life and so here was the birth of my nightmare. I know how *this* story will end. I know how each moment will flow into the next. I hate it. I hate the story and I hate that I have no control of it.

As I struggle through this prescribed exercise, I must fight to restrain myself from throwing this computer against the wall and watching it explode into so many pieces of plastic and transistors and whatever else makes up the guts of this thing. When I am done, when I have printed the last sheet for my dear doctor, I am pretty certain that I will indulge myself in that little fantasy.

Speaking of guts, let's get to the guts of it. Shall we? I was very excited when I received the call from Tom Debart, my agent. Actually, at that time Tom wasn't my agent but one of many that I had sent inquiries to for representation. As I said, I had published several short stories in various magazines, mostly for contributor copies and occasionally for a couple of bucks. I was in the midst of a full-fledged novel and decided I might just have enough success under my belt to attract the interest of an agent. Tom had read a few of the sample works I had sent out with my inquiries and wanted to see more. A few weeks later, after I had sent him the whole of my published works, he called back and we began working out a contract. It was Tom who suggested a compilation of short stories. He said that these books often did well and were fairly easy to sell to publishers, despite what I'd always heard about a collection by a new author being almost impossible to place.

"True," Tom said, "but mostly it's hard to get an agent to pick them up. Once you've won someone like me over, it's not too difficult to find a place to print them up."

For one, he'd said, they were works that had already gotten through someone's approval process, even if it was a magazine with limited circulation, and second, it was his belief that these books sold well because most of America has a pretty short attention span and likes to be able to get the whole of their reading experience in one sitting, rather than investing their time in a complete novel. I can't say that I agreed with him, but getting published is getting published.

"Don't worry," Tom said, "we'll shop the novel once you finish it, but it will be that much easier if you've already got a house spitting out something for you. And it doesn't hurt to have some coin in your pocket in the meantime right?"

It was logic that I couldn't argue with. I had been working as an Automotive Engineer, and while it managed to pay the bills, the thought of being able to walk away from it and write full time, or even to supplement my income with my writing, was like a dream come true. Maybe my wife would be able to quit her part time job, maybe we wouldn't have to worry so much about how we were going to pay our son's tuition at his private school next year.

Things moved much faster than I thought they would. I had picked Tom as my agent primarily because he was the first one that responded to my inquiries. I did get a couple of other letters from some interested parties, but by that time I had already been talking to Tom and we had met twice for lunches. He seemed to really be interested in my work, not just the prospect of money. Of course, he was interested in making money too, for both of us, and that didn't bother me one bit.

Tom had a publisher lined up in less than a month. It was March when he gave me the news. I was even going to get an advance of five thousand dollars. I couldn't believe my good fortune. That was enough to pay the tuition next year, have a nice family celebration and still put a few, desperately needed dollars into the bank account. I was on cloud nine, as they say.

After some editing and formatting issues, handled mostly by e-mail, and then the submittal of a cool cover design, painted by an artist Tom had worked with before, *Tales From The Edge* by Robert Griffith was scheduled for release, in paperback, for August of 2007.

That summer was as long as any I had ever experienced. Every day, as I sat at my desk reviewing prints, mulling over supplier contracts and putting together test reports, I dreamed of my book hitting the best-seller list and being able to leave the world of corporate bullshit behind. At night, and on the weekends, I continued to work on my novel, losing myself in the story and, at least temporarily, forgetting the everyday worries. August came around and a few thousand copies of the collection sold and then a few thousand more. I began to get royalty checks and Tom started setting up interviews. The dream had started to come true.

The first printing had been 10,000 copies, pretty significant for a first time author, and I made a nice chunk of money from that. When Tom called and told me they were going to print again and this time they were going for 100,000 copies, I almost fainted. Besides the money that I was going to receive for this printing, Tom had managed to sell my half-finished novel to the publisher. He struck a deal which included a $100,000 advance. The book would be printed as a hard cover. I had arrived. It was ridiculously fortunate and while I won't feign humility (I do think I write a pretty good story), I knew just how lucky I was.

The money allowed me to quit my job and write full time; at least to give it a go for a year or two. I was energized and the words flowed out of me. My first draft for *The Denizen*, a book about an alien plant life that takes root on earth, causing all kinds of mayhem and death, was completed in December of 2007. I started the book tour circuit in February of '08, in anticipation of a March release.

My life had changed. I had never been so happy, so satisfied. Susan, my wife, was happy. Ethan, our twelve year old son was happy. Life was good. Little did I know that it was the trip to Minnesota, to the Barnes and Nobles in the Mall of America, for a greet and meet with fans and book signings of the newly released, limited edition, hard cover version of *Tales From The Edge*, that would really change my life.

A simple plane ride. A puddle jump from Detroit to St. Paul, with a layover in Cincinnati, would actually end up touching down right in the middle of Hell.

CHAPTER TWO

"Ethan has winter break at the same time I have this thing in Minnesota," I said. "Why don't I take him with me? It will give us some nice father and son bonding time."

Susan was finishing loading the dinner dishes into the machine as I leaned against the kitchen counter, a cup of coffee in one hand and a Marlboro in the other.

"First of all, I wish you would quit smoking in the house. It makes the whole place stink," she said. "As far as taking Ethan with you, that's not a bad idea. He would probably enjoy seeing how famous his Dad is."

There was a little good-natured ribbing in her tone, but I thought I could sense a little pride, as well. Susan had always been supportive of my writing; my biggest fan.

With her back to me, her arms covered in suds up to her elbows, I took a minute to look her over. This is something I did on a fairly regular basis, stealing moments to look at her when she wasn't paying attention, when she was unguarded.

She was still as beautiful to me as she was when I first met her in a second year Creative Writing class at Wayne State University, 18 years ago. She no longer wore her brown hair teased out with her bangs curled under, as was so popular then. In fact, some of that brown was now being replaced with gray that had to be beaten back into submission with the occasional dye job and now she wore it in a fairly conservative style, although she kept it long, at my insistence. Now, as I stared at her, it was pulled back into a cloth covered, elastic band in a hasty ponytail. What did she call that thing again? Oh yeah, a *scrunchie*.

Her body had stood the test of time and the abuse of child-birth. Sure, there were a few more pounds in places she would prefer not to have them, but they didn't bother me. And when she dolled herself up for a night on the town, she could certainly turn a few heads. I could feel a tingling down below as I stood there gazing at her and felt myself becoming slightly erect.

I moved behind her and slid my hands to her stomach, slipping them under her shirt and pushing my groin against her ass, "How do you feel about doin' a famous author?"

She grinned and looked over her shoulder at me, "Well, I have always had a bit of a thing for Grisham."

I slapped her on the ass, laughing, and moved back to my coffee and cigarette, "Guess I'll just have to pick up one of those hot, young writer groupies."

"With that kind of stuff on your mind, maybe I should make you take Ethan on all of your trips," she countered.

"I'll call Tom and have him set up two plane tickets," I said.

It would be fun to take Ethan with me. I really did enjoy hanging out with him. At twelve, I was pretty certain I wouldn't have too many more years left where he would enjoy hanging out with me. He would reach that teenage phase where just the word "parent" would be enough to depress him. I'm pretty sure that's a hormonal thing with teenagers.

Ethan was in bed and Susan was curled up on the couch in the living room, with her latest mystery book, as I took my shower later that evening. As I worked the shampoo into my hair, I dreamed of success yet to come. I imagined sitting next to Jay Leno and discussing my latest work. I saw myself at the Playboy Mansion, rubbing shoulders with other famous people; actors and writers and women wearing next to nothing.

I visualized a big house, somewhere in the country just outside of a quaint, little town. There would be an office there, the walls lined with books and lots of stained oak throughout. I could see myself sitting at an expansive desk, my computer glowing warmly in front of me. Glancing over the top of the screen, I could look out the picture window at a deep yard that faded away into the trees. It is winter and the tracks of rabbits and deer are visible in the otherwise undisturbed snow. A fire burns in the corner of my room, crackling and hissing, the smell of it mixing with the aroma of some unknown baked good wafting from the kitchen. Susan must be in there making cookies or maybe a pie. There is a large pile of paper next to me and the printer continues to hum, click and whirl as more of whatever masterpiece I am working on spews out of it.

I see myself walking with Susan and Ethan through the little town. It's the type of town where old men meet at the barber shop even though they don't need haircuts. Where you can walk into the General Store and get most everything you need or just sit by an old wood stove and watch a game of checkers being played. And, of course, everyone knows me. They call me Rob or Bob, and they wave to me and the family. When they talk to their family and friends they comment on what an ordinary, down-to-earth sort of guy that I am. Nothing like you might expect.

The shower curtain ruffles, startling me and snapping me back to the present. Susan is standing there, naked, and I let the fantasy roll down the drain with the soapy water. She steps into the tub and pushes her body against me, "You know, I think maybe I can think of another famous author, besides Grisham, that I might like to spend some time with."

We made love in the shower, a task which is actually much more difficult than the movies make it out to be, in my opinion. I am probably lucky that I didn't slip and break my hip in the midst of it all. Still, it was the kind of spontaneous sex we rarely had after all these years, especially since Ethan came along, and I enjoyed it immensely. It was fun and playful, sex for the joy of sex.
When we had finished, Susan kissed me and said, "I'll let you know how Grisham compares."

I slapped her on the ass as she got out of the shower and we both giggled. She threatened to steal all the towels and I jokingly begged her forgiveness. It was the last time we had sex and the last time we laughed together. It's my fault. I'm the one that can't move on from that nightmare.

It haunts her as well, I know, but she is stronger than me. I would have never said that before all of this, but now I can see it clearly. Maybe someday I will find that kind of strength and then my heart will have a place for love again, a place for joy and playfulness and soapy sex in showers.

Maybe.

Stepping out of the shower, I recall looking in the mirror, needing to wipe the steam off with a washcloth. I could see the gray in my own hair and remember thinking that I must have somehow "caught" it from my wife, like a cold, probably from sleeping too close to her. I recall debating whether I should make my own appointment for a dye job or if the gray would give me the more sophisticated look that a successful author should have. I grinned at the reflection, thinking that I still looked pretty good for my age, young even. A little gray fighting its way into the sandy blonde notwithstanding, I was fairly wrinkle free, my eyes still holding a twinkle of youthful expectation within their blue, and I had only increased my waist size by a couple of inches since college. I turned sideways to check my figure. No beer belly, really no excess fat at all. I was, in fact, quite fit. Certainly I could stand to firm up a little but, all in all, I looked pretty good.

Despite the smoking and caffeine excesses, I felt pretty good too. I still played softball with some friends in the summer, a bit of pickup basketball and bowling in the winter and I was active in my son's activities. *No slowing down for this old dog*, I thought as I checked myself out and tapped my belly with my palm. Yes, life was good just then. It was as good as I ever could have hoped for.

The early part of February 2008 may well have been the best time of my life. In fact, I'm certain it was. A beautiful, loving wife was by my side. We had a well-behaved, bright son. My career, the career I had always wanted, was growing in leaps and bounds. We had gone from "getting by" to "being comfortable" in less than a year and it looked like "living well" was right around the corner.

I'd spent some time in Australia during my Engineering days and recall a phrase they had. Tall Poppy. It was meant to describe someone who is a bit full of themselves and in need of being "cut down"; given a reality check, we might say. I guess, now that I am looking back at it, hindsight being 20/20, that's about where I was, a prime candidate for a swift kick in the pants right out of left field. A reality check.

Some people call it Karma, others will say it is God's way of keeping you humble, these reality checks. Whatever the case, there are a lot of ways it could have manifested itself that I think I could have dealt with, things that I might have even been able to look back on and say, "Yeah, I kinda had that coming." Maybe a bout of cancer brought on by the Marlboros, or some blood pressure or cholesterol problems that required a diet change and exercise regime. I could have taken a less than successful run for the novel or even a flat out end to my writing career.

I don't think I've ever come right out and said it, and I suppose the good doctor might call this a breakthrough, but dying would have been better than what I got. Even now I sometimes wish for death to silence the nightmares. There you go, Dr. Rocher! I wish I was dead. There's something you can keep me on the couch for. Something we can use to drag out the therapy for years to come. You'll probably be able to get that beach house in the Keys by the time we're all said and done. Unless, of course, I just put a gun to my head and splattering my brains all over this fucking computer. That would take a chunk out of your income I suppose, a chunk out of me too, I guess.

I don't think I have the balls to do that, though. I don't have the courage it would take to pull the trigger. I can almost hear you saying it already, "Robert, it takes courage to go on. You are braver for facing these demons. Suicide is the coward's way out."

Well, maybe I am not cowardly enough. Would that be right? I'm not a big enough coward to kill myself? I guess that remains to be seen. The pain I feel as I write these words is immense. It's as if my heart and soul are being pulled right through my chest. I know as I go on, as I delve deeper into the memories, it will only get worse. Maybe that will kill me on its own.

CHAPTER THREE

Saturday, February 16th. Susan dropped Ethan and me off at the Delta terminal for our flight. We would arrive at the Minneapolis-St. Paul airport, after connecting in Cincinnati, around 5:00 p.m. I was scheduled to be at the Barnes and Nobles from 9:00 a.m. through noon on Sunday. After that we planned on browsing the Mall. The Mall of America is, apparently, the largest mall in the country. A dubious honor, if you ask me, but an honor just the same. It has its' own amusement park, complete with a roller coaster inside and, I would imagine, just about any store you can think of. Our plan for Monday was to return to the mall to visit the Aquarium. A mall with an aquarium, ya got that? And this is no chintzy little thing. It comes complete with sharks and everything.

The highlight was that Tom had managed to score a couple of NBA tickets for us. We would sit courtside to watch the Timberwolves battle the Los Angeles Lakers tonight. Neither one was a favorite team of mine (I'm a true blue, bad boy Pistons fan), but with Ethan being nearly as big of a sports fan as I am, I knew we'd have fun. Besides, it's hard to beat courtside and Kobe Bryant.

On Tuesday morning we would fly home. I would go back to working on my book and Ethan would get to enjoy the rest of his winter break. When he returned to school he could tell his friends all about how famous and cool his Dad is, how awesome it is sitting courtside at an NBA game and, no doubt, how many hot chicks he saw at the biggest mall in the country.

As we sat on the tarmac in Detroit, waiting to taxi on to the runway, I looked at Ethan sitting next to me. He had his eyes closed, the earbud headphones from his iPod stuffed into his ears, lost in whatever music he was into this week. It was a moment for me to steal an observation of him, just the way I would with his mother. I guess that is something I do with everyone. Sneak a peek, so to speak. Nice little rhyme there for you, doctor.

He seemed to fill the seat more than I thought he should and I couldn't remember when he had grown so tall. He wasn't especially tall for his age, I supposed, but he was taller than I thought he should be. He was a teenager, or nearly, and I guess you don't notice those sorts of things as they come along. One day you just happen to look at your baby and notice he has become a toddler, walking and talking. Then you peek in on him sleeping and see that he is a full-fledged little boy. A day or two later, it seems, and you glance over at him as he sits in the airplane seat next to you and god damn if he hasn't morphed into a teenager.

I wanted to hug him then. To squeeze him to me while he was still willing to accept my hug, wanted to ruffle his blonde hair (which had grown to a length that was likely to get a note sent home in regards to a haircut, when he returned to school), to plant a kiss on his forehead before he grew anymore and reached that age where only high fives and pats on the back are shared between "real" men. I knew that next week or the week after, at least it would seem, I would see him walking out the door with my car keys in hand and I would realize he was practically an adult.

My thoughts were brought back to the moment as the speakers crackled to life.

"Hello, ladies and gentlemen. This is your captain speaking. Welcome aboard Delta flight 4504 to Cincinnati. We'll be taxiing into position shortly for takeoff. You will notice the De-icing trucks pulling up to either side of us, for a quick spray down. Just a routine job there. There are no weather concerns in our route and we should be reaching Cincinnati in about 47 minutes once we are in the air."

It was a remarkably monotone speech. I imagined that the pilot was on the verge of falling asleep. I wondered if they actually practiced removing emotion from their voices.

He continued, "Should you need anything, please don't hesitate to ask our flight crew. We'll be happy to assist you."

I glanced back over my seat and then up toward the front of the plane. We were on a CRJ50, according to the little info sheet in the seat pouch. It held 50 people, two seats on either side of a very thin aisle. I had only seen one flight attendant and I wasn't sure you could fit a second one in here if you tried. Flight crew, I thought, was a generous description unless the pilot intended on serving some drinks himself.

I glanced out the window as a big yellow truck settled into position next to us. An arm extended from the top of the truck like you'd expect to see on a telephone company vehicle. Instead of a bucket at the end there was a man encapsulated in what reminded me of a machine gun turret on the bottom of a World War II bomber.

As the gunner began shooting spray on the top of the plane, a worker on the ground pulled a nozzle from a boxy contraption mounted to the front of the Freightliner. As he walked toward the belly of the plane, the hose connected to the nozzle played out, obviously on some sort of reel. The worker on the ground disappeared from my line of sight as the spray from the gunner speckled my window. I saw four heavier drops of the de-icing fluid swell to life at the top of my window. They bulged until their weight gave way to gravity and they started to wind their way downward. They moved slowly, appearing thick, and for some reason their pale, pinkish color, coupled with their apparent viscosity, made me think of blood mixed with milk.

It seems like an odd thought now, almost like an omen. I think that you must remember, however, that I am a writer. More than that, I am a writer of fiction, the type of fiction that makes you leave a light on in the bathroom and makes your ear sensitive to the creaking and croaking of your house. I have trained my mind for years to think of things in that sort of way. Rarely can I look at something, anything, and just enjoy looking at it. More often I think of how I would describe whatever I am looking at. How would I phrase it so that someone would understand exactly what it looks like, feels like, to me?

I don't look for stories. It's more like the stories look for me. They are already there. Someone just needs to write them down. Something as simple as the de-icing fluid rolling down the glass of an airplane window could be the catalyst for a story. When the words find me, like they did at that moment, I always hope I can remember them and usually find I can't. For that reason, I started carrying notepads with me. I pulled the notepad (one of the small, spiral deals) out of my pocket as we sat on the tarmac being de-iced and wrote: *The blood of a rose.* That's what that fluid brought to my mind's eye; a bleeding rose.

I set the notebook between my legs, the pen stuffed into the wire spiral that held it all together. I was sure I would need it again. When the imagery starts coming like that, it almost always comes in waves. It's as if once I open my mind to it, I am powerless to close it again until whatever it is that brings these things to me, is done. They don't always go together. Actually, they rarely go together. Some of them may end up in stories, but rarely the same stories. Some of them become the little piece that begins the whole thing. Some of them are just a nice little description inside the story. Some of them just take up room in one of the many little, spiral notebooks that are piled on top of each other in my desk drawer, the notebooks that I grab at random and flip through when I am stuck for something to write.

When I die, sooner or later yet to be determined, I imagine that somebody will go through those notebooks, probably my wife but maybe someone else. They will see a bunch of disjointed comments like *the sun melting into the lake* and *like Jello that has fallen to the floor and been forgotten* or *The Devil's laugh.*

CHAPTER FOUR

The plane finally taxied into position. The engines roared and the g-forces pushed me back into my seat a bit. I'd never flown on one of these small planes and I was struck at how quickly the rumble of the runway beneath the wheels faded away and the plane lifted off. I thought that, despite my sudden success, I had obviously not yet fully arrived. I was pretty certain that an entirely successful author would be enjoying a direct flight in a full sized plane, lounging in first class seating. I would have to talk to Tom about that.

It was overcast when we took off but as we broke through the clouds I was struck by the blue sky and the harsh sunlight. I look down at the clouds, so dark and ominous they had looked from the ground. From above, with the sun beating down on them, they were gleaming white. I thought, and not for the first time, it was something I had imagined before when flying, that if I dared I could drop right out on to those clouds. And despite what I knew, I felt certain that those clouds would catch me; that I would bounce in them like that stupid bear in the laundry detergent commercials. The clouds spread out to the horizon like a bed of fresh cotton and the sky shone as blue as the clearest of beautiful of spring days.

I grabbed my notebook from between my legs and jerked the pen free. I flipped through the pages to my last entry and below *The blood of a rose* I wrote *The sun always shines and the skies are always blue above the clouds.*

I glanced over at Ethan, his eyes closed, head gently bobbing back and forth to the beat of whatever he was listening to. A thought stole through my mind, "Please let that be Van Halen or Bon Jovi or something that's not Hannah Montana or some other Disney crap."

I tapped him on the shoulder and he turned to me, his eyes asking, "What?"

I pantomimed removing earphones from my ears and as he took his off I said, "Look out there," gesturing toward the window. "Remember how dark and cloudy it was when we took off? Look how blue the sky is, how the sun shines."

He looked nonchalantly, gave a little grunt and nodded. He looked back at me, waiting for more.

"That's it," I said. "I just thought it was cool."

"Yeah, I guess," he muttered as he began replacing the earbuds.

"What are you listening to?" I asked.

"My Chemical Romance."

"Acceptable," I said, and Ethan looked at me as if I had worms crawling out of my nose.

I supposed then that those sorts of observations, about blue skies and such, are more for the mature, introspective among us. In other words, us old people.

We landed in Cincy and had a short layover, just long enough for me to have a beer and Ethan to down a Pepsi. Then we were back on another Comair, 50 passenger deal. Chances are it was the same one we had just gotten off. I made a mental note, again, to give Tom a hard time the next time I saw him.

We were seated in row 9, seats A & B. I gave Ethan the window. We were just over the wing of the plane. When the pilot came on, he could have been reading the same speech they gave when we left Detroit, just changing the names and letting us know it would take about an hour and twenty minutes for this flight.

We got up to cruising altitude and I had just settled back, reclining my seat the full two inches for maximum comfort, when Ethan tapped me on the arm.

"You're right, Dad. The blue skies and sunshine thing is pretty cool."

It was nice to know he had been listening and I smiled and patted his leg, "Yeah, pretty cool."

The flight attendant came through with a little basket of snacks. Ethan grabbed some cookies and I took a couple of bags of peanuts and some crackers, sour cream and chives flavor. A few minutes after that she came back through with a little cart and we both got a Coke.

I don't know how long it took me to fall asleep, but I remember waking up to the pilot announcing that we would be diverting to Duluth because of bad weather in Minneapolis. I didn't know how far Duluth was from Minneapolis but I figured I would either be scrambling to get back in time for the book signing, or it was going to be delayed. I also thought how shitty it would be if we missed the Timberwolves/Lakers game.

As it turns out, Duluth is about 150 miles north of Minneapolis. I don't know the route the pilot had to take to get there, maybe a big looping circle around. I later discovered that we ended up some 75 to

100 miles further north of Duluth, right smack dab in the middle of fucking nowhere.

CHAPTER FIVE

The pilot had just announced that we would be arriving in Duluth shortly. The flight attendant announced that she would be coming through one last time to collect any garbage. I had been dozing again and was awakened by the pilot's address. I looked over to Ethan, slumped against the wall of the airplane, apparently catching some Z's of his own.

The flight attendant, a trim blonde, attractive but obviously past the glory days of youth, was moving quickly through the aisle extending a plastic garbage bag to passengers on either side of her. I had gathered the wrappers and empty Coke cans, and was just reaching out as she swung the bag in my direction, when I heard the explosion.

It was actually two explosions. There was kind of a muffled *BOOM!* That seemed to come from right above us and the plane jerked a little to the right. I looked at the flight attendant, her name tag said NANCY and her eyes said, "What the fuck was that?" as she stumbled slightly in the aisle, grabbing the back of the seat in front of me with one hand to balance herself.

I had just enough time to think that the look on her face was not very encouraging, when the second explosion occurred. It sounded like thunder coming from right inside the plane with us and I thought we must have been hit by lightning. The plane listed hard to the right and Nancy fell into my lap, breaking my tray table from its metal supports as she sprawled across both me and Ethan.

Her eyes met mine, "Oh my God," she muttered, not sounding panicked but looking very much so.

The plane righted itself and Nancy scrambled back to her feet, the refuse bag forgotten on the floor. She turned toward the cockpit and managed one quick stride toward the front before the plane seemed to actually stop right in mid-air. It was as if someone put the brakes on and poor Nancy wasn't ready for it. I imagine she was preparing to hightail it up front, maybe to check with the pilot, maybe to get strapped into her seat by the door. However quickly she planned on getting there, she got there much faster. As all of us safely buckled in passengers lurched forward against our seatbelts, Nancy took flight down the aisle. She flailed a bit, looking very much like a rag doll as she bounced off the seats and armrests and came to a sudden stop at the cockpit door with a sickening thud, collapsing to the floor in a heap.

There had been a few gasps and screams at the first explosion, and a few more screams at the second. I may have screamed myself, I don't really remember. The sight of Nancy shooting through the aisle like a human cannonball at the circus, however, really set off the pandemonium.

The plane dropped and I felt my ass rise from my seat. Instinctively, I reached out with my arm to hold Ethan in place. I saw Nancy become momentarily weightless, rising from the floor (arms, legs and head dangling lifelessly) and then thumping back down as the plane caught itself.

For a moment it was quiet, I think because everyone's stomach was now in their throats. The pilot's voice crackled through the speakers, sounding remarkably calm, "We are experiencing a problem with our right engine. Please prepare in case an emergency landing is required."

This little tidbit elicited a new round of screams and prayers, primarily the "Oh God! Oh God!" variety. Ethan was looking at me with a growing fear in his eyes.

"It's okay," I said. My voice was remarkably calm considering my own terror. "Probably just going to be a rough landing."

He nodded, but didn't look particularly convinced, "Did the engine blow up?"

"I don't know, buddy," I told him.

I reached to secure his tray table and felt a stabbing pain in my side. I looked down to see a tear in my shirt surrounded by a red stain. I pulled my shirt up to reveal a nice sized gash in my abdomen.

"Jesus, Dad! Are you okay?"

"I think so," I said. When the plane lurched and poor, old Nancy left my side so abruptly, I had apparently impaled myself on the metal brace remaining from my broken tray table. It didn't appear to be too bad although, now that I knew it was there, it was hurting like a son of a bitch.

"Lean forward against the seat," I said, "Like this."

I demonstrated the classic "brace for impact" position and Ethan followed suit. The screaming had all but subsided to heavy sobbing. Somewhere behind us someone began reciting the 23rd Psalm.

"Yea, though I walk through the valley of death…"

That seemed to goad a few others into action. The Lord's Prayer started, then what sounded like the Apostle's Creed. The psalm made sense to me, maybe even the Lord's Prayer; the creed was questionably. Truth be told, I was thinking that a simple, "God, don't let me die" would suffice. Then, I actually heard someone reciting a dinner prayer.

"Come Lord Jesus, be our guest…"

I actually thought "really?"

I guess that was the only prayer that particular person could remember at the moment. Any port in a storm, I suppose.

The plane nosed forward and I could hear a sickening whine. It was the same sound you hear in war movies when a plane or a bomb is plummeting to the earth. It didn't feel as if we were going straight down but we were sure dropping faster than we should have been. I found myself wondering about the gliding capabilities of the CRJ50.

It seemed like an eternity waiting for the earth to rush up to meet us, and I had no doubt that was what was happening. I had no illusions about the pilot wrestling this plane under control. We were going to crash, plain and simple. The only question was how hard.

I thought of my wife at home, I thought of my unfinished book, I thought of the book signing I was very likely going to miss. I looked at Ethan, his hands and forehead on the back of the seat in front of him, his eyes clenched shut.

I could hear the whine getting louder and realized it was the sound of the ground closing in.

"God, please keep him safe," I whispered, joining my fellow passengers in prayer. "And I wouldn't mind getting through this either."

It was right about then that we ran out of atmosphere.

"Hold On!" It was the pilot, and then his last words, "Oh Fu..."

I don't exactly remember the sound of the impact, only a cacophony of noise; metal twisting, explosions, screaming, thuds and banging against the fuselage. As we hit, I felt the seat in front of me give way. There had been a heavier set man there and it seemed his weight was too much for the bolts holding the seat to the floor. He and the seat flew forward, crushing a twenty-something blonde against the seat in front of her. I reached down and wrapped my arms around my calves, my head between my knees.

I could feel the pressure on the back of my own seat, the weight of the passenger behind me pushing forward. The plane seemed to hesitate and I could feel the tail lifting into the air, trying to out run the rest of the plane, I heard a sickening tearing sound and felt a rush of cold air. And then it seemed that much of the screaming was fading off away from us.

I bounced in my seat, feeling the safety belt tear into my legs and my stomach. The burning pain from the gash in my side melted into the pain the belt was causing. Ethan was screaming, and I imagine I was too, but I took comfort in his screams, a testament to the fact that he was still breathing.

I felt the plane lurch and gravity turned upside down. Then everything was black.

CHAPTER SIX

When I came to, it was dark and cold. I was lying on the ground. I could hear helicopters. It took me a few minutes to remember what had happened. A plane crash. Ethan!

I tried to move and felt a pain, like nothing I had every felt, ripping through my legs. It turns out they were broken. I rolled to my side and could see the plane. Somehow I had been thrown free of it. The back half was a burning hulk resting some hundred yards from the front half. The front was flipped upside down, the top of the plane crushed under its own weight. It was smoking but I could not see any flames. I tried to crawl toward it, yelling my son's name. The pain shot from my legs and gripped my whole body. I blacked out again.

When I next awoke I was assaulted by light. Everything was white. I was in the hospital although, at the time, I could not comprehend that. I heard voices yelling about fluids and vital signs and heart rates. Then I was gone again.

I was the only survivor of Flight 4504. A miracle, they say. Lucky.

CHAPTER SEVEN

I don't know what else to write. I know that I am supposed to find some sort of forgiveness within myself, recognize that it was not my fault that the plane crashed, not my fault that my son is dead.

It's not working. It was my suggestion that he come with me on the trip, a direct result of my actions that he was on that plane. My wife has been strong, telling me I can't blame myself, that it was God's will.

I don't know if I believe in God anymore. If there is a God, He is a cruel son of a bitch.

This exercise has accomplished one thing, doctor. It has made me realize that I will never get over this. I will never be able to lead a normal life. I don't even want to try.

I will print these pages. I will listen to the whirl and click and hum of my printer one last time. I'll put them all in an envelope with your name on it, someone else might read them first and, if not, don't feel any professional responsibility to uphold the doctor/client confidentiality. I don't care who sees them. None of this will be a surprise to anyone.

I am going to smash this computer. I am going to take it out to the garage and pound it to death with a hammer. Then I am going to seal up the garage as best that I can, run a hose from the tailpipe through the car window and go to sleep. I understand that it is a painless way to go. It came to me suddenly, this method, just now as I've been writing. It seems a good option for a coward.

These pages can serve as my suicide note for those looking to understand my actions. I don't expect there will be many questions. There is the single sheet from my notebook, the one I pulled out and am looking at now, sitting next to my computer on my desk. I will tape it to the dashboard of my car. When they find me they will understand it, unlike the many comments that fill the others. My rose is dead. Its beauty snuffed out far too soon.

If there is a God, I will see Ethan…above the clouds…the sun is always shining and the sky is always blue above the clouds.

Author's Notes:

This is one of those stories that started out as something entirely different. I had designs for this story to be a novel which had a very supernatural element to it. The catalyst was still a plane crash but there were to be a number of survivors (most notably, a man and his son) who would be stranded in the wilderness of Minnesota, dealing with some unsavory ghosts and ghouls and goblins and such; primarily drawn from Scandinavian folk lore. As I wrote the story, I had a few issues that I was struggling to work through in a way that I felt was sufficient. I had written something like 20,000 words by the time I decided it wasn't going to work for me but I really liked the plane crash scene, and a few of the other bits, so I went back and rewrote what you have just read.

The inspiration for the story was an actual plane trip to Minnesota, which included a de-icing procedure. I had actually written the "blood of a rose" note on some scratch paper.

Appendix

Above The Clouds. Originally published by Eternal Press – August 2009

Traveling Music. Originally published in Issue 9 (Road Trip) of The Monsters Next Door – November 2009

Observations of an Indifferent Corpse. Originally published in Scarlett Literary Magazine, Vol.1 Issue 1 – Mid-Winter 2011

The Block. Originally published in Scarlett Literary Magazine, Vol. 1 Issue 2 – Spring 2011 and Trembles Magazine – July 2011

Inuit Moon. Originally published in Scarlett Literary Magazine. Vol. 1 Issue 3 – Fall 2011

Do You Make house Calls? Originally published in The Memory Eater anthology - 2012

49558166R00190

Made in the USA
San Bernardino, CA
28 May 2017